THE SPEED OF THE DARK

Alex Shearer lives with his family in Somerset. He has written more than a dozen books for both adults and children, as well as many successful television series, films, and stage and radio plays. He has had over thirty different jobs, and has never given up trying to play the guitar.

'A literary gem . . . stylistically faultless'
Literary Review

'Shearer lets secrets slip at a carefully controlled pace . . . strong on ideas and atmosphere, his novel is sinister to its core'
Guardian

Books by Alex Shearer available from Macmillan

The Great Blue Yonder
The Stolen
Bootleg

THE SPEED OF THE DARK

OF THE

Alex Shearer

MACMILLAN CHILDREN'S BOOKS

First published 2003 by Macmillan Children's Books

This edition published 2004 by Macmillan Children's Books
a division of Macmillan Publishers Limited
20 New Wharf Road, London N1 9RR
Basingstoke and Oxford
www.panmacmillan.com

Associated companies throughout the world

ISBN 0 330 41538 7

1 3 5 7 9 8 6 4 2

A CIP catalogue record for this book is available from
the British Library.

Typeset by Intype Libra Ltd
Printed and bound in Great Briatin by Mackays of Chatham plc, Kent

To Kate (of course)

A stranger here
Strange things doth meet, strange glory see.
Strange treasures lodg'd in this fair world appear.
Strange all and new to me.

Thomas Traherne (1636–1674)

Christopher

Most of these whizz-kids just can't hack it. You see them coming down the road, fresh from college, or wherever they've been, with qualifications hanging out of their pockets, acting like they've got the cure for everything, and answers to all the questions that you haven't even asked yet. But they don't last long. They're mostly like fireworks. They light up the sky for a handful of seconds and then they fall to earth.

Nice and steady, that's my way. Mr Tortoise and Mr Hare, and guess who wins the race? There's more been accomplished by steady plodding than by any flashes-in-the-pan. Which is why I'm still here and working when they've all fizzled out and gone back to where they came from, or off to pastures new.

Seen them come, seen them go, seen them want to come back again, but it was all too late by then. Me, I'm here for the long haul and hanging on in there for the pension. Nobody gets fired here. Not when you've been around as long as me. It costs them too much to get rid of you. And anyway, I get results. Nothing spectacular – bread and butter contributions, you might say, but a steady contribution just the same. And if you don't have the bread and butter work, well, you don't have a sandwich. The jam's no use on its own.

But these whizz-kids, nine times out of ten – correct that, nine hundred and ninety nine times out of a thousand – they just burn out and they're gone.

Sometimes they crack up. Too much is expected and they can't deliver. They were big fish in small pools back home, or back at college. But they come here – well, you're a minnow in the ocean. That's a hard thing to find out when you've been brought up to believe you were Snappy the Man-eating Shark all your life, chewing up those school books like they were sardines and sprats.

Some people can't come to terms with being ordinary. Me, I was born that way, so I never had anything to lose. Anything over and above ordinary was a bonus for me, it was a cheque in the post. Sometimes I wake up and have to pinch myself to make sure that it's not all a dream. I don't know how I got here. I must have got lucky, or somebody confused me with somebody else. Mistaken identity case, I sometimes reckon. But here I am and here I stay, until I get that big, fat redundancy cheque, or I live to take the pension.

I could tell you a hundred stories about the whizz-kids we've had here, the weirdos and the jokers, but what would be the use? You could probably tell better stories yourself, and anyway, you've more than likely heard it all before. They're a penny a dozen, stories like that; you buy one, you get one free. You maybe even know these people, went to school with them.

I reckoned I had heard it all before too, but not this one. This is a prime example, I'd say, of both cracking up *and* disappearing – the whole caboodle all rolled up in one.

He was just a young guy, Christopher Mallan. He was working on the light decelerator, if you remember that, if you read the scientific journals, and I dare say you don't. The whole thing was his idea, but I knew it would come to nothing. You'd never crack the necessary equations on that kind of thing, not even with computers working night and day and weekends and holidays for a thousand years. You'd need to be lucky or a genius – or possibly a lucky genius – to figure it out. Always assuming such a thing could ever be figured out in the first place, which for my money it never could. It was never feasible, not from the start.

But just the same, I wouldn't have had Christopher Mallan down for a disappearing act, and I wouldn't have had him down for a poet either, or writer of any kind, though that was what he turned out to be.

No, there was only one thing he was interested in as far as I could tell, and that was physics and his crazy decelerator idea. The kind of physics he dealt in was the sort which maybe only ten people in the world fully understood. And of those ten who could say even *they* fully understood it, possibly five of them were lying, exaggerating, or trying to pump up the truth along with their reputations.

Chris spent his time working on a problem that he never did solve. He pushed things forwards a little maybe and advanced the cause of science by a millimetre or two, but he never did much more than that – which is probably true for most people who work in science; we try to push this great train along a track. If we all get our shoulders to it and push at once, we maybe move it two centimetres in a hundred years.

And then someone like Isaac Newton or Albert Einstein comes along, and they move the train a mile in a minute, by using just one little finger.

But for most of us, it's just drudgery and tedium, repetition and failure and finally a little success, or maybe no success at all.

Chris was a loner, and a bit lonely too, I thought, and he had a strange attitude to his work. His approach to science was not so much that we were discovering new things, but that we were rediscovering what we had once known, things which had been lost. He seemed to have a kind of 'fallen from grace' approach. As though we were all so many Adams and Eves, trying to get back into the Garden of Eden, trying to remember what we had forgotten, to recover the knowledge we were born with, to regain what we had lost.

He was an acquaintance of mine more than a friend, but there could have been a warmer relationship there, only his work preoccupied him and there was the age difference too. He was young. By comparison, I'm an old guy. But Chris didn't have much time for friendship, whatever your age. He lived for his work. Maybe he sacrificed himself for it too.

I guess that for some people, failure is a hard thing to come to terms with, or even to contemplate. But Chris was so obsessed, so driven, that for him it maybe wasn't even a possibility. He dulled any such qualms with work.

Even God took Sunday off when he made the

4

world, and if a day of rest was good enough for him, it was good enough for me.

But all Chris did was work, work, work.

One weekend I did persuade him to take a few hours off and to come over to the house for a barbecue. It was June and a hot one. The house and the garden were full of friends and their rampaging children, and we'd invited all the neighbours round too so that they wouldn't complain about the noise of the party as they'd be making it themselves.

My wife got Chris in a corner with a drink and a burger and began asking him all the questions that were probably none of her business but he was too polite to say so.

She started by asking him if he'd never thought of settling down or getting married or living with someone or starting a family himself or whether there was someone important in his life. (I knew what she was angling at but I felt that she was wrong, and it was none of her business anyway. It wasn't that he didn't like women, he just didn't seem to have the time for them.)

Chris managed to avoid giving her any direct answer, as he always did. He dithered and evaded, wriggled out of it and changed the subject, but not before implying – as she told me later that night – that he already had commitments, big family commitments, and couldn't afford to take on any extra responsibilities. Only precisely what they were, he didn't go into details.

Which puzzled me in a way. Because in the time that I'd known him, I had never heard him pick up a telephone and answer a personal call. I'd never once seen a card on his office or laboratory window sill either, from an uncle or aunt or anyone, wishing him a happy birthday or a merry Christmas, or whatever the season dictated. The little I knew about his background was the little he chose to tell me, and that was precious little indeed.

I did know some things about him from his CV, his interview (which I chaired) and his exemplary academic record. As a child he had been abandoned. Exactly how or why or what the circumstances were, he never elaborated on, but I heard from other sources that first his mother had gone and then, some years later, his father had deserted him – just walked out and left him alone to take care of himself – and hadn't ever come back, from that day to this, leaving him to be brought up by strangers or some friend of the family. He had just disappeared from Chris's life, turned his back on him.

It wasn't as though Chris had been a small baby back then either, and perhaps wouldn't have known enough to experience rejection. Maybe that would have made it easier, if he had been younger. It would all have been buried too deep then to do any harm.

But it was harder and tougher than that. Chris knew his dad, and he loved him, and after his mother's early death or departure – whichever it had been – his dad had brought him up, right from the beginning. He wasn't conventional, but that doesn't mean he wasn't a decent and caring man. In fact, for honest dealing, give me an outsider any day; it's the ones in the suits you have to watch, in my experience.

His dad had been the one to deal with the nappies and wake in the night and worry about the high temperatures and the fevers and the hacking coughs. His dad had been the one to take him to the nursery and the playgroups – sometimes the only man there amongst the mothers.

So it could only have made it worse. For them to have been so close for so long, and then for his father simply to walk out like that, with nothing – no note, no explanation, no word of farewell. He just completely disappeared.

Of course people do disappear. Maybe that was why Chris did it himself later. Maybe disappearing is in the blood. It's like that with some talents and virtues and vices – they run in families.

In a way, the world's archives are full of missing persons – people who move in and out of each other's lives and are never seen again. Maybe some of them are truly lost, maybe others do not wish to be found. Maybe some fell victim to someone and were murdered, or thrown into a concrete mixer or into the sea. Or they leaped from a high cliff, or took an overdose and lay down in the long grass, able to bear it no more, and never woke up again.

Maybe Chris's father didn't so much disappear as somebody else (person or persons for reasons unknown) disappeared *him*. He lived on the fringes a little, or so I understand, and he maybe knew some unsavoury characters. But try telling that to a child – that the person you loved did not go willingly. As far as a child is concerned, the abandonment is the same. You are lost and alone, abandoned by the one you love. It doesn't matter how or why they went, it's the fact they went at all.

How could you ever see it any other way? How

could you live on after that, other than with the hurt of the rejection, coupled with the never quite extinguished hope that the person you had lost might yet return?

I think – or I like to imagine – that the people who brought Chris up after the loss of his father were good, well-intentioned, kind individuals. But maybe they weren't. Maybe they were strict and brutal. I have no idea. All I know is that he didn't talk much about them and that he didn't keep in touch with them either. If he had any stepbrothers or stepsisters, he didn't mention it. In fact, he didn't seem to have any connections with his past or mementos at all. Except for one thing – the little glass dome.

You know the kind of thing – he used it as a paperweight. It was always there on his desk whenever I went in to see him. We worked on parallel projects for a while and used to collate data and share our thoughts.

I don't know exactly what it meant to him, but it meant a lot. It looked like one of those things you get which are filled up with little snowflakes suspended in some clear liquid. Often a snowman sits on the base, and when you shake it all up, the storm starts and the snow falls. Suddenly it's winter again and it feels like Christmas, right there on your desk.

Only the liquid must have all leaked away or dried up over the years, because you could see it was empty. It didn't have that little air bubble trapped inside, caught between the liquid and the top of the dome.

Of course, the first time I saw it, I didn't know that, or I wasn't looking properly, and as Chris and I were talking, I casually reached out to pick up the dome and to shake it a little, to see the snowflakes fall.

But as I reached out, a change came over him. His face went white. He was normally quite a placid, easy-going man. But I think if he had needed to kill me right then, to stop me touching the small glass dome, he would have done it without a qualm.

His hand shot across the desk and grabbed my wrist. His grip was like a steel cable, a noose tightening. I was genuinely scared. I felt that he had some almost superhuman strength for that moment and he could have snapped my arm in two, broken it like a match. I was really afraid. The way you are when you think an ordinary, normal person has actually been mad all this time and it's taken you this long to notice it.

'Don't you *ever* do that again!' he said. 'Don't you *ever* touch it. *Never!* You move that . . . you shake the dome, and . . .'

I tried to talk calmly. If I was calm, it would calm him down too – I hoped.

'What is it, Chris?' I said. 'What's wrong? What's the matter? I only wanted to see the snowflakes fall. That was all. I'm sorry. I didn't intend any harm to the dome. I won't touch it. It's not important. It's OK.'

He kept hold of my arm for a few moments, and then the anger went from his eyes and he let me go.

'I'm sorry,' he apologized. 'It's just . . . important to me. And it's very old . . . quite old now . . . and very fragile . . . that's why . . .'

Then I realized then that the dome had no liquid in it.

9

'The stuff's all leaked away,' I said. 'You couldn't make the snowflakes fall, even if you wanted to.'

He looked at me blankly, as if he was far away.

'Snowflakes?'

'The snowflakes . . .'

He seemed to understand then, but he shook his head.

'No,' he said. 'There never were any snowflakes. That's not what it is.'

'No snowflakes?'

'No,' he said. 'No snowflakes.'

I took a better look at the dome. He was right. No liquid, no snowflakes – no snowman either, come to that. In fact, it looked a bit dirty, as if there were a few black specks of dust inside.

'So what is it, exactly?' I said.

'It's . . . a souvenir,' he said.

The Dome

I looked at the dome again. But not that closely. I wasn't particularly interested then. I had work to do and my own backs to stab, greasy poles to climb and bills to pay. That's the way it is sometimes in the wonderful world of science. Besides, I was starting to need reading glasses but vanity was delaying my getting any. So I couldn't see the dome that well, although I could see enough to tell me that it was a souvenir all right.

Inside it was a replica of a town. It was the kind of thing you might buy if you were a tourist, I guessed. There was no name plate on it, but I thought I recognized the place. It was a model of a spa town in a quiet part of England, a place steeped in the past and with many historical associations – its cathedral spires, its abbey square, its parks and greenery, its theatre and its mineral, hot-spring baths. It was unmistakeably – well, somewhere. If you've been there, you'd recognize it. If you haven't, I'd prefer not to say. And in a way, what does it matter where it is? A place is a place, where things happen which could have happened anywhere.

It seemed a good replica too, pretty detailed as far as I could make out.

11

'You used to live there?' I asked.

He gazed at the dome for a while before answering, as if looking back into his childhood, into the hurt, the pain and whatever happiness and fond memories there may have been of his past.

'Yes,' he said. 'I used to live there.'

'Got any connections there still?' I asked.

He gave me a look. You know those looks? The ones that can turn water to ice without the intervention of a refrigerator.

'Yes, I've still got connections there, of a kind. Now, what was it you wanted?'

'These equations of yours,' I said. 'On the decelerator. To be honest, Chris, I hate to say it again, but you're wasting your time here. There are other projects . . .'

He gave a thin smile.

'Oh?' he said. 'Wasting my time? Really?'

'I hate to say it, but you're going off in completely the wrong direction,' I said. 'The whole project's a waste of time. A decelerator is just not feasible. I don't think such a thing could ever exist.'

'You don't?'

'No.'

He gave his cryptic, vaguely condescending smile again.

'What if I told you such a thing already did exist?' he asked.

'I'd have trouble believing that,' I told him. (I like to be candid.)

He just ignored me.

'What if I told you that such a thing not only already existed, but that I had seen one.'

12

'I'd have equal trouble believing that too,' I said.

But he just ploughed right on, head down, horns up – a charging bull in search of a red rag.

'What if I further told you that wasn't the problem?' he said.

'What wasn't the problem?' I said, getting a little mystified now.

'Slowing light down to the point where it ceases to be light . . .'

'You're losing me . . .'

'To the point where it turns into . . . what's the best way to describe it . . . when it turns into . . . darkness?'

'How about a coffee, Chris?' I offered. 'White no sugar, that's how you like it, huh?'

'How about if I told you that the problem doesn't lie in *making* a decelerator at all. The problem lies in *reversing* it?' Chris went on, ignoring the coffee offer.

'Reversing it, huh? OK.'

I was looking round for possible interruptions and distractions by now, kind of hoping that someone might walk in, or the phone might ring.

'Otherwise it isn't a thing you can ever tell people about.'

'Why not?'

'Because if it's only a one-way process, it's too dangerous. It's not a machine any more.'

'Then what is it?'

'It's a weapon.'

'A weapon?'

'Of punishment – of revenge. And how could you ever let that fall into the hands of the wrong people?'

'I'm sorry, Chris . . .'

We were in over my head now. Maybe in Chris's

case it was only up to his neck, but me, I needed a snorkel, and I hadn't brought one. I tried treading water.

'See it this way,' he went on. 'There are many wonderful machines in the world. What do they have in common? They can all be stopped. What they do is not necessarily irreversible. But take a gun. It fires a bullet. The bullet kills. There's no reversal, no going back.'

'Second law of thermodynamics,' I said, just to let him know I was back in my depth again and still in the conversation. 'The entropy of a system always increases – in other words, the mess always gets bigger. You drop a glass, it shatters. You drop the pieces, they don't spontaneously join up again and make a new tumbler. You fire a bullet into someone—'

'You can't un-fire it. Exactly. You can't make things un-explode. Only that's what I need to know . . .'

His voice drifted away and he stared out of the window.

'What do you need to know, Chris?'

He turned and looked at me.

'How to un-fire the gun. I need to know how to un-fire the gun.'

I was starting to feel that Chris had gone and joined the crazies now. You ever heard that saying, something about 'great wits are to madness close allied' or something like that? It means the smarter you are, the nearer to crazy you are, as far as I can understand it. Not that I'm a qualified psychologist.

'So you have the gun?' I said. 'Metaphorically speaking? You already have the gun?'

14

'I have the gun.'

'But you can't tell anyone about it.'

'No. Not until I've learned how to un-fire it.'

'I see.'

I didn't. But I'd decided to leave it at that. Only I did casually add, 'I'd really like to see this machine, Chris. Any chance of taking a look at it?'

He gave me his thin, cryptic smile again. It had a superior edge to it. As if he knew more than others, as though there were hidden things which only he was privy to and which we lesser mortals couldn't possibly hope to understand.

'One day maybe,' he said. 'One day.'

But those kinds of smiles don't bother me. I've also seen them on the faces of men with sandwich boards, out on the street; men with pamphlets, men with theories, men with thin yet complicated books which have been published at their own expense; men with soapboxes; men who know the aliens are coming; men who have been whisked away on flying saucers; men who know for a fact that there are conspiracies afoot, and that the Prime Minister is personally behind it all and hushing the whole thing up.

So those thin, superior smiles don't bother me too much. They don't so much remind me of my own limitations as make me think of white vans coming.

'So I can see it?' I said again. 'One day soon?'

He thought about it. He was a great one for thinking about it before he answered your question. This was maybe a good thing up to a point, but it could also try your patience.

'Maybe,' he said eventually.

Such a long wait for so few words.

15

'When can I see the evidence?'

'One day,' he said again.

I was getting a little tired of 'one day'. In fact, I almost thought about cutting his funding right there and then, I was getting that peeved. I couldn't have done it personally, but it would have been no trouble to make a recommendation. Instead I just bit my lip, turned and headed for the door.

'It can't be done, Chris,' I told him as I left. 'We can hardly even gear up the tiniest speck of matter to the speed of light. To do the opposite . . . it's a ridiculous concept. It just can't be done.'

'It can . . .' he said. And I think he added, '. . . and it has,' as I closed the door behind me. But I probably misheard.

I guess that the real scientist, the innovator, the pioneer, needs to have more than mere science in his heart. He needs a touch of the artist too, which I never had. In all honesty, I think I just had a touch of mediocrity. Equally, the real artist has an intuitive understanding of the world around him or her and is – if not by education at least by intuition – a scientist as well. At least, that's what I think. I have never really gone for this separation between science and art. To me they are two complementary parts of one thing, two sides of the same coin. Many great artists were great scientists, and many great scientists were great artists, and that's the truth.

But I never had Chris Mallan down for a writer. Not ever. It didn't come to light for a long time. Not until after he had gone.

There's not a lot else of note to say about Christopher. He was a private, strange, driven man, with his own compulsions and demons. He was a man who worked long hours, who worked obsessively, and who never, if he could possibly avoid it, took a holiday.

He was so driven, it was almost as if he were trying to pay off a debt of some kind, as though he had made a promise once, or people were relying on him not to let them down – as though he were their only hope. As if he were riding to some unspecified rescue.

One other strange thing did happen. It was an incident which convinced me even more that Christopher was not just eccentric, but could be downright crazy when he wanted to be as well.

About a week after the business with the paperweight, I had to go into his office to see him again, about some forms he should have filled in and hadn't got around to. (He had managed to decelerate forms quite easily.)

The paperweight was sitting in the same place as usual. But there was now something different about it.

He had screwed it to the desk.

Three small screws had been put through the wooden base of the dome and had been driven flat into the top of the mahogany. (OK, mahogany veneer, but it was still an expensive desk and property of the institute.)

He saw me looking at it. I don't think it had occurred to him that you weren't supposed to go screwing things on to your desk, not when it was institute property. Or he more than likely didn't give two hoots.

'I was worried,' he said, 'that the cleaners might move it.'

'Ah,' I said.

Then he said something that convinced me that he needed a holiday.

'It would be like an earthquake,' he said.

'Ah huh?' I nodded.

'People could get killed,' he said.

'Right,' I nodded.

'So it's best to keep things nice and tight and all screwed down,' he said. 'Then there can't be any accidents and no one will get hurt. We don't want anyone getting buried in the rubble.'

'No, Chris,' I said. 'We don't.'

I made him take a holiday that year. I went and spoke to Jefferson and we absolutely insisted. I think he travelled around Europe for a few weeks. I peeked into his office while he was away.

The holes left by the three screws were visible in the desk, but he had taken the dome with him. Taken it on holiday, I presumed. Maybe he wanted to show it the world.

When he returned from holiday, he screwed the dome back on to the desk. It remained there until he vanished. I mean, it remained there even *after* he vanished. I'm looking at it right now.

Christopher just disappeared one day. He vanished from his lab. Mrs Evershad in Accounts was the last one to see him. He was coming in late to finish some work just as she was going out.

He was still working on the decelerator project, working on ever more complicated equations on the polarization of light, on the various wavelengths of the various colours, on how to split the spectrum, separate and isolate the colours and to – as it were – fire one wavelength back against another, with the object of slowing everything down and then throwing it into reverse. He made some progress, but he never did crack it as far as I know. In fact, the last thing he did before he vanished was to wreck a fair amount of expensive equipment. There was broken glass and burnt-out circuits everywhere. (It's a good job we're insured.) As for his equations, there were reams of them. They're near impossible to read and twice as hard to make sense of. Maybe it was his big day that day – or he'd hoped it would be – but things went wrong and it was the last straw for him, and he'd had enough, and couldn't admit to his failure.

Of course, yours truly got the good jobs – tying up the loose ends, trying to track him down, dealing with the authorities and the police and the paperwork and the men in suits and all the rest. Then I had to clear out his desk, and that was when I found the manuscript – the one which follows now.

Also lying on the desk was the small glass dome. I couldn't understand why he hadn't taken it with him, as it seemed to be so precious. The glass top had been removed and set to one side. On the desk next to it was this odd, but quite compact, machine, a series of lenses and mirrors and electromagnets. I guessed it was what he had been working on.

In the bottom desk drawer I found his box of writing. On the top of it was a note saying,

'*Dear Charlie,*' (that's me)

'*I guess you'll be the one to clear up after me, and I would like you to have this, by way of some kind of explanation. I guess I owe you that much. You may* wonder why I don't just write this down straight and why it has to be a story. Well, the fact is that no one will ever believe me. They're going to think it's nothing but a story no matter what I do – and maybe you will too – so I may as well write it that way. Also, to be honest, I couldn't write it in the first person. I tried, I started that way, but I couldn't say 'I' or 'me' all the time. It was just too painful to bring everything back. Somehow I had to detach myself a little. So I wrote it all as if it had happened to somebody else. And I tried to be fair to people too, the bad as well as the good. Because it seems to me that often there are no real villains, just people in pain, whose unhappiness makes them do bad things. So here it is. Maybe you will be able to get it published for me one day, maybe not. Either way, I hope this goes some way to explaining things. Thanks for all your kindness to me, and give my love and my thanks also to your wife and kids for taking the trouble of trying to be a friend to me. I hope I didn't seem too distant and unfriendly in return. I just never had the time for friendship. As you'll maybe understand now.

Yours, Christopher.'

No, he wasn't such a bad kid. He wasn't that bad at all.

Anyway, I opened up the box and I found that it contained this manuscript, along with a computer disk – which also held a copy of the same manuscript, as I was later to discover.

The box also contained a few poems he had written. Some of the poems weren't bad, though they were all mostly on the same themes, of love and of loss. I read them through, and although I didn't fully understand them, they seemed to be what poems should be – they made you feel that you could be better than you are, that the world is better than it seems, that there are surfaces only scratched yet, and that no matter how badly the world treats you, it is still a strange, beautiful and wonderful place. They left you with a sense of wonder, a sense of childhood even, of when things were new and frightening and extraordinary, when nobody had told you yet that your dreams were impossible, when you still believed that anything could be done, back when miracles could still happen.

Then there was this . . . the manuscript. I don't know what to say about it. I'm no judge of literature, or even if it deserves to be called by that name. But maybe it has its merits. The way the little glass dome has its merits, as a keepsake and a souvenir.

In a way, this manuscript is Chris's testament and his memorial – probably the only one he will have. He's maybe in a shop doorway now, for all I know, or sitting next to a cash machine, asking for spare change from the people who are able to use it.

He must have written the book in the evenings, as a break from his work on the decelerator project. A page here, a page there, it soon mounts up.

My theory, regarding the manuscript, is that it was a way to cope. Inside Chris there was still this small abandoned child who had lost his parents. He was never fully able to come to terms with that, and the fantasy contained in his manuscript was a way to ease the pain. In a paradoxical way, the fantasy was a rationalization – if that doesn't sound too pretentious.

So here it is. The story is all Christopher's. Only the title is mine. He left the manuscript unnamed and I wondered a long time what to call it – something that would both do it justice and seem apt. I must have tried a hundred titles and rejected them all. And then I remembered that phrase he had used, and which had become the working title of the decelerator project. It was also buried in a paragraph of one of his scientific papers, and it occurs several times in the book. It somehow seemed right and appropriate – a melding of both art and science, of mystery and paradox. I think Christopher would have liked it. He may even have chosen it himself.

So here it is – *The Speed of the Dark*. I'm not saying you have to read on. But if you do want to know Chris's story, in his own words, just the way he wrote it, this is it.

You only have to turn the page.

Poppea, the Dancer

When she first disappeared no one thought or worried too much about it because that was how she was. Always disappearing. Almost like it was a conjuring trick. She was supposed to have gone for a dancing job, but when they rang, they said she had never arrived, and they assumed she had changed her mind.

She had been working at Mr Eckmann's for a while, seeing that it was winter now, and too cold and wet to be a statue any more. But Eckmann said he hadn't seen her. She had just come and gone, like she always had just come and gone, and that was why people loved her and warmed to her. Or at least why Robert did, and maybe Christopher too. She was just so easy to love.

Some people might have said that she had let Mr Eckmann down, when he had expected her to stay longer, but even he didn't seem to see it that way, or if he did, he never said so. It was certainly inconvenient not having her there, because it meant that, as well as creating the exhibits, he had to run the gallery too, all on his own. He had to be at the till to take the money and to point the visitors in the right direction, up into the darkened room, advising them to pause a while and to allow their eyes to get used to the light before peering into the microscopes.

But he didn't seem to mind. He could have got somebody else in, without much trouble. There were always people looking for temporary casual work, especially inside, out of the cold and wet, with easy hours and a chair to sit on, and nothing much to do except answer a few questions and give out the tickets and use the credit card machine.

But he didn't bother. Maybe he liked to think that he was keeping the job open for her, and that she would soon return as suddenly as she had gone. But the weeks went by and there was still no sign of her, nor any word. But he kept the job open anyway. He wasn't that busy in the winter, not like in the spring and summer time when the visitors came from all over the world to see the old buildings and the ancient baths, and to take the open-topped bus tours in the sweltering sun.

There were always some visitors, of course, even in the very depths of winter. But much fewer. It wasn't so good to be a statue then either, with a silver-painted face, in a silver-sprayed tutu, covered in car-paint, or maybe wrapped up in foil like the Tin Man from *The Wizard of Oz*, only moving when somebody pretended to wind the key and dropped a little money in the tin to make the music start.

There was good money in the summer, and Poppea was one of the best statues you had ever seen. She could stand still forever.

When she worked at the gallery, she was out of costume, of course, and her hair was tied back, the way ballet dancers often tie their hair back, to keep it out of their eyes so it won't bother them. She wore a T-shirt and faded jeans and sandals and had no make-up on at all. But she still looked beautiful, just the same – at least she did to Mr Eckmann.

Everyone called him Mr Eckmann. ('Probably even his mother,' Poppea had said once.) He dressed formally in two or three piece suits, not the way you would expect, not for an artist. His home was in one of the old Regency houses, where the crescent curved above the park. But he didn't spend much time there. He was usually in his studio above the gallery, way up in the attic, alone there with his working tools, his microscopes and his telescopes and lenses.

From here he could see the moon and the stars. Or if he angled the telescope down, he could view the whole city. He had a little camera obscura, which he had made himself. This was a kind of telescope which projected a circular image of the city on to a white-painted piece of steel, shaped like a large bowl, about two metres in diameter.

You could make out the figures on the street, as small as insects moving across the curved, white-painted screen. It was like watching a world in miniature, and that was maybe why Mr Eckmann liked it. It was as if the tiny figures were his creations, their destinies were in his hands, and he was like some divine being, high up in an ivory tower. Here he was no longer small and overweight and unattractive, nor waddled when he walked.

But then who would have chosen to be who they are and how they are? Who wouldn't like to change maybe one or two things?

And that was where it all started.

*

25

Down by the shadow of the cathedral where the tourists went you could see them – summer, winter, autumn and spring.

There weren't so many tourists in the winter, nor so many performers either, but even on the coldest and most bitter days there was always someone trying to make a few pounds, a few pennies, a few foreign coins – whatever might be thrown into the plate.

Often the gathered crowd would begin to drift away as it sensed the act was coming to an end. That was the time to pass the hat round, before they all escaped. Many people didn't like paying for what they thought of as free entertainment, and were happy to slope away and leave the paying to somebody else. After all, nobody asked the performers to do it, and yet they had to make a living. Apparently.

But you couldn't pass the hat round while you were still juggling or riding the unicycle or walking on the wire or whatever you did, so it was useful to have an assistant, a partner maybe, a friend, or a child. Or to somehow – as Poppea did – manage to obtain payment in advance.

Beneath the energy and high spirits of the entertainers (because who wanted to watch a dreary clown or a glum-faced juggler?) there also lurked something else, something colder, harder – a kind of fear, maybe, a desperation. Perhaps it was the fear of the artist who worries that his talent will not be appreciated, that his invention will flag, that his antics will no longer amuse.

The street performers were mostly young. Once they reached thirty, they seemed to move on. Maybe the cold got into your bones one winter's day, and you could never get it out again. Maybe there was a bad fall to contend with, a clumsy backflip, an awkward landing. Maybe your reactions slowed down and you missed the clubs, choked on the fire, couldn't spin the plates, dropped the diabolo. Maybe you simply lost the ability to entertain; you had done it too long, and had got too old, sad or disillusioned, and nothing seemed frivolous any more.

And then what?

On that Saturday afternoon a bleak grey cloud covered the abbey and there was the threat of imminent rain. But there was sunlight too, and some warmth in the air. It was, for that time of year, typical English weather.

Postcards stood in racks outside the souvenir shops, and the tourists thumbed through them. An opentopped, double-decker bus drove past, offering 'Tours of the City in Five Languages', one of which sounded like Japanese. The diesel engine roared as it pulled the bus up a sharp hill and headed for an elegant crescent of Regency buildings in pale limestone.

Below the crescent was the park, and below that again the abbey, and in front of the abbey, the flagstone square where the performers jostled and negotiated for space and time and for the right to establish themselves as regulars with the privileges that brought. Not that they were really supposed to be there, and sometimes they got moved on, or fined.

A small cluster of people surrounded a young woman who stood in the centre of the square upon a box. The box had been painted silver and the girl was dressed in the costume of a ballerina. She wore a pink tutu, pink tights, pink shoes with pink straps, and her

27

hair was tied back with a pink ribbon. Her face was made up to be very pale, with dark lips and darker eyes, and with two pink circles of blusher on her cheeks. Falling from her eyes, down along her face and into the circles, were painted tears.

The tears had been painted on with considerable skill. They started off quite small at the corners of the girl's eyes, and widened out as they fell. The girl maintained a completely blank, expressionless face, and the make-up did all the work for her. Her appearance was that of a large mechanical doll, like one of those tiny dancers who stand atop a small mirror on a musical jewellery box, and who spin in slow pirouettes when the key is wound up and the music plays.

Which is just what she did.

In the side of the box on which she was standing was a large silver key. Next to the key was a slot for money. Onlookers who wished the dancer to dance went up to the box, made a show of turning the key (while their friends and relatives took photographs) and then dropped money into the slot.

As the money fell, some contrivance within the box set off a concealed tape player and music would begin. The piece was usually, though not always, the 'Dance of the Little Swans', from Tchaikovsky's *Swan Lake*, or sometimes the 'Waltz of the Flowers', from *The Nutcracker Suite*.

When the music began, the dancer would revolve. She was elegant and graceful and must, at some point in her life, have studied dance with a view to a more serious career than balancing on a box for the entertainment of tourists.

It was difficult to know precisely how old she was

under her make-up, but from her figure she seemed to be still quite young, if not in the very first bloom of youth, and she was, in her way, rather beautiful.

It was not exactly a conventional beauty, however, and some people might have disputed that it was beauty at all. But to those who had an eye for the unusual and the idiosyncratic, it was a beauty as rare as a desert flower.

As the music played, the ballerina continued to dance, revolving upon her small stage for exactly one minute. After sixty seconds, the gadget hidden in the box cut off the music, and the dancer froze just as she was.

In some ways her ability to maintain her position at the end of the dance was the most remarkable part of the performance. She could hold a pirouette for minutes on end, without any visible effort. Or if, at the end of the music, she found herself balanced upon one foot, with her arms outstretched, then she could hold that same position too, seemingly indefinitely – or at least until some kind onlooker took pity on her and wound up the key again and dropped some more money into the box, so that she could move.

Her audience, not unexpectedly, consisted mostly of tourists. The locals had seen it all before and would no doubt see it again, want to or not. They passed her by as though dancing statues were the most common thing in the world. Some of the locals knew her, but would not dream of calling to her. She was, after all, at her profession, and not to be interrupted while at work. Behind the tutu and the make-up lay the economic imperative; even one as beautiful as the dancer with the tear-drop eyes still had her bills to pay, her rent to find, her food to buy, and all the usual harsh realities to deal with. Life made no exceptions just for looks – only allowances.

But one spectator was not a tourist, and although he had seen the performance many times, its novelty had yet to wear off. He watched the dancer almost every day, with undiminished fascination. Yet for all that he was so entranced by what he saw, he had so far held back from personally stepping forwards, making the show of winding the key and dropping the necessary coins into the slot. He preferred to leave that to others and to remain on the sidelines.

He maybe had good reason for this. A less self-conscious man might not have been so bothered, but Ernst Eckmann was constantly aware of the abnormality of his appearance and did not wish to be reminded of it by the eyes of others. He had had quite enough of that at school. He didn't like children – well, as individuals, maybe, but not as a species. When he had been a child, they had made his life misery, and now that he was an adult, they sometimes continued to do so with their frank, open-eyed curiosity and their uninhibited, unguarded remarks.

'Mummy – why is that man so *funny?*'

Or worse. Even from adults too sometimes, as he walked home from the gallery, along the alleyways and streets, through the arcades and the parks, passing crowds of merry-makers, some the worse for drink, some the better for it, but not many.

'Hey, look! It's a garden gnome!'

There was no fatuous insult that he hadn't heard before. The general imagination didn't seem to run to much originality. Nor was his lack of height his only

30

handicap, though he was not actually that small. What made him appear so was that he seemed stunted, unfinished. His neck barely seemed to exist and his overly large head seemed to grow directly out of his chest.

It was useless to say that none of this was his fault. It was of no help for Eckmann to know that his misfortunes were a mere accident of birth. Knowledge of causes doesn't make pain go away. Nor was there much consolation for him in his awareness of his own unique and considerable talent. If anything it made it all worse.

A man of his genius should have been revered, respected. But he felt that his work was not taken seriously, and he felt himself reviled. He perceived himself as repugnant and assumed that he created revulsion in others, even when he did not. Many people treated him with kindness, and would have treated him with friendship. But that moment of shock, of surprise, of first encounter was always there. And it was something he could never forgive them for.

But she was different. The girl on the box. She had never once looked upon him and recoiled or turned her eyes away from him as he stood there in the crowd. It was almost as if she hadn't even seen him, and yet he knew that she had, that she saw him every time he was there.

Most men would have taken the dancer's failure to react to their constant presence as a rebuff, or at least as a sign of indifference. But Eckmann was encouraged by it, and took her failure to be repelled as something more positive. On occasion, even as an actual sign of affection for him.

He even indulged himself in the notion that she somehow found him attractive. Or that she would find him attractive, if she only came to know him better. It would be quite ridiculous, of course, for him to expect her or anyone ever to love him for his appearance. But for someone to love him for his talent, for his unique and unquestionable genius . . . yes, that was surely possible.

Weren't there precedents for it? Many precedents. Beautiful women in the arms of plain, even ugly men. Ugly men of considerable wealth, or ugly men of indomitable personality, of great fame, or of unique and undeniable talent and achievement. And it was in this latter category which Eckmann, with some justification, placed himself.

And they had something in common too, didn't they? Weren't they both outcasts? The possessors of unconventional talents and abilities – the artist and the dancer? And wasn't it true that to an extent everyone who stepped outside the normal boundaries was excluded, was even to a degree despised, reviled? Even someone as beautiful as her.

A rumble of thunder split the cloud and rain began to fall. The crowd dispersed and the drops of rain fell upon the solitary dancer. People scuttled for shelter, but she remained where she was, immobile, like a statue again, waiting for someone to wind the key, to drop the money into the box.

A feeling of pity filled Eckmann's heart, pity mixed with tenderness. He wondered at first why she didn't stop her act, come down from the box and get out of the rain. Maybe find a raincoat from somewhere – she must have had a bag of belongings, concealed under the box.

Then he understood why she carried on: she hadn't earned enough money yet. Not enough for the day. And soon another street performer would be along to claim his time and place, and she would have to leave. And that would be it until tomorrow.

So rain or no rain, she held on, determined to do her hour, in the hope that someone else would wind the key and pay the coin, and she would earn the money for that day.

The rain fell more heavily; the square emptied. The waiters came out with hooked poles and pulled down the canopies to cover the tables. Here and there the canvas was split and the rain dribbled through and plip-plopped on to the zinc tables and into the empty glass ashtrays.

Still the dancer stood, alone and unmoving. The rain trickled down over her, seeming to mix real tears with the painted ones. A solitary drop fell from the end of her nose, but still she didn't move.

Eckmann watched her. They were quite alone now. He was a solitary spectator, an audience of one. His heart felt bigger than he was, and pity filled every part of it. It welled up in him – the tragedy, the pathos of the scene. That one so beautiful should have a drop of rain falling from the end of her nose – that was the tragedy and the pathos.

He felt in his pocket. He took out his wallet and looked to see what was in it. There was no short-age of money, anyway. He extracted two notes of large denomination, folded them into a taper, and self-consciously walked across the square towards the frozen dancer on the music box.

It was agony for him, a kind of mental torture, this walk across the square, this deliberately putting himself forwards as an object of attention. The customers in the cafés watched him absently – a welcome distraction as they waited for their drinks.

He tried to walk calmly, but his heart pounded and he could feel sweat running down his back. He swallowed and tried to control the trembling in his hands as he neared the dancer. He stopped by the large, pretend key in the side of the silver box. The wings of the key were within his grasp.

Feeling immensely foolish, he turned the key a few times. Why he went through this performance, he didn't know. It wasn't necessary. He could simply have dropped the money into the box. And yet it was necessary too. It maintained the integrity of things. It meant that things were properly done, that the dancer was treated in the prescribed and respectful way.

He let go of the key. He looked up. The ballerina's costume was heavy with rain now. She went on staring ahead of her, seeing, yet not seeing him, letting his squat ugliness make no difference.

He raised the folded banknotes, wanting her to see that it was not a coin he had, but something more, something special.

'For you,' he whispered. 'For you.'

And he dropped the banknotes into the box.

And waited for the music.

But it did not come.

Of course, of course. The weight, the weight. The

mechanism needed the weight of a coin to trigger it. Of course. Obvious.

Frantically, he searched in his pockets for a coin. Would you believe it though. Nothing there. Nothing in his coat either. No small change at all. Just more banknotes. A wallet full of credit cards and bank notes and not a single, solitary coin.

He felt himself blush. He burned crimson with shame and apology. Wrong. It had gone wrong. Across the square he could see faces, watching him from under the shelter of the canopies. Were they laughing? Laughing at him again? At the funny little man who stood in the rain.

He looked up at the dancer. Did she know? Did she realize that he had put the money in? That it wasn't his fault? Maybe in trying to be too generous . . . that was all. If she didn't know, she wouldn't dance for him . . . but she couldn't dance until the music started, that was the way it was done.

He tried to catch her eyes, but her gaze seemed set on some distant view.

'I'm sorry,' he whispered. 'I'm sorry.'

Then, still burning with his own sense of shame and clumsiness and of things improperly done, of conventions broken, he turned to walk back across the square, across the acres of vast, empty paving, watched by all the eyes.

But as he went, the dancer started to move. She came alive for him, and revolved upon the music box in a wonderful arabesque. She danced in the silence and the rain, and it was the most wonderful thing, the most superb, beautiful and wonderful thing he had even seen. The loveliest moment he had ever had.

It was as if behind a glass wall somewhere, other people watched them. But really there was only the two of them in the whole world. He, and she, the marionette upon the music box, dancing in the silence and the rain. He heard the squeak of her slipper, he felt the rain soaking his face. And then she had stopped. She was frozen again, awaiting the next coin.

'Thank you,' he said. 'That was beautiful. Thank you very much.'

And not really knowing why, not knowing if she was in his debt or he was in hers, he gave her a small bow, and then he walked off across the square in the direction of the abbey and towards the cobbled streets behind it, where he kept his studio and his gallery.

As he went, he kept muttering something to himself, the same thing, over and over.

'She danced for me. She danced for me. She really danced for me. For me.'

He seemed to have quite forgotten that she danced for whoever put their money into the box, that she had danced for him only as a marionette dances for a customer, not as a woman dances for a man.

'For me! She danced for me!'

And he rubbed his hands together with a kind of schoolboy glee. As he came to the door of the gallery he took keys from his pocket, unlocked the door, went inside, and changed the *Closed* sign to *Open*.

As he reached up to turn the sign round, he looked like a small boy struggling to do something that really ought to have been left to somebody taller and older. Yet he wasn't a boy. Hadn't been for a long while. He was an adult, with the mind of an adult, and with

36

the feelings and passions and thoughts and desires of a man.

In the abbey square, the clock rang the hour. The bedraggled dancer got down from her music box as a young man in spangled tights and a T-shirt with stars upon it approached across the flagstones.

He exchanged a few words with her as she up-ended the box she had been standing on and counted up the money she had earned.

'Good session, Poppea?'

'Not bad.'

'Let's hope the rain stops.'

'It will. It's easing off already.'

'See you tomorrow then.'

'Bye.'

The dancer had put a coat on to cover her costume. Her box – which she had made herself and was rather proud of – turned out to have wheels fitted to it, so she pocketed the money she had made and wheeled her equipment away.

She made a rather bizarre spectacle, with her box on wheels and her tear-dropped face and her pink tutu puffing up under her coat. But nobody paid much attention to her. She seemed quite ordinary in her eccentricity.

She stopped off at a bakery on the way back to her flat to buy a roll for lunch. Once home, she ate, changed, washed the make-up from her face, and got ready to go to her other job – teaching dance in a local academy to ballet-struck schoolgirls.

She counted the money again before she went. It had been a good morning. Somebody had given her a lot of money. But that happened sometimes. It wasn't so unusual. Oh, and the music mechanism must have got stuck again. It didn't start up once, did it? She'd look at that this evening.

She took the money with her. She'd do some shopping later on her way back. As for Eckmann, she had already forgotten him.

In the square the juggler picked up a machete. He demonstrated its sharpness by slicing through a piece of paper with its blade.

People started to get interested.

'Stand back if you would, sir, madam. I wouldn't want anyone to get hurt.'

He took up two more identical machetes and began to juggle with all three of them. The silver blades flashed and glinted in the sunshine. The clouds had gone now, the rain had stopped.

People stood and watched the juggler. Some wondered if he might accidentally catch one of the machetes by the blade instead of the handle. He might even slice his hand off. So they went on watching as he went on juggling. They just couldn't seem to tear themselves away.

Like the rest of us, they lived in hope.

Robert, the Artist

In the evening a warm glow of twilight came and the abbey square began to change. Summer brought long evenings. The sun didn't suddenly dip and vanish as in the far south; here, with the approach of evening, long shadows would streak the courtyard, while the towers and spires and gargoyles lay in elongated silhouette upon the ground.

In autumn and winter, gas burners were lit in the restaurant courtyards and in summer the diners swatted the insects away with their menu cards.

The entertainers had gone, and in their place came others, small traders with suitcases which turned into tables and which were filled with homemade jewellery. Vendors sold chilled drinks and beer. Women with selections of coloured thread set up chairs and offered to braid your hair for a moderate fee. The takers were usually teenage girls, or foreign exchange students, whose friends and boyfriends waited patiently and watched with admiration as the braider wrapped and wove colour into the girl's hair.

People walked past, going nowhere, just strolling aimlessly, absorbing the atmosphere. They stopped at a café, drank an espresso, ordered a beer or a tumbler of wine.

Three men appeared with a suitcase. They opened it and rested it on a wooden spike. Inside the case was a green baize interior. One of the men threw three cards upon it, two tens and a red queen. He flipped the cards over, skilfully moved them around and then challenged the second man to guess where the queen was, while the third man kept watch from a distance.

A tourist came by. They involved him in the game, and after letting him win a few times, fleeced him for all the money in his wallet. They cleaned him out. He started to wonder now, began to ask questions in his imperfect English. Maybe these men weren't as friendly or as honest as they looked. Maybe they were all in cahoots. Maybe . . .

The third man let out a short whistle. Two policemen were crossing the abbey square. In seconds the baize table was a suitcase again, the spike was a walking stick, the tourist was left with empty pockets and the men had gone – all part of the night-time entertainments.

Some shops remained open, even at this hour – jewellers, the confectioners, the perfumers, the postcard shop. Others had long since closed; their owners had done the day's accounts, balanced the books and gone home.

The doors of Eckmann's gallery were locked, the sign read closed, but the light in his studio still burned. Sometimes he crossed to the window and looked down into the streets from his elevated height, or gazed at the picture of the city upon his camera obscura.

His stomach gurgled. He was hungry now, but hunger meant he had to go out into the world. He had to go out to be small and insignificant again, whereas here he was neither of those things. Here he was accepted, looked up to even, admired. Here his genius was recognized and appreciated, in the apparently bare and empty studio. No one talked to him. He talked occasionally, but it was really for his own benefit, just to drive the silence away.

Every minute or two he did a little more work. He could only do so in short bursts, the work was so fragile and delicate. The moment had to be just right, or a week's work could be ruined by one sudden, miscalculated move.

In the abbey square the bats flitted from one side to the next. Mothers told their children to be careful as they walked, to hurry or the bats might become entangled in their hair. But of course it never happened, and probably never had or would. The bats were too agile and alert, with eyes and radar. Pigeons pouted among the breadcrumbs and waddled under benches looking for scraps.

In the abbey itself, a small orchestra was playing and a choir singing. Admission was by programme only, but someone had left a door open and the music wafted out into the square.

Darkness began to settle and a handful of artists appeared with their chalks and easels and sketch pads. They carried folding chairs with canvas backs, and small stools for their sitters to perch on while their portraits were drawn. There was also an extra chair for a friend to sit in, to chat, to smoke a cigarette, maybe wait to be the next as the drawing was done.

They set up the examples of their work. Some worked in charcoal, some watercolours, a few in

41

acrylics or oils. The specimens they displayed tended to be of famous and celebrated people – pop stars, Hollywood actors, sportsmen, icons from thirty, forty, fifty years ago: Marilyn Monroe, James Dean, a young Marlon Brando, Che Guavara, Bob Marley, the Beatles. Their portraits had been copied from photographs.

The promenaders circulated amongst the artists. Very few put themselves forward as subjects for portraits, much as it may secretly have been what they wanted. They had to be urged and cajoled by their friends and loved ones, or by the artist himself.

Each artist had his own means of persuasion. Some were great extroverts, full of jokes and flattery, both delivered with such good humour that they would have a sitter in the chair in no time. And they would keep them amused all the time the portrait was being painted, and send them away smiling and happy, even if the likeness was not all that wonderful.

Others had no gift of the gab. They worked in silence, or with minimal conversation, concentrating on the job in hand. But their portraits were as good, and anyway, it was not every sitter who wanted to be talked at, some preferred to sit in silence.

Among the portrait painters were a few caricaturists. They immediately latched on to one or two of their sitter's dominant features – a snub nose, a collection of freckles – and used them to great effect, enlarging, distorting them, making them bigger than life. Although sometimes grotesque, the results were nearly always appreciated. The sitter's friends and relatives would sneak looks and emit guffaws and sniggers while the cartoon was being done. The sitter waited impatiently, trying to hold the pose, but dying to see the picture. Then there were gasps of mock outrage, howls of laughter, but seldom, if ever, any real anger. For whatever the artist may have done to their faces, he had flattered them just the same. He had affirmed their individuality, turned them into personalities.

A man appeared now and set up his chairs and easels among the rest. He must have been around thirty years old. He was above medium height, but not tall. He was quite broad-shouldered and thick set. His eyes and complexion were dark, his hair was black and curled, and although his face was pleasant, even good-looking, in a slightly unkempt, unshaven way, he had the aura of one prone to melancholy, of occasional pessimism even. He seemed like a man of moods.

He nodded to one or two friends and acquaintances, artists like himself.

'Robert . . .'

'Hello, Robert . . .'

'I'll move up, make some room for you . . .'

Although the artists were in direct competition with each other, in the summer at least, there was enough business to go round for everyone, so they could afford to be friendly. In the winter, things weren't so cosy.

What distinguished Robert from the others, however, was not so much his appearance as the fact that he wasn't alone. He was accompanied by a child, a young boy, who, from the look of his curly dark hair and dark eyes, was plainly the artist's son.

The boy helped his father to carry the necessary

43

equipment, and on arrival at their designated spot, which by tacit agreement with the other artists was reserved for him – as their spots were for them – he helped him set up the chairs and easels and the samples of work.

These few square feet which the artists worked from would be allowed to stand empty for two successive nights. If, on the third night, the artist did not appear to re-stake his claim, then the spot was regarded as a free area and up for grabs to anyone who might regard the vacant spot as better than his own.

Should the original occupant of the spot re-appear on the fourth night, he would have to accept a place somewhere out on the periphery of the square, away from the main passage of tourists, and where the light was not so good; from there he'd have to inveigle his way back in again.

Should he attempt to take his spot back on that fourth night, he would be opposed by all. Fist fights had been known to break out over such matters, but the aggrieved party always had to back down in the face of universal opposition. It was their mutual way of acknowledging that all artists had a right to live but that the world owed none of them a living.

When it came to attracting customers, Robert Mallan was plainly too taciturn a man to cajole passers-by into availing themselves of his portraiture services.

Not for him the well-used joke, the tried and tested shaft of humour which had served well and proved successful so many times before. Not for him the ingratiating word, the attempt to charm. There was in

44

him the deep stubbornness of his ancestry. His origins were in the moorlands and the hills, where poverty and pride once went hand in hand, where each man had his dignity, and often his own inner anger against some unspecified aspect of an unjust world. Rebellion was in his blood, and his attitude towards his potential customers was that they could take it or leave it. And if they did not want his services, then the loss was theirs.

Coupled with his pride, and to a certain extent inflaming it, was his contempt for a world too blinkered to recognize his talent – and he was an unusually able artist. But his strength was also his weakness. He was too unique, too individual, too quirky and uncategorizable. He would never please the gallery owners, the magazine publishers, the arbiters of artistic taste. He knew it, and was both angry and proud of it. He was proud of his independence, of his refusal to compromise, and yet he was unhappy too, knowing that his work would never be recognized in his lifetime, and that on his death it would be swallowed up and forgotten.

In the meantime, he made a living. He set his own hours, he earned his own money, he called no man his boss. Not even those who sat for him. A client, after all, is not an employer in an artist's eyes. The dialogue between artist and sitter is more a conversation of equals. If either is superior, the artist thinks it is him.

When the man looked at his son, however, his face changed. The edge of hardness vanished, his patience became almost infinite. It was hard to know if he loved the child for himself alone, or for the look of his mother in him; if it was two people he loved there, or

45

one. But were you to ask after the child's mother, or to wonder how it was that the artist was bringing up his son alone, or whether she might be returning soon, you would have been told to mind your own bloody business. And it was advice you would probably have taken.

From some deep sadness in both the son's and the father's eyes, you may have thought that she was indeed forever lost to them, and they grieved for her deeply. But nobody knew for certain if the mother had died, or if the relationship between the parents had simply disintegrated and she had moved away, or had fallen in love with another, or had wanted more from life than a husband and child, or what had happened. But no one expected her imminent return. That was just how it was.

Once the easels and chairs were set up in the square, once the paints, charcoals, brushes and the samples of work were ready, the same routine was followed every time.

The boy, Christopher, would sit on one of the canvas stools and open a book. He was a great reader, and had a different book with him every night, sometimes two or three. The public library could never keep pace with him, so his father might buy him a dozen or so tattered paperbacks from the second-hand bookshops which operated at the fringes of the square.

They weren't always books entirely appropriate for a child of his age, but he read them anyway. They weren't always fiction either. There were books on science too – medicine, biology, astronomy, everything. His father always took a look at the blurb on the back cover first, just to make sure that it was nothing too racy. But his definition of 'racy' was fairly broad.

The boy was not just a reader though, but a re-reader as well – from inclination as well as from necessity. He returned to the same books over and over – classics, modern favourites, science fiction, children's adventure stories.

Once or twice there had been complaints from well-meaning busybodies about the father keeping the boy up so late, out in the square. Social workers had called at the house, child welfare officers had investigated.

Robert had always been extremely polite and co-operative. He may have had his pride and his temper but he also had the sense to see that any outburst from him would only have exacerbated the situation and might even have provoked the bureaucracy he despised into taking the child away from him. He knew they had the power to do it, and so he would smile and nod and welcome them in, offer them tea and co-operate in every way.

He showed them his son's school reports, and they would have to admit that he was doing well, that his reading age was well in advance of his contemporaries, that he seemed happy and well cared for and that there was no evidence of any mistreatment or neglect.

And besides, as the father pointed out, what else was he to do? He couldn't afford a childminder, he couldn't leave the boy on his own, and he had to work. He tried working during the day on occasion, but usually the business was simply not there, or not enough of it for him to earn a living. People weren't in the right frame of mind in the daytime. They had sights to see, places to visit, open-topped double-decker bus rides in five different languages to take. People needed to feel well fed, relaxed, reflective, at leisure, before they would sit and have a portrait done.

So he made a few promises, murmured an apology or two, and the well-meaning bureaucrat would go away. Then he rattled the dishes in the sink, cursed the do-gooders and the nosy parkers who had brought this trouble upon them, which they could well do without. And all the while the boy would just sit in the corner and read his book with an unflappable good humour which he must have inherited from his mother, if anyone at all, because his father seemed so singularly lacking in it.

But then the artist would look across the room, and when he saw his son sitting there, glued to his book as he always was, with his tousled hair that neither a comb nor a brush could ever straighten out (not that they were often given the trouble of trying), for some quite illogical and impenetrable reason, he would collapse in laughter. And soon, the two of them were wrestling and rolling and tickling each other and hooting like they were both children, like brothers rather than father and son.

Quite why the boy could make him laugh and draw him from his moods and make him feel suddenly happy for a while without so much as a word or a gesture, the man couldn't tell. And quite why his father could make him feel so loved, the boy couldn't have told you either. Except that he *was* loved – both were, each by the other. It was a simple, unstated fact.

Sometimes, though, when the night's work was

over, and the boy was asleep, the father would peer into his room and wonder what would become of his son if something should happen to him. Who would care for him? Look after him? Love him? Poppea maybe. Could he ask her? Would that be too much of an intimacy, an imposition? What would such a request imply?

Worry and weariness would descend on him then, and the small hours of the night would bring fear for the future and all their gloomy intimations of mortality and age, of poverty and infirmity. But then morning came, and the child woke, and everything was well again.

So out in the square now the easel was set up, the chairs had been put out, the samples of work were on display. The boy opened his book, the artist took his sketch pad, picked up a crayon and began to draw his son.

He had done this innumerable times, and yet no two of the portraits were ever the same. As Robert drew, passers-by would stop to linger, to watch over his shoulder as the portrait took shape. His style was not entirely naturalistic. He did not draw an exact likeness, yet was somehow able to capture it – the essence of the sitter. It was a wonderful talent, it made people smile with delight. The portrait was, representationally, not quite right, yet it was more accurate, more truthful and revealing than any photograph.

'Yes, that's it. That's it. That's absolutely right. That's him to a T!'

People would nod, nudge, smile, turn to each other. The portrait of the boy was somehow so utterly and completely *right*.

'Er, excuse me . . . when you've finished . . .'

'Of course, take a seat. I'll be right with you. Christopher, there you are.'

He handed the boy his finished portrait. Christopher smiled, folded it, tucked it away into the pages of his book.

'And now you, madam . . . and you as well, sir? Take a seat there, if you would. Chris, give the man your seat.'

'No, no, that's all right.'

'No, it's OK . . . Chris . . .'

'Sure.'

He took his book and wandered a short distance away to sit on the abbey steps. The son et lumière was underway now. He read by the gleam of the spotlights while his father got to work. Soon he had one portrait completed and another underway. More customers gathered around him.

'And you, my dear? Yes, of course. Sketch or water-colour? The price is there – as shown. You may have to wait a short while. Is that all right? Have a coffee and come back. I'll remember you. Yes, twenty minutes or so. I'll know your place in the queue.'

Soon he had sitters all stacked up, like planes waiting to land. He could go on all night, until the last of the bars closed its doors. But he kept an eye on his son and on the time and he wouldn't work beyond a certain point.

'Sorry, sir, last one now. I'll be here tomorrow if you're still here. Yes, OK. Sorry about that.'

Christopher closed his book. The son et lumière had finished. The spotlights were extinguished, except for one or two which remained on all night. The pale

50

yellow pavement lights illuminated the gargoyles. The boy yawned and looked about. He stood and stretched. From where he was, he could see the attic rooms of Mr Eckmann's gallery. A light was on up in the studio, but it abruptly went out. Then a light came on in the stairwell. Then that light went off as well. Mr Eckmann must have finished and be going home too.

The last portrait was done and paid for. Robert rolled up the drawing and slid it into one of the cardboard tubes that were included in the price.

'Stop it getting crumpled. There you go.'

'Thank you.'

'Good night.'

The tourists went. The hour rang out on the abbey clock. Christopher helped his father pack his things away, to collapse the stools, take down the easels, put the tops back on the tubes of paint.

'How are you, stranger?'

Christopher turned and smiled. A young woman had come up behind his father and put her arms around him.

'Poppea!'

Christopher didn't know if it was her real name or not. It probably wasn't. Most of the street performers had made-up names, as if they didn't much like the ones they had been given, or as if they were trying to leave the past behind, and a change of name would help them to shake it off, or prevent it from following them.

Robert swivelled, saw that it was who he had expected it to be, embraced and kissed her.

'How are you? I called round earlier. You weren't in,' he said.

51

'Working. Hi, Chris.'

Christopher smiled shyly. He liked her. His dad liked her, he knew that and went along with it. She wasn't like the others, the rich ones, the tourists, who would take them out for dinner on the balcony of the Grand Hotel sometimes, when he had to put his jacket on and watch his manners and wonder about all the forks.

Poppea was different. Poppea was nice. She was like them. Lived on her wits. Dad had done her portrait once. Christopher wasn't supposed to have seen it but he did. She didn't have any clothes on. She didn't care. She even let his dad put it in for the exhibition. He sold three paintings that day. He could have sold the one of Poppea with no clothes on too, but it wasn't for sale. You wouldn't have realized it was Poppea if you didn't know her. Her face was in shadow. He could easily have sold it though. It was called *The Dancer*. Mr Eckmann had wanted to buy it. He'd wanted to take it home, he said, not put it in his gallery. He wanted to buy it for himself.

And here he came now, Mr Eckmann himself, waddling along penguin style across the square, heading for his customary table in the restaurant, where he would eat a late supper before going to bed, or returning to his studio to work.

'Hello, Mr Eckmann.'

He looked up, saw the boy, and smiled.

'Christopher!'

They liked each other, the boy and the little man. They were about the same height, though maybe Eckmann just had the edge on it, but not for much longer, not at the rate Christopher was growing.

52

Eckmann also liked the boy because he had no judgement or condemnation in him, no aversion, no recoil. His mind, like his father's portraits, seemed to see only the essence of people – not the superficial exteriors, but the truth inside.

'How are the sculptures, Mr Eckmann? How's the gallery?' the boy asked.

'Fine, Christopher, fine. Busy, you know, busy, yes, yes.'

'Any new ones?'

'Soon, soon.'

'Can I see them?'

'Of course.'

'When?'

'When they're finished.'

'Can I watch you make them some time?'

'Maybe, maybe. I need to concentrate . . . I can't be distracted.'

'Please.'

'Maybe. We'll see.'

Eckmann stopped in his tracks when he saw her. There she was, the dancer, talking to the boy's father. Eckmann blushed crimson with embarrassment to the very roots of his hair. But who cared? Who was interested, who would even notice in the dark?

He recovered his composure. Would she remember? Would she acknowledge him? Would she recall how he gave her the money, the folded-up banknotes? How he dropped them into the box, only they didn't set the music off, but she danced for him anyway, in the silence and the rain.

Yes, how she danced for him only. And as she had danced, he had pictured her, as she'd been in the portrait he had wanted to buy. The unusual and yet strangely beautiful picture which captured not only the beauty *of* her, but the beauty *in* her. The one in which she had nothing on.

She had danced for him, in that public square, and yet he knew – and she knew, they both knew, surely – that no moment had been more private or intimate than that moment when . . .

'I'd better go then. I'll see you tomorrow, Robert.'

'Yes, OK. Bye.'

She was leaving.

'Bye, Christopher. Oh, bye, Mr . . .'

She waved vaguely to the small man. She knew she ought to know him, but she had forgotten his name. She then kissed the artist, ruffled his son's hair, and was gone.

They all watched her go. Eckmann was the last to take his eyes off her. He looked up at the other man, and for a second experienced an almost murderous hatred. He hated him not for his talent – which Eckmann's could easily equal and excel. No, he hated him for his looks, for his dark hair, for his brooding eyes, for his thick-set shoulders, but more than anything for the fact that the dancer had kissed him.

Robert grew aware of Eckmann looking at him.

'Hello, Ernst. Done for the day?'

The wave of bitter, jealous hatred subsided. Eckmann was himself again.

'Robert. Yes, just off for some supper. And you?'

'Yes. Got to get home.'

'Would you care to join me for a drink first?'

Robert nodded towards his son.

'I would, but I'd better get him to bed.'

'Of course, of course. Another time, maybe.'

'Sure.'

'OK then. I'll be seeing you.'

'Bye, Mr Eckmann.'

'Good night, Christopher. Straight to bed now.'

'You won't forget.'

'I won't forget.'

'You said you'd let me see the new ones.'

'Soon as they're done.'

Hand in hand they crossed the square, trundling their belongings with them. Eckmann watched. The nauseous wave of jealousy engulfed him again. To hold hands like that, with your own child, your own son, to walk along together, hand in hand, side by side. To love. To know you were loved in return. Unquestioningly, unconditionally loved. It was unfair, so unfair. What had he ever done to be denied that? What crime had he ever committed, other than to be born a little different from others? What woman would find him attractive? What woman would bear him a child?

He turned his back on them, bitterly and maybe self-pityingly, reflecting that in turning his back on the world, it was no more than the world had many times done to him.

He crossed the square to the restaurant where the waiters knew him and usually kept him a table. He preferred to eat late not for any digestive reasons, but because there were fewer people around then and fewer curious eyes to stare at him.

But tonight he was unlucky. As he sat at his table and studied the menu, gnawing on a breadstick and sipping a glass of red wine, a family of tourists walked past. A small, tired-looking girl who should long ago

55

have been in bed, caught sight of him. She stopped and stared at him with frank, innocent curiosity.

'Mummy!' she demanded in a loud ringing voice which echoed all round the square. 'Look at that man! Why is he so peculiar?'

The girl's mother did not reprimand her for her rudeness, nor did she offer Eckmann any apology. She merely said, 'Come along. Don't dawdle. It's late.' And dragged her away.

The waiter came to take Eckmann's order. His face registered nothing, but Eckmann knew that he had heard.

'Are you ready to order, sir?'

Eckmann looked out over the top of his menu to where the child was being bundled away across the square. He would never have thought that it was possible to hate a complete stranger so much, especially a child, a guileless, totally innocent child. But he did hate her. He could quite cheerfully have killed her.

The waiter cleared his throat.

'Your order, sir?'

Eckmann gave his order.

'And some more wine,' he said.

'A glass?' the waiter asked.

'A bottle,' Eckmann told him.

The waiter hesitated, as if to say something, as if he were about to proffer a little unsolicited advice. But if such had been his intention, he changed his mind.

'A bottle it is, sir,' he said. 'I'll bring it now.'

And he went to fetch it.

'Maybe better make that half a bottle,' Eckmann called after him.

The waiter nodded imperceptibly in agreement.

Mr Eckmann

The main attraction of the town was the Roman baths, where hot springs bubbled up into pools built nearly two thousand years ago, but which were still as civilized – if not more civilized – than ever.

Then there were the museums to visit: the children's toy museum; the costume museum, where the clothes of rich and poor were preserved in dimly lit glass cabinets, remnants of other eras and of less egalitarian societies.

Next there were the inevitable churches to look at, the abbey and its chapels. When bored with that, there was the old market hall to see, the antique shops, the cafés, the theatres, where ageing film and faded television stars took to the boards in try-outs hopefully headed for the West End.

Then there were the expensive and fashionable art galleries, with swan-like women perched at desks, waving with an elegant hand to indicate that you were welcome to view what was on display, but frankly, my dear, she doubted (if appearances were anything to go by) that you could possibly afford to buy any of it.

Then there were the lesser galleries, where more affordable talents were on display. Here were pen and ink drawings, silkscreens and watercolours of local scenes and landmarks. Proper art, you might say, traditional drawing, painting as a souvenir. Some of the drawings had been turned into cards and postcards.

And then there was Eckmann's gallery which was very different – in fact, unique – and which distinguished itself from all the others in three important respects.

The first of these was that there was nothing to buy, the second was that there was little to see, and the third was that you had to pay to go in and see it.

A gallery with nothing to buy, with little to see, and you had to pay to get in – who could resist it? It did good business all summer long.

The entrance was at street level. Here was a small ticket desk, a cash register and one or two souvenirs for sale.

A painting or two adorned the walls – usually the work of local artists which Eckmann had bought for his own collection. Then a sign, an arrow and a red silk rope suspended between two small posts assisted visitors in finding their way to the cast-iron spiral staircase which led up to the gallery proper.

It was unusual for an artist to own a gallery for the purpose of exhibiting his own work. In some ways it had the odour of vanity, or even desperation about it, that Eckmann had been forced to exhibit his own work as no one else would display it. But that was not the case.

Eckmann was no Bohemian. In his eyes the traditional and legendary financial incompetence of the artist was but a romantic convention. The public, it seemed, liked to have its artists poor. It liked them drunk and dissipated, it liked them up in garrets. It liked them to live out its own fantasies. It liked them to be the way they were supposed to be in the films.

But these were all conventions for which Eckmann had no time.

He had understood even while still a student that the dependency of the artist upon the dealer and the gallery owner was primarily due to lack of confidence and the need for approval.

Artists were often uncertain. One day they believed they were geniuses, the next that their work was worthless and glorious in nothing but failure. Supreme arrogance alternated with terrible self-doubt. And dealership was the exploitation of uncertainty. The gallery owner offered access to the public, the promise of a reputation. He took a huge commission or maybe even paid the artist nothing at all and accepted his work only on sale or return. He therefore stood to gain much and lose little, and of the price in the catalogue, the artist would receive but a small proportion.

In his early days, Eckmann had trundled his work around the galleries, like any other young artist. He had shown his portfolio, he had had the odd piece accepted, but he had soon seen that there was no future here. He saw that he would have to go into business for himself – for he had nobody else to rely on.

Eckmann's name was of Dutch origin, but he was thoroughly English, as was his accent. His grandfather was from Amsterdam. His father settled in England and married his mother, an Englishwoman. He gave his son the name Ernst in honour of his own father. But he was always disappointed in him. Ernst was never what he had wanted. But that was in the past. Both of his parents were dead now and Ernst Eckmann was quite alone.

Eckmann's work was painstakingly done. The time and labour involved were extensive, his failure rate high. It took him so long to produce a piece he was satisfied with, that had he merely sold it, it would not have brought him sufficient income. He would have run out of money before he produced the next work.

So he hit on the idea of not even trying to sell his work at all. Instead, he would charge people to come and see it.

When Eckmann first went to the bank to borrow the money with which to open his gallery, the woman behind the Small Business Loans desk treated him with extreme suspicion.

Here was this strange, small, overweight man in front of her, perched on the edge of the chair like a well-scrubbed schoolboy in his grey, special occasion suit and sober tie. He had his business plan, he had his silver pen. He claimed to be an artist – and she had seen her fair share of those before. They usually came along with vague plans for building castles in the air and just needed to borrow the money for the foundations.

But this was different. Eckmann had no portfolio of work with him. No leather folder containing his sketches and paintings. And yet he leaned forwards and asked, 'Would you like to see a sample – of my work? It's very specialized, you see. Quite unique, even if I say so myself.'

The manager did not wish to see his work, but politeness demanded that she nod her head and say, if brusquely, 'Of course. If you think it will make any difference.' Implying by her tone that it would not, and as soon as she had seen his work, she could get rid of him with a clear conscience.

But then Eckmann reached into the pocket of his grey jacket and took out . . . well, nothing.

At least nothing of any apparent importance. Just a small glass dome on a black plastic base. It was the size of one of those novelties which contain things like Christmas scenes and snowmen and snowflakes suspended in some clear viscous liquid, so that when you shake the dome, the snow languidly falls.

Once the snow has settled, you shake the dome again to ensure it wasn't a fluke the first time. Then you do it a few more times. Then you get utterly bored with it, put the thing on a shelf somewhere, and forget all about it. Until you rediscover it, years later, when the liquid has all leaked out, or evaporated. And you hold it up, and think about the past.

He pushed the dome across the desk, inviting the bank manager to pick it up for her own inspection. She did. The dome looked empty. There seemed to be nothing particular there, except perhaps for a grain of sand.

Eckmann smiled. He reached into his other pocket and took out a jeweller's glass, a thick heavy lens, which you could screw into the socket of your eye. He placed that on the table and invited the woman to take it.

Hesitating, she reached out and picked it up. The magnification of the lens was as intense as that of a small microscope. She fitted the jeweller's glass into her right eye, picked up the small glass dome and peered at it through the lens.

For a second she could still see nothing. Then she gasped – in wonder, in amazement, at the sheer impossibility of it. Yet it was possible. It was there, right in front of her, at first invisible then suddenly clearly visible, but just as impossible as ever.

It was an incredibly minute, yet entirely wonderful and exact sculpture of the Taj Mahal of India. It was the size of a grain of sand.

She looked at the odd man on the other side of the desk.

'You did this?' she said.

Eckmann nodded.

'It's beautiful,' she said. 'Absolutely beautiful.'

She peered through the lens again.

'But more than beautiful – wonderful – I mean, in the real sense, the real way – it makes you wonder – how anyone could do this, how anything like this could be accomplished.'

Eckmann smiled and nodded, in polite and gracious acceptance of her admiration. She looked at the dome again, then she called in her assistant to see it.

'It's so . . . so beautiful,' she said. 'I mean, I've never seen anything like it. Why, you'd pay to see a thing like that. Wouldn't you? Don't you think?'

So Eckmann got his money, rented his premises and opened his gallery. He called it The Gallery of the Art of the Impossible.

Which, in the circumstances, seemed fair enough.

As that summer progressed, Eckmann got into the habit of always being in the square at some point during the hour when Poppea, in her marionette make-up, her dancer's costume and her painted tears, stood stock-still upon the music box, waiting for somebody to wind her up and drop a little money into the box.

Eckmann still thought of her as beautiful, wonderful, talented. The fact that she stood on a box for a living did not indicate to him that her talent was second or even third rate. She could dance, yes, up to a point, and whether it really was the talent she lacked or the ambition to do anything with it, who knew?

Art, like it or not, was a competitive trade. And the world of dance was no exception. It took not only ability but fierce dedication and determination to reach the top. In all honesty, it took considerable ability and dedication just to be mediocre.

Maybe the life had been too hard and regimented; maybe a life in the chorus simply hadn't appealed to Poppea – melting into the background only leading to more melting into the background, until even melting into the background required a younger face. And yet maybe she'd known she was not and never would be a prima ballerina.

Better to be a statue on the square.

Eckmann invariably dropped a coin or two into her collecting box as he passed. He did it hurriedly, not pausing to wind the key, but just putting the money in. The sound of *Swan Lake* or the 'Dance of the Sugar Plum Fairy' would echo behind him as he waddled on across the square.

Occasionally he would look back to see if she was dancing. And yes, she always was. For as long as the music played, the marionette upon the music box would revolve, whether she had been properly wound up or not. But Eckmann felt that he couldn't go through that rigmarole again in full view of the tourists and everyone else.

To drop some money into the box was a small act of generosity; to stoop to wind up the key, struggling to turn it, was somehow humiliating, possibly even degrading, and certainly ridiculous.

Eckmann didn't have the small, ordinary, human amount of acting ability which was needed to carry such a gesture off successfully. Everyone, to a greater or lesser extent, is an actor when in a public place. But some are better, and less self-conscious, than others.

Eckmann thought about Poppea more and more – when he was behind the ticket desk of the gallery, talking to his assistant; when he was alone, up in his studio on the top floor. He went and looked her name up in a book of names, but could only find variations of it and not the name itself.

He knew that she taught in the afternoons, and had sometimes seen her, out of costume and make-up, hurrying on her way to the dance studio to teach basic pirouettes to stage-struck ten year olds.

'What a waste,' Eckmann would think. 'What a waste.'

He felt, rightly or wrongly, that she had a difficult time, that it was hard for her to make ends meet, that she was permanently in debt, that her rent was overdue, that there had been some sadness, some tragedy in her past, which had brought her to this present way of life.

And in all these opinions and amateur psychologies, he was totally wrong. Poppea was, in fact, quite happy with her life, and had no real ambitions beyond it. She came from a good and prosperous family who would bail her out when things got hard. She enjoyed the theatre of the streets; she enjoyed acting the part of the music box marionette. Sometimes she might get work in a show: a winter pantomime or a summer musical. But Eckmann seldom went to the theatre. He hated the crowds, the bodies around him gave him an imminent sense of being crushed.

As for the tragedy in Poppea's life, there had been none of that either. Yet.

Hand in hand with his pity for her imagined predicament, Eckmann soon began to picture himself as her saviour. He saw himself as her anonymous benefactor whose generosity would one day be inadvertently revealed to her – and suitable gratitude would ensue. Yes, once his true character was known – his tenderness of feeling, his generosity of soul and nobility of purpose – her gratitude for his kindness could not fail to follow. And where there was gratitude, there might be affection, and where there was affection, there might, possibly, one day . . . be love. And where there was love, there was blindness to the defects of the loved.

He stepped up his contributions.

He did it surreptitiously. It began in a small way, with a five pound note. Every day he palmed a tightly folded five pound note into the slot in the music box, dropped a coin in after it, and went on his way as the music started and the dancer began to revolve.

He always folded the money in the same way too, so that she might know that it had come from the same person. But others did sometimes make equally generous donations. In fact, one day Eckmann saw a tourist push a folded ten pound note into the slot in the box. He felt momentarily enraged, as if some stranger were trying to abduct a personal possession, trying to outdo him and muscle in on his territory.

The following day he upped his contributions again. He put a twenty pound note into the box. He did this again the next day, and again the day after. He did the same on the Friday.

That evening, when he was closing up, she came to his gallery.

'Mr Eckmann?'

He looked up at her, momentarily lost for words.

'Ah yes. Good evening. How can I help?'

She took the four twenty pound notes from her coat and placed them on the ticket desk.

'I'm sorry – and it's very kind of you – but I can't take this.'

'No, really, really . . .'

'It's too much.'

'No, really . . .'

'It's too much. Far, far too much. I really can't take this. It's kind of you, but I'm sorry, it just feels wrong.'

Eckmann could feel himself grow hot and embarrassed. Faced with the reality of her, his fantasies seemed insupportable. If only, if only . . . he could just somehow address the important issue. If only . . .

'So thank you, but really, I'd rather not. It is kind of you, but it just makes me feel . . . well . . . not very nice.'

Eckmann's face clouded.

'Not very nice?'

'I mean awkward.'

'My money makes you feel not very nice?'

'I just mean – embarrassed.'

'Is that my money – or everyone's money?'

'The tourists are different. I'm a novelty. You . . . us . . . well, we see each other every day. We're . . . I don't know . . . on the same side.'

'The same side?'

That was different. If they were on the same side.

'Yes. I mean, in a way, we earn our money from them – not from each other. Do you understand?'

'Of course, but by that same token, from one artist to another . . . each must help each . . .'

'No, it's very kind of you, but I'm fine. I can manage. I like to feel I've earned it, whereas I feel . . . this is . . . charity.'

'Charity?'

Which it undeniably was. Or something more than charity. Patronage, perhaps. A gift given in the tacit expectation of some kind of return.

He picked the money up from the desk.

'Very well, if you feel . . .'

He returned the notes to his wallet.

'It was kind of you. But I'm fine. I'd better go now. Bye.'

'Wait. Have you seen the exhibition?'

But the door was closing behind her, and she was already gone.

It was only much later, when the winter settled in, that he thought to offer her a job in the gallery. She seemed to have forgotten all about the money by then. It was too wet and cold to stand like a statue in the abbey square, and the teaching had dried up, so she was glad to take the work. It was only part-time anyway, four or five hours a day, a few days a week. It would tide her over until the start of the pantomime season and the next dancing job.

She seemed to think that she was helping him out; freeing up his time so that he could get on with his sculptures. It didn't seem to occur to her that he could have employed anyone. It didn't cross her mind to ask what had happened to his previous assistant and why she had left.

The truth was that Eckmann had fired her. Paid her off and sent her away, told her she was no longer needed now that the takings had dropped with the end of the tourist season. He would manage on his own now.

It didn't occur to Poppea for one moment that Eckmann had got rid of her predecessor merely in order to have a job to offer her, to have her under his roof.

The Exhibition

A camel, slowly heading through the eye of a needle, was frozen in motion, and the boy watched it intently. His mouth hung open slightly. Not with idiocy though, but with sheer, unadulterated wonder.

According to the Bible, what he was seeing was impossible, or at the very least highly improbable.

'It is easier for a camel to pass through an eye of a needle than for a rich man to enter into the kingdom of God,' Jesus said.

Well, it was good news for rich men. Mr Eckmann had evened up the odds for them there a little.

'You like it, Christopher?'

He already knew the boy liked it. He just liked to toast his hands at the warmth of Christopher's admiration. Adults didn't admire like that.

But Christopher just admired and stared and wondered in open delight. There wasn't a gram of envy in him. He didn't even think of Eckmann as the man who had made this astounding creation. It was as if it just existed and they were admiring it together.

'How was it done, Mr Eckmann? How did you do it?'

'Ah, hah!'

Ah, hah. That was what they all said. Tricks of the

trade. And the truth was that Eckmann didn't actually know how he did it. He just knew that he *could* do it, and that was all.

He had started as a child, short, overweight and lonely. He sat out in the back garden and began to make furniture for ants. Swings and slides and garden tables – chairs they never sat in, utensils they never used. Work, work, work. The ants swarmed heedlessly over the things he had made, mere obstacles in their way. And then it rained. The small, intricately carved pieces got soggy and disintegrated over time. But Eckmann just left them out there. Ruin was an occupational hazard, it gave him a reason to carve some more.

Where the talent to make these delicately carved, miniature pieces had come from, he did not know. The ability seemed to have come to him like a cuckoo to another bird's nest. Maybe the talent wasn't really his at all; maybe he was just looking after it for somebody else, who would claim it at a later date.

Eckmann's father was in business, his mother ran a small shop selling maternity clothes. His father was a disappointment to his mother, for his lack of sensitivity and his endless infidelities; she was a disappointment to him for other reasons, and Ernst was a disappointment to them both. Too short, too fat, too slow. And there was only the one of him, when they had wanted more children, and anyway, they would have preferred a girl. As for his artistic ability, it was too quirky, too useless, not real art, more a sort of freak show, put on by a sort of freak. How was it possible to boast about something which you could barely see?

70

He carved the ants' furniture from tiny offcuts of wood; the table-tops might be wood shavings; the legs, split matchsticks. He never used glue back then. All the joints were carved out and slotted together. It was as much carpentry as sculpture, as much craft as art.

He carved with pins and penknives for his tools. In the beginning, he used only the naked eye. His sight was extraordinary. But as time went by and the sculptures became smaller, he began to use magnifying lenses, mounted on stands, the kind used for macramé or in the creation of illustrated manuscripts. Then there were jewellers' glasses, and then, finally, microscopes.

The studio workroom was full of them, large and small, new and old. One was linked up to a computer screen. Others must have been over a hundred years old – they were heavy and robust, built to last, made of dull, unpolished brass.

Eckmann could work without blinking for hours on end. His eyes would become red and inflamed, and he would need to bathe them afterwards, to wash out the dirt.

As the lenses he used got thicker, the carving tools grew smaller. A shard of broken glass, glued to the head of a pin, now served as the sculptor's chisel. He would carve in any material: wood, metal, glass, wax, sugar. One of his prize exhibits was a pyramid of Egypt, carved from a single grain of sand. Then there was the Empire State Building, carved into the tip of a pencil-lead, where the tiniest King Kong the world had even seen scaled the side of the building, with the tiniest woman a gorilla had ever abducted clutched in one hand.

Eckmann worked when it was quiet, in the still of the night. Or he might leave the gallery and go away for a week or so, to somewhere remote and quiet, a small island he knew, where there were no cars.

The slightest vibration could ruin a piece; the shudder of the building as a lorry went past; the tremor from the wheels of a train. The smallest error could destroy a month's work. He cut between heart-beats. That was all the time he had. If he tried to carve at any other time, his hand would tremble slightly and everything would be lost.

Sometimes he made mistakes. There really was only that split second in which to make the cut. Sometimes he gauged it wrongly and would chop off an arm from a sculpture, or destroy the symmetry of what had already been done, and turn a beautiful face into an ugly one.

He worked standing up, leaning his shoulder against the wall, the microscope and the carving tools set out on a high table. He could stand there all night, quite unaware of time passing, as if in a trance. He might work for hours and only make two cuts. But as long as they were the right ones, what did it matter?

The camel had taken him three months to finish. Two other camels had been lost on the way. One had inadvertently had its hump chopped off. The other had been lost.

Eckmann had forgotten to hold his breath as he leaned over the microscope to make the cut. The draught of exhalation from his nostrils had blown the sculpture off the slide and the camel had tumbled to the floor. It was so light and weightless it had probably sailed down, like a mote of dust. But which mote of dust? And where had it fallen? It could have floated anywhere in the room, like pollen drifting over a field. Of course, maybe it hadn't been his breath at all. Perhaps it had been some build up of static electricity which had caused the camel to leap from the slide.

He had taken a magnifier and gone looking for the sculpture. Weeks of work had gone into it. He covered every inch of the room. He even laughed silently to himself, thinking of the answer he would have given to anyone asking him what he was doing, kneeling on the floor, peering through a magnifying glass.

'*I'm looking for a camel.*'

He never did find it. Occupational hazard. He hadn't let the cleaner into the studio for a week. He wouldn't let her in anyway until everything was securely locked up and under glass. But she wasn't allowed in at all now, and while she moaned and groaned about the dust, Eckmann went on gazing at it and sifting through it. Eckmann the stargazer now Eckmann the dustgazer.

But the camel never did turn up.

Who stole the camel?

'*Who's got my camel!*' Eckmann shouted to the occupants of the dust. '*Who's stolen my camel? Is one of you riding around on it down there?*'

Then he would rock with laughter, a solitary voice in the still of the night. He would laugh until he wept sometimes, thinking of tiny people living in the carpet, riding around on his camel. He imagined his own reaction if a camel suddenly fell out of the sky and landed in his garden, in his world. You'd look up and scratch your head. It's raining camels. Why would it be raining camels? Maybe that's what meteorites were – some great sculptor's camels, falling from the sky, dropped from his microscope to the tiny world beneath.

It would have been good to have had someone to share things like that with. He could have told them how it had all started, years ago. How he had carved a tiny horse and had lost it and begun to cry. And then the horse had turned up, floating in one of his tears.

A horse floating in a teardrop – how bizarre, almost funny.

Poppea would have liked a joke like that. Poppea. If only she knew. If only other people knew. That was the point, wasn't it. If only we knew what lay underneath the surface. Not simply the things about someone which can be seen with the naked eye, but the other things, the inner things, the things a person is, what they hold inside them, what they dream. All the invisible things. The things you need to get close to to see. Just the way you had to get close to the sculptures to see them, to appreciate their beauty. And even then, close was not enough. You needed a lens, magnification, you needed your eyes to be opened in a special way. You needed someone to hold your hand, to guide you.

If she only came a little closer, surely it would all become clear. Take the lens, focus the microscope, and it was no longer a small, ugly man you saw. It was someone else, the artist inside, the maker of the beautiful creatures, the creator of the wonderful world.

Then Eckmann would laugh again, thinking of

another of his jokes. What if God was a short, fat man with an ugly face? What a joke that would be. If the creator of the whole universe and everything in it was a short, fat man going thin on top, with his hair combed over to make it look as though he wasn't.

Ha! What would the worshippers do then? Would they continue to believe as before and still come to church on Sunday?

The camel never did turn up, so he just had to start all over again. More weeks of work, of endless patience, of carving between the beats of the heart.

After each work session he was always exhausted. When a sculpture was finally finished, he might sleep for a whole day or more. It felt like a kind of jet lag, like the exhaustion after returning from a long journey to a foreign land in a different time zone.

Eckmann didn't work every day, or even every week. Sometimes he was content just to sit behind the counter at the gallery, answering questions, handing out pamphlets, ringing up the money on the till.

There was a notice on the desk which read, *Admission Cost Refunded If Not Truly Amazed.*

He had never had to give anyone their money back. Except once. And that had only been a couple of teenagers daring each other. He knew they had loved the exhibition and had been overawed by it, just as everyone was. It was impossible not to be. It was like drawing a bow across the string of a violin. How could it fail to do anything other than to play a note? The tiny sculptures were the bow; the instrument was the human capacity for wonder.

And yet . . . he was always dissatisfied too. The

sculptures lacked one thing. It was something he was unable to do, one quality he was quite unable to give them – motion. If only he could do that. If only it were possible.

It took three and a half weeks to remake the camel. Once it was finished he was then faced with the intricate and delicate task of mounting it in the eye of the needle.

Space wasn't the problem. The camel was so small relative to the needle that he could have fitted two camels and a llama in there and still have had room for a yak.

The problem was how to secure the camel within the needle's eye and how to get it there. If he used the point of another needle with a spot of glue upon it to hold the camel in transit, there was a danger that the glue might solidify and the camel wouldn't come off, or that in trying to remove it, he might break the sculpture itself.

Eventually he did it with a hair. He put a tiny spot of glue into the eye of the needle. Then he took a hair from his collar, brushed it along the arm of his coat to give it a small electrical charge and moved it towards the camel on the microscope slide.

He was worried that the camel might be repelled and had his free hand ready to catch it if it jumped.

But the charges on the shaft of hair and on the sculpture were opposite. The camel slid across the glass and attached itself to the point of the hair, like a shard of metal to a magnet.

Eckmann picked up the needle with his left hand, holding it by the point. As he stared into the microscope, not even daring to blink or breathe, he moved the hair across and carefully inserted the camel into the needle's eye.

Damn!

The hair twisted. It was now upside down. The camel's head was hovering over the tiny spot of glue, not its feet. What sort of exhibit was that going to be? The amazing upside down camel going through the needle's eye?

He slowly twisted the hair back, praying that the bond between it and the sculpture would hold.

It did.

He righted the camel. He set its feet into the minuscule puddle of glue. As he watched through the microscope, he could see the glue begin to congeal. He counted to five, a long, slow five. Then he tugged at the hair.

At first the camel came with it. It leaned over to one side. It seemed as if it might plop out of the glue. But then the hair parted company from it. The sculpture wobbled, then righted itself.

For some reason Eckmann put the hair back on to his head. As if he didn't want to lose it. As if he hoped it might possibly reattach itself.

Finally, there it was – *The Eye of the Needle*. The new exhibit for Eckmann's gallery – The Gallery of the Art of the Impossible. Admission Cost Refunded If Not Truly Amazed. (But everyone was truly amazed. Everyone.)

'Can I see it again, Mr Eckmann?'

'Yes, Christopher. Of course you can.'

He stood out of the way and let the boy look down

into the microscope. As the boy watched, Eckmann watched him. He envied him his life. He envied his father his child; he envied his father his relationship with the dancer; he knew she spent half of her evenings with them, that one day she and the boy's father would probably marry – or if that was too conventional for them, simply live together. Then maybe Christopher would have a brother, or a sister, or both. Then they would grow up and grow old and achieve nothing much, except, maybe, to be happy.

They would just live, the way people like that did. The casual portrait painter, the dancer who stood in the abbey square, dressed as a statue. Time would go by and youth would leave them. One day a tourist would look at the statue in the square and remark to his companion, 'Bit old for that, isn't she?'

What happens then? When the make-up is applied only to cover the cracks. And the boy's father? What of him? When the cold seemed to chill him to the marrow of his bones? When he couldn't sit out in the square so long? When the tourists chose to have their portraits sketched elsewhere, by one of the other artists, someone younger, not so dour. When the art you practised became drudgery, what did you do then?

'Can I go and look in the gallery too, Mr Eckmann?'

'There's nothing new, Christopher. This is the only new one.'

'I'd love to see them again, just the same.'

He never tired of them. So Eckmann led the way. They left the studio and went down to the gallery. It was empty. The sign in the window had been turned so that *Closed* faced the street. Christopher had got into the habit of dropping in on his way home from school. He knew better than to do so in the summer when the gallery was crowded and he would be in the way. But the winter was a different matter.

The gallery walls were painted in black, as was the ceiling. Some dim strip lights provided faint illumination. It was like entering a cinema, and it took a few seconds for your eyes to become accustomed to the gloom.

The gallery comprised two rooms, a larger and a smaller; you entered by one and exited by the other. Some information boards were on the walls and ambient music played. But there were no pictures here.

Around the periphery of the room was a series of glass domes, mounted on plinths which came up to average chest height. Fixed into each dome – depending on the size of the object inside – was either a single magnifying lens or a laboratory microscope. By the plinths were small steps, for children to stand on, so that they could view the exhibits independently and without having to be held up to see them by an adult.

A small name plate gave a brief description of what was inside. It did so in five languages. English, Spanish, French, German and Japanese.

'Look, Mr Eckmann! Look!'

Eckmann smiled. He hardly needed to look. Why would he look? At his own creations? He knew their every feature, from memory alone.

But he looked anyway. The boy stood aside and let him take a turn.

'See it, Mr Eckmann? See it?'

He smiled wryly. 'Yes, I see it, Christopher. I see it.'

Perched upon a fragment of a leaf, a grasshopper played a small guitar and sang to the stars above.

Christopher had already moved on to the next.

'Look, Mr Eckmann!'

This one was wonderful. It was an iceberg, carved from a single granule of sugar, and basking upon the iceberg was a walrus with ivory tusks, and next to it was a penguin, a little black and white waiter, all smart in his evening coat.

But you could only see it with the microscope. Because if you looked with the naked eye, there was really nothing there at all inside the glass dome. The whole thing was a swindle. There was nothing to see but a shapeless, worthless, translucent speck.

'Do you see it, Mr Eckmann?'

See it? He had made it.

Next, under another dome, a herd of hippos was basking on the rim of a thimble of water. And that was not a real thimble, but a Tom Thumb thimble, the tiniest thimble ever seen.

But let's not split hairs . . .

Only talking of which, here was one, split straight down the middle, the splittest ends you had ever seen, and holding the two strands apart was a strong man in a leopard skin, with muscles like footballs. The strongest man the world had ever known. But if he sat on your sleeve, you wouldn't even brush him off, because you wouldn't even know he was there. He was no bigger than a speck of dust.

They went on, around the room and into the next. There were some thirty-five or forty exhibits in all. The boy hurried from one to the next, Eckmann following behind. There was the boy's delight and Eckmann's delight in it; they made a complementary pair. Here were more wonders and marvels – a palace in a flower petal, with a castle and a moat. Here was the Grand Canyon, carved from a pencil lead; here was a cathedral in the head of a match. Here were replicas of famous places and works of art, cut and carved into toothpicks or from shavings of soap. It was art, and yet not art. The wonder was not so much in the quality of it, but that it had ever been done at all.

Here, in a fragment of a garden pea, an owl and a pussy cat were setting out on a voyage, while watching them from the top of a nearby needle was a piggy wig with a ring in his nose.

Some of the exhibits were under continuous illumination. But Eckmann was concerned about the effect of constant light upon some others, and so had installed a timer button which had to be pressed in order to illuminate the exhibit for thirty seconds.

Christopher went from one to the next. Pushing the buttons, sometimes holding them down.

'Christopher . . .'

The abbey clock was chiming.

'I think maybe you ought to get home now.'

'In a minute. One more minute.'

Eckmann made himself be patient. He didn't want the boy's father coming round, suspecting him of whatever. It wasn't like that. Not at all.

'Where's Poppea?'

Christopher looked up from the Leaning Tower of Pisa.

'Poppea?'

'Isn't she working here?' Christopher said. 'I thought Dad said she was working here.'

'For a while. The odd half day. It was quiet so I let her go early,' Eckmann explained.

'Too cold to be a statue now, I guess.'

Eckmann nodded.

The boy went to look at the elephants, trunk to tail, moving across the vast savannah of a sliver of grass.

'You like Poppea, Mr Eckmann?'

'She's very nice.'

'Dad likes her.'

'Ah.'

'She stays with us sometimes.'

'Yes.'

He looked up from the Great Wall Of China, all the miles and miles of it, contained on a space the size of a thumb-nail.

'I like her too.'

'I'm sure everyone likes her.'

'She's mad.'

'You think so?'

'She's a statue.'

'Ah.'

'You'd have to be mad to be a statue.'

'It's a living.'

'Most people aren't statues for a living.'

'No.'

'Eccentric then. Not mad but eccentric.'

Christopher looked for a while at the Eiffel Tower, studying it, full of contemplation. Every single girder was just as in the real thing.

'Mr Eckmann, why don't I know any normal people?'

He laughed. 'Normal?'

'At school they're normal. Me, my dad's an artist and Poppea is a living statue. I don't know anyone normal.'

'Ah well, what's normal?'

'I don't know.'

The boy paused to admire the Taj Mahal and then moved on to Mount Everest, where a team of climbers, in masks and carrying oxygen cylinders, was about to reach the summit.

'Mr Eckmann . . . do you think Dad and Poppea will get married?'

A pang of something less like envy and more like grief.

'I don't know. Why do you say that?'

'I don't know. Just wondered.'

Christopher reached out and pressed a button to illuminate the Sistine Chapel.

'Mr Eckmann?'

'Yes?'

'Why do you think my mum left? Didn't she love me?'

Eckmann realized that he was holding his breath. It was just as if he was sculpting, about to cut between the heartbeats, afraid that if he made the slightest error, he might do untold damage.

'I'm sure she loved you, Christopher. Very much.'

'Then why did she leave? Why do people leave?'

'Sometimes . . . people are unhappy together. Nobody is to blame. It's just how it is.'

'I was happy.'

'Maybe.'

'And even if she had been unhappy, couldn't she have stayed for my sake?'

The light went out upon the Sistine Chapel. The abbey bells had stopped ringing outside.

'You'd better ask your father, Christopher.'

'I did. He avoided it.'

'Maybe one day then, he'll explain.'

'People don't like to tell you much when you're young. They say you won't understand. But that's not it really. They're more likely afraid that you *will* understand and then get upset and they won't like that. It's themselves they want to look after. They just want to avoid it all.'

'You might be right.'

'That's what I think.'

'You're a clever boy.'

'At least I'm normal. Don't you think?'

'Yes.'

'Are you normal, Mr Eckmann?'

'No,' he smiled. 'I'm a mad artist too.'

'And a scientist.'

'It's an interest.'

'I'm going to be a scientist one day. Not a mad one though. A sane one.'

'Not an artist?'

'No, too cold, and you never have any money. Well, *you* do, Mr Eckmann, but not most artists. Dad never has any. Not much. Can I see the telescopes now? And all the lenses and the other things, up in the studio?'

'No, not now. You'd better go home, Christopher. Your father will be wondering.'

'Where will you put the camel, Mr Eckmann?'

'Right here. It will be the last one you see as you leave.'

'Do you think you'll ever need a bigger gallery?'

'Maybe. Maybe not. I can move things around. Some in store, some on display. That way it's always different. This is a good size. Any more would be too much to take in. Even wonder is a thing people can tire of. Too much of a good thing.'

He walked Christopher to the door and made sure he had his school bag.

'Any luck yet, Mr Eckmann?'

'Luck?'

'With the other thing? Making a sculpture that can move?'

'Try and fail, Christopher.'

'That's what you always say.'

'Try and fail and try again.'

'And then get it right.'

'Maybe. Here. Don't forget your coat.'

'Thanks. Think you will?'

'It's very difficult.'

'You can if anyone can.'

'I share your optimism. I share your hope. But your faith in my abilities, I'm not so sure.'

'Homework then, Mr Eckmann.'

'That's it. Got to do the homework!'

'Try and fail.'

'No, for you – try and succeed. You'll get good marks.'

'Goodbye.'

'Goodnight.'

'Can I come back?'

'Check with your father first.'

The door opened and he was gone. A swirl of winter came in through the door. Eckmann hastily shut it out again.

He turned off the lights in the gallery and went up to the studio. He glanced at the camel, still there, immobile in the eye of the needle.

Immobile. Yes. That was the problem. Still, he'd make up a name card for it and set it up in the gallery tomorrow. Poppea could help him. There wouldn't be much else to do. A dozen visitors a day sometimes, and even then you would be lucky, at least until the winter holiday and then the place filled up again.

Immobile. How to get over that? Things could go on getting smaller and smaller, at least up to a point. Yes, smaller and smaller was one thing, but if only he could make things move. If only the camel could walk, not just stand in the eye of the needle but walk through it, and down along the length of the needle, back up the other side and through the eye again.

If only that were possible. If only you could sculpt motion. But how? Some tiny, infinitesimal clockwork mechanism, so small that it would actually fit inside the camel itself? But how could that ever be made? How could the legs of the sculpture be articulated? Even if you could make and fit such a tiny clockwork engine, how would you power it, wind it, keep it in motion?

A computerized version then? Some printed circuit, some tiny chip? At some point in the future maybe, but not today. And even if you could make it, how to power it, wire it, place it inside the sculpture?

There was always the other idea, of course, the one which he had worked on and had kept to himself for so long. But there didn't seem to be even the remotest chance that that would ever work, for all his time and effort.

Eckmann left the sculpture and turned his attention to another dome. Under the glass his most ambitious project was taking shape. It was a tiny city. A replica of the very town outside his windows, the city of which he was a part.

He reached up and turned the mounted telescope in the attic studio around so that it projected an image of the city on to the white dish of the camera obscura.

There was his model. There was his template.

He moved the lens slightly and brought the abbey into sharp focus. There were its turrets and spires, its buttresses and gargoyles.

Eckmann brought the model over, lifted the glass, and took his sculpting tools from their case. There were tiny needles and pins and probes; there were shards of metal, fragments of glass. There was medical equipment, scalpels, tools used in fine and delicate eye surgery. There were special tools which were even finer, made to his own order and specification.

He took up his jeweller's glass and screwed it into his eye. He picked up one of the cutters and prepared to do some more work upon the fascia of the abbey.

But then, on the surface of the camera obscura, he saw movement. Figures were crossing the square.

One was a child. He recognized Christopher. The boy was walking and then running across the surface of the camera obscura. He was running with his arms wide, ready to be embraced, towards two people in the abbey square who were walking together, arm in arm. They separated at his approach, and one of the figures opened its arms and held the boy as he dived into them, and then the figure held him tight and spun him around and around.

Eckmann watched until the spinning stopped. Then watched as the boy slipped between the two adjoining figures, taking the hand of each. They all walked off together, briskly, happily it seemed.

Only as they walked, a finger came down from the sky. Or more precisely, Eckmann's thumb. He placed it on the head of the image of one of the figures on the camera obscura screen. And he ground the figure under his thumb, squashed it flat, like an insect.

But out in the square, the man whose image he had just squashed walked on, oblivious, with Poppea and his son. He did not know that he had just been eradicated from the face of the camera obscura, and carried on about his business.

The figures left the square. Eckmann got the abbey back into focus. Then he took up a scalpel. He glanced from the camera obscura to the model. Then he decided on which cut to make. He raised the scalpel and made the incision, swiftly and accurately, between the beats of his heart.

The Proposition

In the quiet season, Robert would stay at the flat, sketching and drawing, sending off illustrations to publishers in the hope of winning a commission to illustrate a book. But the competition was stiff and he was an unknown provincial artist. Why should they employ an unknown, a tedious train journey away, when there was some tried and tested illustrator with a good track record who could be relied upon to deliver what was wanted bang on time, and who would be willing to change things without creating difficulties?

Other days he would paint in oils – when he had the money for the materials – abstracts sometimes, or things from memory. He could simply have painted local well-known scenes and sold them from a stall in the precinct. But for him there would have been no satisfaction in it, and besides, others were doing it already. Even here the competition was fierce.

Some mornings he would walk Christopher to school. Other times the boy wanted to go on his own and Robert would let him. He believed in freedom and in willingly accepting the danger that came with it. For without exposure to danger, how did you ever learn, or grow, or become skilled in its avoidance?

You lived in a cocoon, swaddled up like a baby, never to be released from your bindings until it was too late for you ever to grow properly. You emerged like one of those old Chinese women, a victim of the foot-binders, forever hobbling through the rest of your life with tiny, diffident, uncertain steps, never able to run from danger, always reliant on the protection of others.

He preferred that Christopher should learn to look after himself. And besides, the dangers of childhood were, in Robert's opinion, greatly exaggerated.

The flat was neither large nor small, but adequate. There was a living room, incorporating a kitchen and dining area, two small bedrooms and a bathroom.

Robert moved around and set his easel up where the mood took him. Sometimes he worked in the living room, other times the bedroom. If the weather was fine he might move his chair and sketch pad out on to the small balcony. Like Eckmann, he too had a good view of the city – if from a less salubrious district. From their balcony he could see the abbey and the Roman baths and the crowds queuing up to get into the museum.

Some days Robert would gather up a few of his pictures and go around the galleries in town, trying to interest the dealers in hanging a few of his canvases on their walls – on a sale or return basis, if nothing else.

But he tended to be sullen and surly and lacking in persuasion. He also resented the dealers for the extortionate mark-ups they put on the paintings and the commissions they charged. He would be lucky to get half of the proceeds from a sale. Neither did his work sell well or often. It was good but it was unusual. It had appeal, but only to a minority – one which Robert liked to regard as discerning.

Christopher would usually make his own way home after school. By then, depending upon the time of year and the weather, Robert might already have gone to work in the abbey square.

If his father was working in the afternoon, Christopher would let himself into the flat, watch some television, then do his homework, maybe even cook himself a meal. Poppea had her own key and would sometimes be there when Christopher came home. Some nights she would stay, other nights she would go home. As he lay in bed reading, Christopher would hear the murmur of their voices out in the living room. He didn't quite understand the relationship between them, if they were all going to live together one day or what they would do. But in other ways it didn't matter, he was happy enough with things as they were, and it was security of a kind.

Now and again Poppea would go for auditions. She was a good, competent dancer, though she didn't really practise enough. The productions she got parts in tended to be small, local affairs, neither well-paid nor particularly spectacular.

Christopher had been taken to see her once, when she danced in the chorus line of *Jack and the Beanstalk* at the Theatre Royal. She looked glamorous in her tights and costume and Christopher had clapped loudly at the end, as though it were the best thing he had ever seen, maybe hoping that she would hear the sound of his hands above the sound of all the others, and know that it was him and his father, and that she was special to them.

To his surprise, he had glanced down from the front row of the upper circle where they were sitting, to see Mr Eckmann, down in the stalls. He had a good seat, near to the front, at the end of a row, by the middle aisle, with nothing to impede his view. Christopher had thought it a bit sad for Mr Eckmann to be all on his own at the pantomime.

Pantomimes were for families really. Adults didn't go to them on their own. You needed a child to take with you to enjoy it properly, that was the truth, as far as he saw it. And if you didn't have a child of your own, sometimes you borrowed one, like a friend's, or your own children's children.

You saw that a lot at the pantomime – grandparents who had borrowed their grandchildren for the afternoon or the evening, so that they could take them to the show, to cry out 'He's behind you!' or 'Oh no it isn't!' when they said 'Oh yes it is!', and to hiss loudly whenever the villain appeared – and maybe, for a little while, to be young again, surrounded by ice cream and darkness.

But there was poor Mr Eckmann, all on his own, looking a bit like a child himself, small and plump and nicely scrubbed and wearing his best clothes. It was always slightly strange to see him out of the gallery, where he seemed to belong. He was a little like a fish out of water, gasping for air.

Christopher felt sorry for Mr Eckmann and he wished that Mr Eckmann could have had someone with him too – maybe Mrs Eckmann on one side and the little Eckmanns on the other. Mr Eckmann would have been happy then, happy ever after.

But instead, he loved Poppea, and she was hardly

even aware of his existence. To her, he was just the man who ran the gallery and who had put too much money into her music box when she was working as a living statue outside the abbey. He wasn't the first who had done it, and probably wouldn't be the last. In some ways, it was an occupational hazard. Public figures had to put up with this kind of thing, even when they were no more than humble statues in the square.

In time, Poppea soon knew, or at least half suspected, why he had offered her the job in the gallery, but she couldn't see the harm in it, and she certainly didn't encourage him in any way; she made that plain from the outset. Business only. It was strictly a business arrangement. Besides, he needed someone in the gallery, didn't he, if he wanted to work and do other things?

Robert didn't like it much – or like Eckmann much – but maybe that was jealousy. Say what you liked about him, call it art or call it micro-engineering, Eckmann certainly made a good living out of it, and that was more than most artists did. There was probably only a handful in the whole country who actually made a living from their art and art alone. The majority held down other jobs, or taught in colleges or waited on tables, or compromised, or simply gave up and went and did something else.

The days were quiet when Poppea first went to work at the gallery, which, being gregarious and sociable, she didn't much like. They livened up briefly when the school half-term holidays came, but soon reverted to as before.

The proposition had been that she would look after

the cash desk while Eckmann went up to his studio and got on with his sculpture, but things didn't quite work out that way.

Instead of locking himself away for hours or even days on end, which he was quite capable of doing, Eckmann found reasons and pretexts to abandon his work. It wasn't going well; his back was aching; his eyes were sore; his concentration was flagging; the inspiration (not that he believed in it, but he knew that others did) wouldn't come. He would suggest coffee, he would even go and make it. Poppea was glad of someone to talk to for a while.

'How does it pay here? It's so quiet now,' she said.

'In the winter, yes. But the summer is very busy. The same as it is for you statues.'

'I suppose.'

'Hand over fist!'

'You make a lot of money?'

'Hand over fist, hand over fist . . .'

And somehow he wanted her to know it. So he said it again. 'Hand over fist!'

She sipped her coffee and looked at him curiously. She would dearly have loved a cigarette, but she daren't light one. For one thing dancers were ill-advised to smoke, and for another Eckmann hated the smell of it in the gallery, though at home he smoked an occasional cigar.

'Mr Eckmann . . .'

'Ernst . . .'

'Ernst . . .'

But then a customer came in – one shortly followed by another, both Americans, but unacquainted up until then, and glad to have found a fellow countryman so far from home. They bought tickets and went on into the gallery together, to wonder loudly and vociferously at the statues in miniature.

'You were going to ask me something?'

She had forgotten what it was by then. She had only been making conversation anyway, maybe going to ask him about his foreign-sounding name when the rest of him was so English. By the time she remembered, it barely seemed worth pursuing.

So Eckmann asked her something, only he did it indirectly, by way of a series of musings and suggestions, which led to their own inevitable conclusion.

'I was wondering about my next sculpture,' he said.

Poppea tried to look interested but she kept thinking about that cigarette. She was trying to give up too, which made it worse, and she'd sworn that she'd never get addicted. She tried to focus on the moment.

'Do you really need any more?' she said, rather tactlessly.

Eckmann looked at her, astonished. It was a question he had never put to himself and the answer to it was plainly no. He didn't need any new exhibits. And he never would. At least not until the existing ones began to show signs of wear and tear and required replacement. But the matter was more complex than that. Eckmann was an artist, or at least regarded himself as such. If he did not create anything, what was he then? He was a gallery owner. If an artist does not exercise his art, what is he, what has he become? If he stopped, what would he do with his time, with his life? If he wasn't himself, who was he?

'It's as well to keep working,' he said. 'Who knows,

I might open another gallery, in another town. Or maybe begin to sell the odd exhibit or two.'

'Weren't you working on something? I thought you said . . .'

'The miniature of the city, yes. But that's such a grand canvas . . .'

Poppea almost giggled. It seemed so absurd for Eckmann to talk of his 'grand canvas' when it was no bigger than a Christmas snow-scene, hidden under a little glass dome.

He insisted upon showing her his work in progress one afternoon. He took her up to the studio, following her up like a little dog, all but wagging an invisible tail. He showed her how to focus the microscope, just like a proper little gentleman, never imagining how this would irritate her. As if she couldn't focus her own microscopes – as if she needed it explained to her.

There, under the dome, was the replica city. She felt Eckmann's breath upon her cheek as he explained the difficulties he had experienced in constructing everything. For a moment she felt uneasy at his proximity. But Eckmann was a gentlemen, every inch of him. There may not have been many inches, but gentlemanly conduct occupied every one.

'Such a grand canvas . . .'

Maybe it was to him. To her it was just a tiny city under a glass dome. All very nice, all very good, all very clever, but so what? It wasn't life, was it?

They headed back down the stairs.

'Too much to complete all at once,' Eckmann said as they went. 'I need to do something in between . . . I did wonder . . .'

'What?'

'Just an idea. But maybe a dancer.'

'A dancer?'

'Like yourself.'

'Oh?'

'A tiny dancer, perched on the tip of a needle.'

'The tip? You mean the top, don't you? The eye? The blunt end?'

'No, no. The point.'

'The sharp end?'

'Yes, the sharp end.'

'That small?'

'Yes. A ballerina – in a dress, a tutu, with make-up and a frozen tear, and a painted smile.'

'Like me?'

'Sorry?'

'Like me. The living statue.'

'Yes, yes. Why, of course. Yes, that's right. That must be where the idea came from. From seeing you in the square.'

Poppea smiled. Did he expect her to believe him? But just the same . . . she was flattered.

'I don't suppose . . .'

No. He left the question hanging in the air. It remained unasked and unanswered.

The visitors emerged from seeing the exhibits in the gallery, blinking their way into the light.

'Marvellous!'

'Wonderful!'

'Truly amazing!'

They signed the visitors' book to that effect, and then they were gone, off to the next attraction – the costume museum, or the now cold and draughty open-topped-bus tour, or perhaps to take tea in the

Pump Rooms, to the sound of a trio trying their best to make well-known classical favourites sound fresh.

'Where were we now?' Eckmann asked when the visitors had gone. As if he had forgotten. 'Ah yes. Maybe that would be quite an attraction. And not only a sculpture of a dancer, but for her to move as well . . .'

She looked at him.

'Move?'

'To see her dance.'

'Dance? Actually dance? How?'

'Well, rotate.'

'Rotate?'

'Spin round and round. Maybe mount the needle on some mechanism, which can slowly move around, and then . . .'

'Ah. For a moment I thought you actually meant, well . . . to actually dance.'

'That would be difficult.'

'Yes.'

'Wonderful, but difficult.'

Eckmann spread his hands out in a deprecating, rather apologetic gesture, as if to convey how sorry he was that he couldn't quite manage that yet, as if the existing wonders of what he did weren't already wonderful enough.

That was the most wonderful thing of all about it – how rapidly a wonderful thing ceased to be just that, how quickly people took it for granted, and looked for something new. What, after all, was more banal than the moon and the stars and the sun in the sky – daily miracles, taken for granted, barely given a second glance.

Poppea looked at him and suddenly saw him in a different light. She had always taken him for something of an innocent, but now she wasn't so sure. It was his stature which misled you, his small, rotund, childlike figure, a Peter Pan of a man who had never grown up – just outwards a little. The small, fleshy hands were smooth and clean, and they folded themselves, one over the other, reminding her for some reason of a plate of oysters, or a nest of newly born mice.

Maybe he wasn't the innocent she thought. He was a man, after all, not a boy, and who knew what he did after he had eaten his meal at the café table in the abbey square. Maybe he didn't always go straight home, or back to his studio. Maybe he went somewhere else first. After all, he wasn't short of money.

She demurred, as was in her nature. She had always preferred postponement to commitment, as Robert well knew; it was a trait they had in common. Now was always more important than tomorrow; enjoyment of the moment more necessary than the formulation of future plans.

'Oh, I don't know . . .'

Eckmann detected a note of possibility.

'It wouldn't take long . . .' he said.

She thought otherwise.

'All that standing still . . .'

'But you're a professional statue.'

'That's what I mean. I don't want to do it when I don't have to.'

For a second Eckmann thought of offering payment, but rightly decided that any such offer would seem rather tawdry and only turn her against it.

'Oh, I don't know,' she said again, and she put her hand up to stifle a yawn.

He glanced at his watch. He made something of a display of it, giving her time to notice the discreetly expensive timepiece on his wrist.

'Well, perhaps you could think about it,' he said. 'I'll see you later on. I have an appointment now.'

'OK.'

'I'll be back this afternoon.'

'Fine, Mr Eckmann.'

'Please – Ernst.'

But she didn't call him Ernst, at least not on that occasion, and he went off to his appointment – if he had one. Or maybe he just said he did, but actually spent the afternoon roaming the streets, looking in jewellery shop windows, and then walking by the river, sitting on a bench, eating a sandwich, peeling parts of the crust off and throwing them to the birds. Maybe, as he fed the birds, he sat and swung his legs under him, like a child on a swing, and then when he had finished his lunch, he hopped down to solid earth and walked on.

He tried to get back to the gallery before the schools finished for the day. The teenagers on the streets made jokes about him sometimes, loudly and callously, as they passed by, on their way to pile into the news-agent's shop to buy chocolate – adolescents, but still children at heart. Their ties were askew, their shirts pulled out, some of the girls looking as if they had outgrown their skirts, but their parents hadn't realized

100

that it was time to buy them new ones. Or maybe money was tight.

When he returned to the gallery there was the smell of stale cigarette smoke in the air. He sniffed and scowled with disapproval. Poppea gestured towards the exhibition room.

'Someone was in smoking earlier,' she said. 'I had to ask them to put it out or to leave.'

Eckmann shook his head in annoyance.

'It's not as if they can't see the signs,' he said. And that was true. But maybe people never saw what they didn't want to see.

Eckmann moved on and headed for the door marked Private, which led up to the top of the building, to the store rooms full of files and accounts, and ultimately to his studio in the attic.

'By the way,' he said casually, as he turned the handle of the door, 'did you have any more thoughts?'

'About what? The statue?'

'Yes.'

'How long would it take?'

'Not long. I'd do some sketches and make a rough sculpture first, you know, in clay – something to work from. Then when we had that, I'd use it to model the miniature on.'

'Oh. You wouldn't do it directly?'

'Too difficult. Just a rough model, and then maybe a final session for the finishing touches.'

'I'll think about it,' Poppea said.

'OK,' Eckmann said. He smiled and let the door close behind him as he went on up to his studio.

He didn't work on any sculpture that afternoon,

but interested himself in the camera obscura, and watched the life of the city as projected upon it.

Life unfolded before him as people came and went, without discernible objective. It was like watching a TV drama, without the sound, without any apparent plot, and – come to think of it – without any drama. How odd that life should seem so disorganized, so aimless, plotless, pointless, random. But still life.

Drama seemed more real than reality.

Later, he heard Poppea call goodnight to him from downstairs, and he called back, and heard her close the gallery door behind her.

Darkness came early that day. It was a heavy, gloomy winter darkness of greys and browns and sodium yellows, and a drizzle of rain.

Eckmann reached up to the telescope section of the camera obscura and changed the lens, slotted some filters into it and then refocused the image upon the dish. Next he took some prisms of glass and laid them on the surface. The light fragmented and shot off in all directions, now broken up into its component colours.

Richard Of York Gained Battles In Vain – once learned, never forgotten and as strangely meaningless as ever. But it helped you to recollect the colours of the spectrum. Red, Orange, Yellow, Green, Blue, Indigo, Violet.

All the colours in between too, all the subtle nuances. As if there were only seven colours in the world, when there were really more like seven thousand; or maybe the truth was that the shades of colour were infinite. Colours were like numbers, infinitely divisible. Count them as you would, you never got to the end. There was no end to get to.

102

The broken colours jutted out from the prism at odd, jagged angles. They almost seemed like limbs with too many joints in them.

Eckmann stared at the colours for a long time. Then he took out a notebook from a drawer, turned to a page covered in formulae and equations and began to add to the scribble, making more notes and alterations. As he worked he gave out little grunts, almost as if to say, 'Yes, yes. That's it now. Quite so. Quite so.'

The work absorbed him, and he no more noticed the time pass than he did when at work on his sculptures. The emptiness in his stomach finally told him it was late. He was hungry and thirsty now and tired of being alone, so he got his coat and the hat he sometimes wore, locked up the gallery behind him and headed for the café on the square.

The gas burners were lit and the canopies were up to keep any rain off, but hardly anyone had chosen to eat outside. The couple who had, however, had selected Eckmann's favourite table. The waiter showed him to another and swatted imaginary crumbs away from the perfectly clean tablecloth.

'What will it be tonight, sir? Your usual?'

Eckmann nodded. It was good to be known, for people to be aware in advance of what you needed, to have a 'usual'. After all, Eckmann was a paying customer here, a dependable regular, a valuable asset to the restaurant's business. He was money in the bank.

The waiter brought him his half bottle of wine and poured out a glass. Eckmann nodded and sipped at the wine. He smiled. He looked up towards the attic window of his gallery where he had left a light on.

Yes. It had been a kind of breakthrough really. He could almost see how to do it now. Others didn't see things in that way, the amalgamation of science and art and how much one was an intrinsic part of the other. But look at da Vinci, look at the great architects of the cathedrals and pyramids. Look at the science in the art, the art in the science. What were plans without execution? Ideas without practicalities? What were dreams without the knowledge and ability to make them real?

Having no one to clink glasses with, Eckmann turned, on a sudden impulse, towards the couple who had taken his customary table.

'Your health!' he said, raising his glass in a toast.

'Er . . . your health,' the couple responded, somewhat bemused.

'It's a lovely night,' Eckmann said, though it patently wasn't. But the couple agreed with him anyway, the way people do when they suspect talkative strangers of being either unbalanced or drunk, and decide that it is best to humour them in the hope that they will soon shut up or go away.

The next day, Poppea said that she had been thinking things over and that maybe she might do it after all – pose for the sculpture of the dancer.

'It's quite flattering in a way,' she said, 'to be the model for a statue. Even when you do need a microscope to see it.'

Eckmann told her how pleased he was.

'You won't regret it,' he said.

'I expect I'll need my costume,' she asked him.

Eckmann agreed that she would. He asked her to bring everything: make-up, shoes, leotard and dress.

He looked forward to getting to work.

He could hardly wait.

A Trick of the Light

Poppea decided not to tell anyone (Robert being the *'anyone'*) as people could be funny, and get jealous over nothing, even if – or especially when – there was no need to be. Besides, you had to have some independence, some other life, all of your own. Maybe that was the glue that held you together anyway, allowing each other freedom and some privacy and some individual life.

Like milk on a doorstep, love left unattended just went sour. You had to keep things fresh and alive.

So she didn't say anything or tell anyone, not for now. Once it was all over and finished they would be able to see it for themselves, and that would be soon enough. Was it the kind of thing you put on your CV? *Model for exhibit in the Gallery of the Art of the Impossible. The Tiny Dancer – that was me.*

No, maybe not.

Still, it was better than sitting at the cash desk all the time. Though even that wouldn't be for too long. Soon it would be the pantomime season again, and with luck that would mean six to eight weeks of solid work, and then it would be February and a well-earned couple of weeks away somewhere warm, and then it would be spring and time to be a statue once more.

She would get the costume out and clean it up, or change her image and make a new one. Maybe she would change her make-up too. She might not even be a ballerina next year, but a different kind of statue altogether.

So the spring would pass and then the summer, and maybe a summer show, and then some teaching or some casual work, or maybe back to Mr Eckmann's or some teaching in the evenings, and then the pantomime again.

You didn't have to be famous. You didn't have to dance Juliet in *Romeo and Juliet*, or Odette in *Swan Lake*, or the little girl in *The Nutcracker*. You just had to lead your life and be yourself and let the time go by. That was fulfilment, wasn't it? That was life.

And then, one day, one year when spring came round again and it was time to be a statue, maybe she wouldn't be a statue. Maybe she would look into the mirror and get a sense of time passing and think that she wanted a baby now, a child of her own. And maybe she and Robert and Christopher and the new baby could all be together and happy.

So that was her overall plan, as far as she knew it or thought about it – which wasn't much. She knew it more instinctively than anything else, but it was still a kind of plan anyway, expressed or not. Just give life a free rein and let it trot on down the road, until it came to the place you wanted it to be.

And until then there were Robert and Christopher, work and friends and occasional secrets and surprises, like this one with Mr Eckmann. It was life, that was all, going past the way it did when you were still young.

So she took the costume along with her when she went in to work the following Monday. In the afternoon Mr Eckmann announced that he was closing early as it was such a bitter day outside and he couldn't see business getting any better or many customers coming along. He hung the closed sign on the door, clicked the latch on the lock and then led the way upstairs.

'Can't we do it here?'

'It's the light,' he explained. 'It's better up in the studio – the quality of the light. And besides . . .'

But he didn't finish and *besides what* she never did find out.

She followed him up the narrow staircase, past the floor with the files and ledgers, and on up to the attic studio.

'What am I going to do if he tries it on?' she asked herself. But no, that was ridiculous. Anyway, even if he did, she towered above him. The only person in danger was Mr Eckmann – in danger of a painful rebuff if he made any advances in that way.

She needn't have worried. Eckmann was the perfect gentleman still. He left her alone in the studio while she changed into her costume and would only re-enter when she had called out, 'OK! Ready!'

He returned to the room somewhat shy and embarrassed, not immediately ready to look at her. When he finally did, professionalism took over. He requested a few adjustments to her posture and her dress. But he wouldn't touch her. He just sculpted the air with his hands, demonstrating how he wanted things, letting her do it all, though it would have been quicker if he had adjusted them himself.

Once her clothes and position were right, he made a few preliminary drawings on a sketch pad for future reference, and when he was satisfied with those he took some clay and made a small model, no more than eight or ten inches in height.

'I'll need to make some others,' he said, as Poppea, tiring and unable to hold the pose for much longer, visibly began to wilt. 'In repose and . . . from . . .' he hesitated to say it, so she finished the sentence for him.

'The rear?'

'The back.'

They settled on Wednesday evening after work as the time of the next sitting. Eckmann didn't want to close the gallery too often. Once in a while didn't matter so much, but you get a reputation for unreliability and erratic opening hours, and people don't even bother to seek you out any more.

He offered to pay overtime for the next sitting, but Poppea refused. It wasn't work, after all, it was a favour. Immortality for her, of a kind.

Eckmann left the room again while she changed back out of the costume. She asked if she could leave it there, and Eckmann raised no objection. He found a hanger for it and put it up in the window, where it dangled from the curtain rail, looking limp and lifeless, like some great dead butterfly hung up to dry.

'Perhaps,' he said tentatively, 'next time . . . the make-up . . . ?'

Poppea nodded.

'Of course, yes, I should have thought. I meant to bring it, but I forgot.'

She promised to bring the make-up box with her and to put on the painted tears, so that Eckmann would know how to do the same thing for the Tiny Dancer, when she was finally complete.

On the Wednesday evening, after the second sitting, Eckmann felt that a third sitting might be necessary, possibly even a fourth. Poppea was non-committal. She felt that this was enough now, and besides, she was starting to feel foolish standing there in the ballerina dress and make-up, with the painted-on tears on her face.

But Eckmann persisted and wheedled and maintained that detail was everything and he had to have it all just right in his head before he could start on the miniaturization. So she agreed to one more sitting, on the Friday night, and then she announced that she would also be leaving at the end of the following week.

Eckmann looked startled. More than that – shocked. He recoiled physically, as if he had been struck in the face.

'Leave? What do you mean?'

'I've been offered some work, in the chorus, you know, for the winter season.'

'But the gallery . . .' Eckmann objected.

'It's so quiet,' Poppea said. 'You don't really need me. It was only a casual arrangement anyway, wasn't it? I can find someone to fill in for me if you want. I can't turn down the dancing job, can I?'

'You don't like working here?'

'Yes, I do. But that's not the point. I'm a dancer. If you're a dancer and you don't dance – what are you? I mean, you're not a dancer any more.'

Eckmann nodded, but his face was pale, and his lips were compressed into a thin line, as if he was trying to hold back anger or hurt.

He carried on putting materials away and tidying up, then he went to wash the clay from his hands. Two small clay dancers now sat on his work bench, Poppea in motion and in repose.

Poppea looked at them. They were good. Each was an excellent likeness. She said as much and Eckmann smiled. Then she wandered over to the camera obscura and looked at the dish and the image upon it of the city outside.

'So this is what you do,' she said. 'Spy on everyone.'

Eckmann took the joke earnestly. He flushed crimson and began to protest.

'No, no, not at all.'

'I'm only joking. Don't take everything so seriously. May I?'

She reached up. Eckmann nodded. She moved the lens around and a different part of the city came into view, an area of shops and sparkling lights. The first of the Christmas decorations were going up in the windows, though there were still weeks to go.

'It's wonderful,' she said. 'Like having your own little world.'

Eckmann nodded. He plucked up courage and suggested:

'I'm just about to eat. Would you care to have dinner with . . . that is . . . a bite to eat . . .'

Poppea looked at her watch. Robert was working and then taking Christopher with him to the cinema. She was at a loose end. She could have dinner with Eckmann and go round to the flat later.

111

'OK.'

The sudden and simple acceptance wrong-footed him. He didn't expect things to be so easy. Was there really this world where men and women went to dinner together, and it really was that casual, that straightforward, with no formality, no courage required?

They got their coats and went to the café in the square.

'Do you always eat outside?'

'No. Not when it gets too cold. But for now . . .'

It was somehow atmospheric and romantic to sit out under the gas burner, warm in the cold, your breath a mist in the air. The waiter appeared, impassive as ever.

'Good evening, madam, good evening, sir . . .'

He brought two menus tonight, and it was just as if Eckmann was always bringing attractive young women to have dinner with him, just as though it were a normal, ordinary course of events. The waiter didn't even remark on it.

They ordered food and drank their wine and talked and even laughed a little. But what to Poppea was just one ordinary meal with a passing acquaintance was to Eckmann something far more. It was a landmark, a watershed, a defining moment in history. Such a thing had never happened before. He felt at least six feet tall.

When the bill came, she reached for her purse, intending to pay for her share of it, but Eckmann wouldn't have it and for a second grew almost belligerent. The wine had affected him, and she could see it, so she let him have his way. He put his credit card down on the dish with a flourish, and the waiter went off with it.

'And now what . . . ?' Eckmann said expansively, rolling the brandy around in his glass, as though the night were still young and theirs for the taking. 'What will it be?'

'I really have to go now.'

The brandy glass stopped moving. His hand grew still.

'You have to go?'

'Yes, I'm expected.'

'But . . .'

'It was a really nice meal. Really nice.'

Only that didn't seem adequate somehow. Not to Eckmann. 'Nice' was not good enough. Simply not good enough. And 'really nice' was little better, almost an insult, in fact, a kick in the teeth. You paid, you always paid. You tried your best, you did your best, and this was what you got, always what you got. They took and they gave nothing. Same thing, same story, all your life. You gave and they took and they gave nothing back. Over and over. As an artist too. You gave all that you could. And what did you get for it in return? Nothing. No proper recognition, just contempt.

No one saw the art in it, the *real* art in it. Yet it was as subtle and as beautiful as anything anyone had ever done. A freak show, that was all it was to them. The camel in the needle, the Empire State Building carved into the tip of the pencil lead, the cathedral on the head of a match. Yes, it was all so very interesting. Now let's go and see some real art.

The thoughts rampaged through his head. But all

113

that Poppea saw was a little man, a bit drunk, whose mind seemed to have drifted off on to other matters.

'Oh, right, yes, of course. Well, if you have to go . . . if you're expected . . . Yes. Well, I'll see you tomorrow . . .'

She picked up her bag and her coat.

'Yes, of course. And thank you again – for dinner.'

'And one more sitting?'

'Fine.'

'Next Friday? Before you leave?'

'Friday it is.'

She smiled and walked away. He watched her cross the square. She walked like a dancer, elegantly, precise, with seemingly effortless grace.

'The lady has gone, sir?'

The waiter was back with his credit card.

'Yes, the lady had to go . . . has gone.'

He scanned the waiter's face for signs of pity or contempt, but there was nothing readable printed on such a blank countenance. His thoughts were all in invisible ink.

'Your card, sir.'

'Thank you.'

'Thank you, sir. Have a nice evening.'

Eckmann crossed the square, walking with his characteristic waddle, which, try as he might, he could do nothing to get rid of or improve.

He may as well go back to the studio. There was nothing else to do.

So that was where he went. He went up to the attic and turned the lights on, and there it was, Poppea's ballet dress, hanging from the rail. He went up to it and felt the garment with his hand; he pressed the material to his face and inhaled the perfume, the scent of her.

To think, to only think . . .

He reached into his coat pocket and took out a small red jeweller's case. He opened it, and inside was a bracelet made from diamonds, multi-faceted, sparkling, twinkling like stars.

What made the diamonds sparkle was the speed of the light. Contrary to common belief, the speed of light was not constant. In a vacuum it was. But not in a diamond. Within the stone the light moved at varying speeds, refracted and reflected from facet to facet, from cut to cut. This was what gave the diamonds such magic – the varying speed of the light within.

And to think, just to think . . .

. . . he had been going to tell her that he loved her.

He laughed. In truth, he snorted, and as he did so some mucus spilled out from his nose. Then he began to cry, a vicious hateful grieving, and he beat his small body with his hands. Then he grabbed at himself, took up handfuls of flesh and pulled and twisted at them, cursing at himself and shouting, 'I hate you, I hate you, I hate you!'

Then he sat weeping upon the chair by his work bench, and the mucus ran from his nose worse than ever and the tears spilled from his eyes. And all the while he held the diamond bracelet in his hand, and the light sparkled through the blur of tears as though those tears were diamonds too.

Finally, all the anger and passion subsided. He tore off a piece of kitchen towel, blew his nose and wiped his face.

And then it came to him. That was the one missing piece in the jigsaw. The speed of the light. Of course. Now he could do it. It was obvious, so obvious, and had been all along. That was how to make the creations move, to give them life and motion. That was it.

The speed of the light. The way it moved at different speeds. The way it could be slowed, and the difference that made.

He took the bracelet and crossed to the window. He set up his arrangements of prisms and filters and trained the light from the telescope upon them. Then he set the bracelet down and watched as the light entered through the largest of the diamonds and how it emerged.

Yes. Yes.

That was right.

Of course, it was going to take a little more than that. It wouldn't be quite that simple. You would need to create an electric field, powerful electromagnets too, and there was always the danger that the whole thing would burn out and shatter before . . .

But in theory, yes, in theory it ought to work. There was no reason why it shouldn't. He hurried to get his notebook and opened it at the pages of formulae.

And to think, only to think, that he had been going to tell her that he loved her.

The shame, the hot burning shame of it, and what she would have said about it when she got home, and how the two of them would have laughed. The boy may even have woken up and heard their voices in the adjacent room and the two of them laughing. Poppea and Robert. Laughing. And making love too.

At his expense.

So he had until Friday. Well, it wasn't long, but it was long enough.

To think that he had been going to offer himself up for ridicule like that. To her, to them – to a second-rate dancer and a third-rate artist.

To think that he had ever deluded himself that he could . . . she could . . . a woman like that . . .

To think that he had been going to tell her that he loved her.

He must have been mad. Maybe he still was.

Because, even now, he loved her still.

The Tiny Dancer

'Mr Eckmann?'

Eckmann was sitting by the cash till in the gallery. He looked up from the newspaper he was reading and peered over the desk.

'Christopher?'

'Anything new?'

The boy stood there in his uniform, straight from school, dragging a backpack by its strap behind him, letting it trail along the floor.

'Anything new?' Eckmann repeated. He folded the newspaper and put it down.

'I was only passing.'

For some reason, Christopher hadn't liked to call in when Poppea was there. But now that she had gone, he felt at liberty to start visiting the gallery again. She and his father had quarrelled, the day before she was due to leave for her rehearsals. So she had gone without saying goodbye, which had disappointed him. But he knew they'd make it up again, they always did. A quarrel over nothing, a sulk for a few days, each waiting for the other to ring, and then one of them would apologize and it was all done and forgotten – until the next time.

'Anything new? There can't be new things every day, you know.'

'No, I know that, Mr Eckmann.'

'You know how long it takes to make one, just one sculpture . . . ?'

'I know. I do. But you're always working on something.'

'That's right. I am. And why?'

'Because you're an artist.'

'That's right. And if an artist doesn't work, what is he?'

'He's not an artist any more.'

'You already know that?'

'Dad says the same thing.'

'Ah.'

Eckmann's face clouded over.

'Can I look in the gallery at the old things then?'

'Of course . . . but wait a moment . . . you want to see something?'

'Something new?'

Eckmann nodded. 'Maybe.'

'Finished?'

'Maybe.'

'Where?'

'I don't know if I should show you.'

'Why not?'

'It's a first – a prototype – still, well . . . maybe not quite perfect.'

Christopher became more animated, excited, anxious even.

'Is it different?'

Eckmann nodded solemnly. In truth, there was something of the showman in him. He liked to build up tension and expectation, to create the illusion that marvels were about to be revealed before the eyes of an unsuspecting world.

He beckoned Christopher nearer. He leaned over the desk. Eckmann looked around to ensure that they were alone in the gallery and not in danger of being overheard, looking first to the right, then to the left, like a man about to cross the road, checking that it was clear and free from traffic.

'This one can move,' he said.

The boy looked at him, open-mouthed.

'Move? You mean it's on something that moves it round?'

'No, no. It moves . . . of itself.'

'But how?'

'Ah ha!'

The showman again. So much revealed, but something withheld, and thereby, curiosity maintained.

'Can I see?'

'Come on. It's in the studio.'

Eckmann put the closed sign on the door and led the way up. Christopher followed him. Eckmann waddled up the stairs like a duck and stopped to get his breath on the way. Then he tackled the next flight and they came to the studio.

'What's that?'

Things had changed. Where the telescope had once pointed up to the sky, there was now an elaborate sequence of lenses and filters, and beyond them a circular metal chamber of some kind, and around that, coils of wire and glass tubing, and what looked like a laser.

Eckmann glanced at the apparatus, as though it

were something he had forgotten about, or had intended, but omitted, to conceal.

'Just an experiment,' he said. 'Over here.'

He led Christopher over to the workbench where a small glass dome sat, similar to those on display down in the gallery, and maybe just waiting for a few details to be tidied up before it joined them.

'Here now.'

Only this dome was different. It was in darkness, half covered in black paint. Next to it was a timer switch, which had to be pushed to illuminate the sculpture within. The illumination time lasted for precisely sixty seconds, then the sculpture was plunged back into darkness again.

'What do I do?'

'Look into the microscope and press the timer.'

Christopher stood at the workbench. The microscope needed no adjustment. He and Eckmann were exactly the same height now. Eckmann smiled to see it, but he knew the boy would soon outgrow him. What did children feel then, when they outgrew the adults who had once looked down on them? Could you look up to an adult who was smaller than you? Or did their dignity suddenly disappear – if they ever had any to start with?

'This button here?'

'That's it.'

'What's it called – the sculpture?'

Eckmann hesitated. He licked his lips then said, 'The Tiny Dancer.'

'The Tiny Dancer?'

In his echoing of the phrase there was a note of wonder.

'Go ahead,' Eckmann said, as eager to witness the boy's reaction as Christopher was to see the sculpture. 'Press the button.'

The way he said *press the button*, it almost sounded like *pull the trigger*.

Press the button, pull the trigger, and never be the same again.

Christopher pressed the button and looked down into the microscope.

Light.

A tiny figure stood on the tip of a needle. Not on the top, not above the eye, but on the very *tip*, the very *point* of the needle itself.

It was a dancer, a little marionette, dressed in ballet shoes and tutu, with a ribbon tying her hair back tightly, severely, in a disciplined way.

'It's wonderful, Mr Eckmann, it's wonderful!'

Eckmann smiled. Yes, yes. It was wonderful. He knew that. But all the same, it was good to have it confirmed.

'How did you ever do it?'

'Tricks of the trade, tricks of the trade.'

Christopher kept his eyes to the microscope. Eckmann watched him carefully, waiting for the reaction that had yet to come.

There it was. The boy's whole body stiffened. He pressed his eyes closer to the microscope. It had started.

'Oh, wow, Mr Eckmann! Oh, wow!'

She was dancing. Revolving on the tip of the needle. Dancing in a slow, graceful revolution, just the way Poppea used to do in the abbey square, when someone dropped a coin into the box and set the music off.

'Oh wow, Mr Eckmann! Oh wow!'

As the tiny figure revolved, Christopher saw that there was complete perfection in every detail of the sculpture. It was the most amazingly lifelike of any of the sculptures which Mr Eckmann had ever done. Even the dancer's tiny eyes seemed to move, to be alive with light and fire. Mr Eckmann had even painted her face the way a marionette's face ought to be painted, both expressionless and yet somehow sad. And under each eye, he had painted two artificial tears, and under them, some larger tears.

On she danced, slowly circling. It wasn't a static, rigid, clockwork kind of dance either. Not like a dancer on a music box or a jewellery box, with frozen limbs and arms without gesture, who simply revolved. No. The dancer's arms moved too. There was real, fluid movement in every joint of her body.

'Oh wow, Mr Eckmann! How did you do it?'

And then she was plunged back into darkness.

'Can I see it again?'

His finger was already on its way to press the timer button, to re-illuminate the dancer and set off the mechanism to make her dance again.

'No!'

Eckmann's hand shot out and grabbed Christopher by the wrist.

'Ow! Mr Eckmann! You're hurting me!'

Eckmann released him immediately.

'Sorry, Christopher. Sorry. My fault. I should have said. You musn't press the button again straightaway. You have to let . . . to let it rest. The mechanism, you know. Or it might overheat. Early days, you see.

That's it. Yes. Early days. Can't put too much stress on a thing like that.'

'Oh, OK. Sorry.'

'No, no. My fault. Come on, let's go down. You can see the gallery.'

'OK. Only how did you do it, Mr Eckmann? Get it to move?'

'Ah hah. Tricks of the trade, Christopher. Tricks of the trade.'

'No, but how? Really? Computer chips?'

'Maybe, maybe. Trade secrets, you know.'

'She's so small. I mean, so tiny, and yet to have a mechanism inside, to make her move . . .'

'This way now. Let's go. What is the time? Will your father be expecting you home?'

'I'm OK for a while. Anyway, I've got my own key.'

'Here we are now. Take a look around the gallery. You'll have seen it all before, of course, but if you want to . . .'

'Yes. Thanks. What about the Tiny Dancer? Are you going to put her on display?'

'Yes, maybe. I'm not sure. I'm a little worried about . . . well . . .'

'What?'

'Well, you know – overdoing things.'

'Wearing her out, you mean?'

'That's right. Here. Do you want a biscuit? I have some biscuits. Or a chocolate bar? You like chocolate?'

'Thanks. Are you worried she'll wear out then?'

'Well . . . as I say . . . anything new . . . experimental . . .'

'It would be a great attraction, Mr Eckmann.'

'You think?'

'Oh yes! Everyone will want to see it. Everyone! I mean, all the sculptures are so fantastic, but one so small, that can move. People will be queuing up, really. All round the block. They'll be pressing that timer button and putting the light on all day long.'

Eckmann seemed suddenly heavy and subdued, worried, preoccupied.

'Yes. I'm sure you're right.'

'Are you not having a biscuit, Mr Eckmann?'

'I had one earlier. I don't know. Maybe I should just keep this sculpture in the studio.'

'For yourself?'

'Yes . . . for myself.'

'And friends and special guests.'

'Yes, maybe. Maybe.'

'For private viewings?'

'Maybe, yes.'

'Can I see her again one day?'

'I expect so.'

'You know what she reminded me of, Mr Eckmann?'

Eckmann stiffened. His voice became suddenly curt, almost rude, anxious for the conversation to be at an end.

'She reminded you of what?'

'*Toy Story.*'

'*Toy Story?*'

'You've never seen *Toy Story*?'

'I haven't. No.'

'It's a film, computer animated, and the toys all come alive.'

'Ah, I see.'

'I'd recommend it. You can get it on video. And there's a second one too – a sequel.'

'I'll try to see that. Well, thank you, Christopher.'

'Thanks, Mr Eckmann. Can I come back again?'

'Of course.'

'I won't come back too often. I don't want to be a nuisance. You just tell me if I'm in the way.'

'I'll tell you. Don't worry.'

'It's better if people tell the truth, don't you think, Mr Eckmann. I mean, there's no need to take offence.'

'Absolutely. None at all. Have you seen enough now? I'll maybe close up.'

'Yes, OK. Thanks. Just get my bag.'

'Yes, don't forget that bag. Here. By the cash desk.'

'Thanks.'

'I'll see you out.'

'You know, Mr Eckmann. I was thinking about your sculptures, and you know what I thought?'

'What?'

'It made me think about how much life is worth, and the way people look at it.'

'Oh?'

'The smaller it gets, the less people value it. Have you noticed that?'

'Yes, I have. You're right.'

'A whale, or an elephant – everyone wants to save them. They're so big and beautiful, so magnificent and grand. And if you took a gun and killed an elephant . . .'

'It would be a terrible crime.'

'Yes, everyone says so. But you take a mouse, or a fly, Mr Eckmann, or a mosquito . . . and you could

126

crush it between your fingers, or break it between your fingernails without a second thought.'

'That's right.'

'And people do. Because people don't look on it in the same way. People who would never kill an elephant would quite happily kill an insect, or buy a mousetrap, without giving it a second thought. And you know what I thought then, Mr Eckmann?'

'No, Christopher, what did you think?'

'I thought, what if an elephant was the size of a fly? Or what if a person was the size of an ant? Because say you wanted to get rid of somebody, Mr Eckmann . . .'

'Christopher! I don't want to get rid of anybody! What a bizarre imagination you have!'

'No, I don't mean you, Mr Eckmann, I just mean any of us. I mean take me, now I like most people, but there are people I don't get on with, some people at school. And sometimes I think, I could kill them. Of course I don't mean it. It's just an expression really, isn't it? You'd never do it, never. Because to take the life of another person would be the worst thing ever. Don't you think?'

'Yes, yes. Of course.'

'That's the worst of all, isn't it, Mr Eckmann, to take another person's life.'

'You're a moral boy, Christopher, a very moral boy. With a conscience. Some people, they say children today . . . but me, I don't believe that. I believe that most children have very high standards. I have faith in the future. It's in good hands.'

'Anyway, what I thought, Mr Eckmann, was what if a person was no bigger than an ant? I don't think it would seem the same. People would value that life less, just because it was smaller. I don't even think they would see it as murder any more. Because if you kill an insect, it is a kind of murder, isn't it? But no one really cares.'

'Some do. Some religions. A sect called the Jains, I think, they won't even kill a mosquito.'

'But for most people, Mr Eckmann, it's all to do with the size. When life is tiny, people don't care if they take it or destroy it. They just don't seem to have any conscience about it at all or value it in the same way.'

Eckmann opened the door.

'Yes, well, that's food for thought, Christopher.'

'Well, thanks, Mr Eckmann.'

'Goodnight.'

'See you again.'

Christopher left and Eckmann turned all the lights off in the gallery. He went up to his studio and approached the small dome containing the Tiny Dancer. He pressed the button to illuminate her and to propel her into motion.

But she didn't move. She just remained immobile on the point of the needle.

Something must have gone wrong with the mechanism.

Eckmann began to talk to her; urging her to dance, almost as if she were alive and able to hear him.

But even if she had been alive, what sense would those tiny ears and nerve endings have made of that great rumble of a voice, which would have come as a thunder of indiscernible words, like the grumble of a storm in the sky.

She still didn't move.

Eckmann lifted the glass dome and, taking a pipette in his hand, he dropped a tiny drop of water on to the needle.

Most of the water ran down the side, but a small spot remained, clinging on by surface tension to the metal point.

But it was hard to see what good a drop of water was going to do.

If there was something wrong with the mechanism.

The Fall

Robert refused to call her. Let her call him. She was the one who had gone, after all – who had let her work take her away, when it didn't really have to.

Maybe it was all a pretence anyway – a great pretence that they all put on, one of feigned indifference, as if things like jealousy and envy and insecurity and need and love did not really exist. There was a kind of affectation that it didn't matter, that nobody owed anyone anything, or had any claim on them in any way. All that was just too conventional and petty, just too nine to five, when none of them was like that – in theory.

So let her call him. He'd been the one to call last time and break the silence. It was her turn now, and he could be every bit as stubborn as she was. Even more so.

'Heard from Poppea, Dad?'

'Not yet.'

'Expect she's busy.'

'Yes.'

As if anyone could be that busy, so busy that they couldn't pick their phone up or send a text message or an e-mail. No one was that busy.

In the end he cracked. He sent her a text on

Christopher's phone but got no reply. Then he rang and got the answering service. So he sent one more text and left it at that. Now it was up to her. If she had met somebody else, someone in the theatre, some member of the company, well that was it. Nobody owned anybody. But she at least ought to say.

It was a shame for Christopher, that was all, because he liked her and missed her and she had no business doing that, letting Christopher believe that it was different this time and that it meant something when it didn't. OK, if you were an adult, well, that was your business, that was the risk you took in getting involved with anyone or feeling affection for anyone and you knew – or ought to have known – what you were doing.

But children, that was different. They didn't know. And you shouldn't make a friend of them and make them like you and start to depend on you being there and then disappear and say nothing. It just wasn't very nice. Children didn't know about the small print in the invisible contract which came with every relationship. No one warned them it was there; they operated unconditionally.

After another week, Christopher began seriously to wonder. His father's girlfriends had come and gone before, but this time he thought it was different, permanent. His father wouldn't talk about it, but Christopher knew he missed Poppea and was hurt that she hadn't been in touch.

He wondered if Mr Eckmann might have heard anything and decided to call in one afternoon on his way back from school again, and maybe ask him, indirectly, and maybe get to see the Tiny Dancer again.

It was dark early now and a fall of rain made the pavements glisten. People passed with umbrellas, some of the passers-by wearing overcoats, which smelled of damp wool. It was hard to remember the summer now, or warmth at all. But inevitably the summer would arrive again and you'd have a hard job recollecting the cold and what it felt like, unless you put your hand in the freezer. Which was better? To be hot and need cooling down? Or to be cold and need warming up?

Christopher separated from the usual friends he walked back from school with and turned up along the lane which led to the gallery. He passed bright windows and Christmas goods on display. There were reds and golds, warm colours to counterbalance the cold outside. He passed a shop with a sedan chair in the window. It wasn't a real one, just a replica, and it was draped in fabrics for sale.

Mr Eckmann was visible through the glass panels of the gallery door. There he was, by the cash register, perched on a high stool, hunched over a drawing, a pencil in his hand, his jeweller's eye glass in his eye, as he sketched some fine detail. He looked up as Christopher entered.

'Hello, Mr Eckmann.'

'Hello.'

He seemed subdued today. Moody and withdrawn. Christopher knew it was artistic temperament. He knew because his father got like that too. And his teachers. In fact, practically everyone he knew.

That was the thing about artistic temperament, you didn't have to be an artist to have it. Either that or all people were artists.

'Can I look?'

'Yes, sure. Of course.'

He went back to his sketch.

'Can I see the dancer?'

Eckmann looked up. He kept the jeweller's glass in his eye. He almost seemed like a pirate of some kind.

'Yes. All right.'

'Is she in the gallery now?'

'No. Up in the studio still.'

'Can I . . . shall I wait?'

Eckmann glanced towards the gallery. He had some clients in there, who were taking their time to get round everything. He could hear their 'Gees!' and 'Wows!' and 'Look at this-es!' and 'Amazings!' as they drew each other's attention to what they had seen. They seemed in no hurry to go.

'You go up. You know where it is. But just the dancer.'

'Don't worry, Mr Eckmann, I won't touch anything else. I know how to be sensible.'

At least that made him smile.

'I'm sure you do, Christopher.'

'Old beyond my years, Mr Eckmann.'

'Who told you that?'

'You did.'

'You're right. I'd forgotten.'

'Can I go and see her?'

'OK.'

He went towards the staircase then paused.

'Any news of Poppea at all, Mr Eckmann?'

He glanced up again, the eyeglass still in his eye, like some kind of alien growth.

'No. Not a word. Your father not heard from her?'

'I don't think so . . . I'm not sure. Not as far as I know.'

'She's probably busy working.'

'Yes.'

He went on up to the studio alone.

It was slightly creepy, and special too, to be alone in the attic room at the top of the house.

Small, silent figures moved across the face of the camera obscura. They came and went, came and went, oblivious to being watched. Even the security cameras in the streets outside were unaware of such observation.

Christopher put his bag down. He reached up and moved the lens of the camera obscura. The abbey square came into view on the dish. There was his father, sitting at his easel, painting the portrait of a Japanese girl, as her friends stood nearby, watching the progress of the picture, occasionally laughing and smiling their approval.

Robert was wearing gloves with the fingers cut off to keep his hands warm while he worked. He had set up his easel near to the outdoor gas burners of the café, so as to steal a little heat to work by and to make it warmer for the sitters.

Christopher left the camera obscura and went to look at Mr Eckmann's array of lenses and filters and containers and drums and electromagnets and . . . well, he didn't really know what the rest of it was. Something complicated. He wondered what it was for.

Then he saw the dome with the tiny replica of the city. It had come on a long way since he had last seen it. Mr Eckmann had done a lot of work. There were gargoyles now, on the fascia of the abbey, and signs on all the shops.

Then there was the Tiny Dancer, in her own glass dome, now with a little name plate by it. There she was, concealed in the darkness, waiting for someone to turn on the light.

He put his eyes to the microscope and pressed the button. The light illuminated the dome. There she was. On the tip of the needle. The light seemed almost to take her by surprise. And then she was dancing, just like before, this minuscule figure, as small as a full stop on a page, small and beautiful and perfect, in her marionette make-up and costume and painted-on tears.

Christopher watched enthralled as the dancer circled and pirouetted. Until with a sudden click the light went out, and the minute was over.

He wanted to see it again.

He pressed the button a second time. On came the light. The dancer danced just as before. That is, more or less as before, but not precisely the same. It was fascinating. How had Mr Eckmann done it? To program such a tiny figure with movement, but to have it vary the movement as well.

The minute passed. The light went out.

He wanted to see it again.

He pressed the button a third time. He had forgotten about not constantly turning the button on. The dancer resumed her dance. But she seemed tired now, it seemed an effort for her to hold the pirouette. And then, after ten or fifteen seconds, she began to wilt, to droop, like a flower closing at nighttime. She seemed to grow limp and ineffably weary.

And then she fell.

Down, down, down. All the way from the point of the needle to its base, secured on a small platform in the dome. Down she fell, but slowly, as if she weighed so little that the ordinary rules of gravity could not apply. As she fell, she drifted, and then suddenly hit the wooden base.

And was still. She lay there, limp as a rag doll, as though all her limbs were broken into a thousand tiny pieces.

Christopher stared down at her through the lenses of the microscope.

He felt suddenly cold, right down to the pit of his stomach. Cold and responsible and somehow to blame. And yet he hadn't done anything. Had he?

'I didn't do anything. It wasn't me!'

He knew what a hollow ring it had, and yet it was true.

No it wasn't. She was dead. He had killed her.

But that was stupid. She was a model, a sculpture, she wasn't alive.

He'd broken her then.

But that wasn't true either. He hadn't done anything. She'd fallen. All he'd done was put on the light . . .

. . . three times in succession, each immediately after the other.

But what difference could that possibly make?

He felt something else too, besides the cold. Fear. Fear of Mr Eckmann getting angry and not believing him. Fear of what Mr Eckmann might say. Mr Eckmann was only small and usually very nice most of the time, but you got the feeling that if you ever crossed him, or interfered with his sculptures . . .

Only he hadn't interfered with it. Not really. He hadn't done anything. Just pressed the button.

The timer light went off.

He pressed it a fourth time. She was still there. Lying spreadeagled at the base of the needle. An equivalent fall would have been for the statue of Nelson in Trafalgar Square to have toppled from its column.

He ran down to the gallery.

'Mr Eckmann, Mr Eckmann, Mr Eckmann!'

He ran down the stairs, clumping and banging, the wood echoing hollowly.

'Mr Eckmann! Mr Eckmann!'

Down the next flight, and the next. There he was, just closing the door behind the last of the departing visitors.

'Mr Eckmann . . .'

'Christopher. What is it?'

He was breathless, panting. He couldn't speak, except to say the name again.

'Mr Eckmann . . .'

'Yes? What is it? Take your time.'

Christopher stopped, swallowed. He managed to say it now.

'She fell.'

'Fell?'

'The tiny dancer. I didn't do anything. I didn't touch anything. But she fell. All the way down. She's just lying there. Not moving. I was only looking. I promise, I didn't do anything!'

Eckmann didn't say a word. He just turned and

hurried up the stairs. Not knowing what else to do, Christopher followed him, occasionally repeating the mantra 'I didn't do anything,' hoping for a response which would excuse him, disappointed that he didn't get one, wanting Mr Eckmann to say, 'That's all right. It wasn't your fault.'

But he didn't say anything.

Christopher felt afraid. As if he had broken something valuable but hadn't meant to, hadn't even done anything to break it, or maybe hadn't been told how fragile it really was.

They came to the studio. Eckmann hurried to the dome, pressed the timer button to trigger the light and peered down into the microscope.

His hunched shoulders relaxed. He looked around at Christopher.

'It's all right,' he said. 'No real damage. No harm done.'

'She just fell,' Christopher said yet again. 'I didn't do anything.'

'It's nothing that can't be fixed,' Eckmann said. 'I'll see to it later. Now . . .'

He was plainly anxious for Christopher to go. The boy hesitated. He would dearly have loved to look down into the microscope again, to see the tiny figure, lying there like a doll. How did Mr Eckmann know that there was no real damage, that it was nothing that couldn't be fixed, that there was no harm done?

'I'm sorry, Mr Eckmann.'

'It's all right. You're a good boy, Christopher. A good boy.'

Eckmann was walking towards him, ushering him to the door by the stairs.

'I didn't mean anything.'

'I know.'

Eckmann was approaching, making gestures with his hands. Christopher turned and headed for the staircase.

'It doesn't mean I can't come back any more?'

'We'll see, we'll see. Let's not worry about that for now. We'll see.'

He walked down the stairs; Eckmann was directly behind him. He would have hesitated, but Eckmann bore down on him. He wasn't hostile, but firm and determined. It was time for the boy to go.

They got to the ground floor. Eckmann handed him his school bag.

'There. Not to worry.'

'Mr Eckmann . . .'

Eckmann was on his way to open the door.

'The only thing I did do . . .'

'Yes?'

'Was to press the button.'

'Oh?'

'Three times. One after the other.'

'Ah.'

'Maybe that was wrong.'

'You weren't to know. You must have forgotten. I thought I told you. Never mind.'

'Maybe it overheated or something. Three times in a row without a pause. I didn't mean to. I just forgot.'

'Maybe. Button your coat up now. It's cold outside.'

A draught came in through the open door. Still Christopher hesitated.

'Mr Eckmann . . .'

'Goodbye then, Christopher. Go carefully. Goodnight.'

Then he was out on the wet pavement, and the door of the gallery had closed behind him. He could hear the sound of the key turning, and the snap of the security bolt.

He buttoned up his coat, pulled his bag up on to his shoulder, and set off for home.

He walked through the evening crowds, past the lines of cars waiting for the lights to change. There were long queues at the tills in the supermarkets. But he didn't see any of it and walked on, letting his feet think for him and instinct take him home.

Inside he had this terrible feeling. It was the possession of a secret. One which you can never confide. For who would believe it? Could you even believe it yourself? Maybe you were mistaken. It had been an illusion, an accident of memory, a trick of the light. Something confused you, made you see what wasn't there.

Yet he had seen it. He *had*. He was certain of it. Just before the dancer fell. As she made that final pirouette, suddenly seeming so tired and heavy and exhausted, frail and fragile, as if she could dance no more, something had appeared, right there, running like two rain drops over the painted-on tears.

She had started to cry.

She had started to weep real tears.

And then she had fallen.

Christopher walked on through the glistening streets, through the home-going crowds and the shoppers and the workers, the families and the friends.

140

Only he wasn't going home any more, but heading for the abbey square. The gargoyles were already illuminated by lights, sunk into the ground. The spire was spotlit. Some musicians were hurrying inside the abbey, carrying their instruments, raincoats on their shoulders, the women in black dresses, the men in ties and tails.

He found his father in the corner of the square by the café, just packing up the last of his things into a faded leather bag.

'Dad!'

'Hi!'

'You going home?'

'I am now. Come on. We'll buy something on the way. Shall I cook? Or do you want fish and chips?'

'I don't mind. You decide.'

He helped his father fold up the easel, and then the two of them went on their way. They walked in silence for a while. Christopher kept glancing at his father, wondering how to tell him, if he even should tell him, what chance there was of being believed.

They stopped at the fish and chip shop and bought two portions and a bottle of tomato ketchup as they had run out at home.

From there it was only two minutes walk to the flat. Carrying the fish suppers usually made you hungry to eat them, a little impatient too, and you could picture the food already on your plate (not that they bothered with plates when it was fish and chips) and the chips all smothered in ketchup and salt and vinegar, and you eating them.

Only . . .

. . . tonight he didn't feel so hungry.

Robert opened the front door. He put his work things down in the hallway and led the way to the kitchen. He set the food down on the table, poured out two glasses of milk, then they washed their hands and sat down to eat.

'Well?' he said.

'What?'

'What's the matter?'

'Nothing.'

'Chris, something's the matter. What is it?'

'Nothing, Dad.'

'Is it something at school?'

'No. Nothing. Honestly.'

'There's something. I know you. Now what is it?'

'Dad . . .'

'Yes.'

They ate for a while. Then,

'I went to Mr Eckmann's tonight.'

'Oh?'

Robert didn't exactly disapprove. He didn't approve either. You had to give people freedom. Freedom meant responsibility, and that was what children needed and had to learn.

'So?'

'And, well . . .'

'Well what?'

'I think I saw someone.'

'Who?'

'Poppea.'

Robert stuffed a handful of chips into his mouth, eating hungrily, almost angrily, then he swallowed half a glassful of milk.

'What do you mean you saw her?'

'At Mr Eckmann's.'

'She's back working there?'

'No. I don't mean that.'

'What then?'

'I mean . . . I mean I saw her . . . only . . .'

'Only what?'

'It's hard to say.'

'Well, you'd better tell me then.'

So Christopher tried to tell him. But he knew from the outset, from the look in his father's eyes and from the way he ate as he listened, angry and impatient, and constantly looking around the room, that he would never be believed.

'I don't know what gets into you sometimes, Chris,' his father said, when he had finished. 'These things you say. These stories you come out with.'

He went off to get on with one of his paintings.

Found

Christopher lay on his bed with his hands behind his head, looking up through the skylight at the moon.

Say there was another planet, he thought, only everyone upon it was gigantic. Not twice your size, or three or four times bigger, but a thousand thousand times larger than you. Even if you spoke the same language, how would you communicate? How could you understand the great rumbling sounds coming from such deep, cavernous throats? How could you read the writing of a hand which formed words from letters which to you were miles long? It would be impossible. It would take you a week just to walk around a single solitary O.

It was funny how in books all the aliens were supposed to be so different from people. Why were they never exactly the same? Only larger? Or smaller? Living in worlds within worlds? In fact, maybe that was where all the other worlds were? All the possible forms of life. They weren't out there, light years away, on the borders of time and space, but right here, contained within us.

What if the universe was a whole collection of planet-sized molecules and atoms, whirling and colliding. And if you could stand far enough away, you

144

could see that they all made something – a drop of water, a grain of sand on a beach, a mouse, a whisker, a tie.

And say the worlds within our world – the atoms and the molecules from which everything was made – made universes of their own. What if on one of the planets within that tiny universe there was life?

You could send a rocket to the moon, a satellite to Mars, but how could you send a rocket to land upon the whirling atom of a grain of salt? And say you could, say you did, what would you find when you got there?

Life?

'Christopher!'

'Dad?'

'Put your light out!'

'You haven't said goodnight.'

'Oh, OK. Coming.'

His father came in. He had cheered up a bit and seemed to have forgiven Christopher.

'Sorry, Dad.'

'No, I'm sorry. I shouldn't have snapped at you. I was tired.'

'I just thought I saw it. That was all.'

'It doesn't matter.'

'Do you think she's all right?'

'I'm sure she is. I'll ring her tomorrow. If I don't get her, I'll ring the company she's working for and leave a message.'

'OK. Night then.'

'Night.'

Robert kissed him briefly on the corner of his lips. Not the way you kiss a daughter goodnight, but the way you kiss a son. A bit abruptly maybe, but with affection just the same. Maybe there weren't supposed to be differences, that was what some people said. But there were differences, just the same.

Christopher closed his eyes and let sleep come to him. When you let sleep come, it all faded away. Everything jumbled itself up, and then it dwindled and dissolved. Sometimes it all fell into place too. Like one of those little wooden toys that small children had, with the wooden shapes which had to match the holes.

It didn't happen often, but sometimes it did. And everything was all right then, and it was all explained. Why Mum had gone and left him with Dad, and what had gone wrong and why she had never come back. Poppea was there too, and they were all sitting at the kitchen table and everything was all right and it was going to stay that way as well, and no one would ever go away again, and they would be all right forever.

He hated it when people had to leave.

Why did people always have to leave?

Why didn't they just stay with you? Why couldn't they be happy with what they had? They made it seem like you weren't enough. So they had to go looking for something else as well. But Dad stayed. It was enough for him. That was all Christopher wanted. As long as Dad was there. He couldn't bear it if he lost him too. But he would always be there.

Wouldn't he? Wouldn't he? Surely Dad would always be there.

Only what if one night, he didn't come home?

Christopher tossed and turned and kicked off the duvet. His father looked in later and saw what he had done, and draped the cover back over him so that he wouldn't wake from the cold. By then the nightmare had subsided, and Christopher's dreams were peaceful. It was like a street after the snow had fallen.

Robert rang Poppea the next day, but once again there was no reply, just the voice of the answering service on her mobile. He didn't leave a message this time, but rang a friend of hers and got the number of the theatre company which Poppea had gone to work for. He rang them and finally got to speak to somebody who knew something about it. She said that Poppea had never arrived and hadn't answered their messages, so they had assumed that she had let them down, and had hired somebody else – you knew what these people were like.

'No,' Robert said angrily, 'I don't know what these people are like, or what people you mean exactly.'

'You know,' the voice at the other end of the telephone said, 'artistes. They're all so unreliable. They get a better offer. They come and go. You simply can't depend on them.'

In Robert's experience, quite the opposite was true. 'Artistes' were the most reliable people in the world, rain, snow, asthma or influenza. When they said they would be somewhere, they were there, even when they were sick. After all, they were the ones with most to lose – work, income, a reputation. Who was going to employ an 'artiste' with a reputation for not turning up on time and for letting people down. The show must go on – wasn't that it?

'Thank you anyway,' Robert said. And he hung up.

Eckmann had a buzzer fitted to the gallery door which went off when it was opened, so that he would know if anyone came in, even if he had gone to the toilet or was in the back room making coffee. He could hear the buzzer from up in his studio too, and would hurry down the stairs, calling, 'Coming! Coming! Right with you! There in a moment.'

He could easily have afforded to pay for another assistant to sit behind the cash desk, but for now, while it was quiet, and since Poppea had gone, he seemed happy to run things by himself.

Only this time it wasn't a customer. It was Robert Mallan, the boy's father, looking slightly bedraggled from the afternoon rain. He had an artist's portfolio on his shoulder and was, as Eckmann rightly suspected, doing his rounds of the galleries, trying to interest them in his work.

'Ah, Robert, it's you.'

He tried to sound friendly, but couldn't totally keep a note of slight hostility – or was it rivalry – from his voice.

'Ernst.'

'How are you? Is this a social call or . . .'

He gestured with slight concern towards the portfolio.

'No. Don't worry. I'm not trying to sell you anything.'

'No, no. It's not that, it's just I don't really exhibit . . .'

'I know, any work but your own.'

'Was there anything in particular?'

'No, no, I was just passing. I wondered if you'd heard anything from Poppea at all.'

148

Eckmann seemed puzzled. He shook his head.

'No, no. She left almost . . . two weeks ago. Why?'

'I haven't heard from her, that's all.'

'Ah well . . .' Eckmann spread his hands out in a gesture intended to convey that they were both men of the world together and they understood a few things. '. . . women. You know.'

Robert did know about women. But he didn't know if Eckmann did. Or if he did, to what extent, and with what understanding.

'Sorry,' Eckmann said. 'If she gets in touch I'll pass a message on, of course. But other than that . . .'

'Thanks.'

Eckmann seemed hopeful that he would go now, but Robert looked towards the gallery.

'You know, I've never really looked at your work . . .'

'I was just about to close,' Eckmann said, though it wasn't even three o'clock yet.

'Maybe another time.'

'Yes.'

Robert moved a few paces towards the door, then hesitated again.

'Actually, I may have something that might interest you.'

'Oh?'

'A picture. Of her.'

Eckmann hesitated. His tongue came out and licked his lips.

'Of . . . Poppea?'

'Yes. It's the nude study.'

'You'd consider selling it?'

'Maybe.'

'Why?'

'I might need the money.'

'I'd need to see it again first.'

'Of course. The light's not very good here.'

'Bring it up. To the studio.'

He beckoned towards the staircase.

They walked up to the studio and Robert untied the portfolio and opened it out upon the table.

Eckmann politely leafed through the work, but he was anxious to get to the one painting in particular, and his hands were even trembling slightly.

'What's this?'

Eckmann looked up. Robert had found the dome containing his model of the town.

'Ah, in the dome? It's a replica, of the city. Look through the lens.'

Robert did.

'It's wonderful.'

'Thank you. You have a portrait of her, you say?'

'I'm sure it's in there. Unless I forgot to bring it . . .'

Eckmann went on flicking through the contents of the portfolio.

'I don't see anything.'

'You must have missed it. Look through it again.'

There was another dome. Upon it was a name plate which read: *The Tiny Dancer*. Robert craned forwards, put his eyes to the microscope above it and pressed a small button to trigger the light.

The scene was illuminated.

The tiny dancer was sitting at the base of the needle. She had her arms around her knees. She held her hand up to guard her eyes from the light, almost as if trying to see who it was looking down upon her.

There was a sound from somewhere; a whirr; a drone; the movement of machinery. But Robert didn't hear it. He stared, engrossed, fascinated by what he saw.

'It moves . . . she can move . . .' he muttered. 'She's . . . alive.'

The light went out. He pressed the button again. The tiny dancer stood up. She made a pantomime of gestures. *What do you want? What can I do? What have I done? Why me? Why this? What do you want from me?*

The light went out. Another minute must have passed. Robert pressed the light button again, and this time he held it down. He had forgotten all about Eckmann, all about the portfolio, all about the picture he hadn't brought with him and which he would never have shown, let alone sold, to Eckmann at any price. He had forgotten about the pretence and the ploy and the shallow subterfuge to get into the studio and see for himself.

The last thing he saw was a faint blur in the periphery of his vision, and then there was a sudden blinding flash and an awful, immense pain in his skull. Then nothing, nothing at all. Just the silence and emptiness of oblivion.

And Lost

Christopher came home from school to find the flat empty. This wasn't so unusual – his father often went out in the afternoon, to work, or to visit a gallery, or to buy some artists' supplies. Sometimes he just wandered around 'looking for inspiration' – whatever shape that took. He probably didn't know himself, but hoped to recognize it when he saw it.

Though even inspiration was never enough on its own. Even when you got some, you still had to do something with it. Inspiration was like a lump of dough or a piece of clay that needed moulding. Sometimes inspiration was your worst enemy, other times it was your best friend. It could send you down blind alleyways which led nowhere except to the start of something which you couldn't see how to finish.

Christopher's father usually warned him in advance when he was going to be late. But Christopher didn't worry. He just poured himself some milk and took some biscuits (maybe a couple more than usual, seeing he was on his own) and sat down for a while to watch TV.

He noticed that the easel and the folding chairs – one for the artist, one for the sitter – were lying against the wall. His father wasn't out in the abbey square then, hustling tourists to have their portraits done.

Christopher promised himself that he would start his homework in half an hour, but then another programme started, so he watched that too, and then there was another one. An hour and a half had gone by before he turned the set off. It was past six now. He checked the time on the clock and vaguely began to worry.

He went into his father's room and saw, among the finished and unfinished paintings, that his portfolio was gone. He must be going round the galleries then. They'd all have closed by now, and he'd be back soon. Reassured, Christopher poured another glass of milk and did a little homework.

By seven he was hungry, and anyway, all his homework was done. There were only two subjects today, instead of the usual three, and neither task was particularly difficult – a short history essay and a few maths questions.

He wished his dad had a mobile phone. He'd bought Christopher one, as a safety measure, so that he could ring home, but he hated the things himself and wouldn't carry one.

Christopher went into the kitchen and opened the fridge. He peered into the freezer compartment to see what was there. Maybe he ought to start cooking something so that it would be ready when his father got back. He took out some oven chips, some veggie sausages and some frozen peas and turned on the oven.

Still he didn't come. The meal had cooked. Christopher ate his share, put his father's meal on to a plate

153

and put the plate in the oven, leaving it on a low heat to stay warm but not to dry out too quickly before he got back.

It was nearly eight o'clock now. The worrying began in earnest. It had been there for a while already, but now it came to the surface.

He'd give his father ten minutes – maybe fifteen. Then he'd ring someone, or go out and look for him. He looked at the phone, wondering why his father didn't call.

He went into the living room. He tried to read but couldn't concentrate, so he put the television back on. It was a quiz programme, one he usually enjoyed, but the questions sounded stupid now, and the whole thing seemed pointless and hollow. Why did people want to do it? To get on TV to parade their knowledge or their ignorance? What was it for? What did it prove? That you were stupid, that you were clever? He couldn't see that it really proved anything.

He turned off the sound but left on the picture. He sat chewing at his fingernails. He kept thinking about the Tiny Dancer, the way she had fallen, the real tears he thought he had seen. But he couldn't have seen them, he must have imagined it.

Only how did Mr Eckmann make the dancer move? She was so like Poppea too. He must have modelled the dancer on her – he *must* have done.

Christopher looked at the clock again and went and got his father's address book from the bedside table in his room.

He rang some of the people in it.

'Hello, it's Christopher, I just wondered if my dad was with you?'

No luck.

'Hi, is that Miff? Hi. It's Christopher. Were you in the square today? You haven't seen my dad? No. OK. Thanks anyway. No. I'm sure he's OK. He's just a little late. Yes, OK. If you do. Thanks. No. I'm fine. But thanks for offering. Yes, I'll ring again. No, you don't have to come round, really. I'm OK.'

He wondered if he should ring the police, but on second thoughts, it wasn't that late. Only what if there had been an accident and he was in hospital?

He felt suddenly sick, aware of how alone he was. It was different for other children, with their brothers and sisters and mothers and fathers. They fought and quarrelled and thought that they were having a hard time. But at least they had someone to fight and quarrel with, and to make up with at the end of the day. There was no insurance when you just had one person. When you lost them, you had no one. There was no margin for error, no room for things to go wrong.

He got the note pad from beside the telephone in the kitchen, scribbled a message on it, saying that he had gone out searching, and left it on the door for his dad to see, if he came back in the meantime. Oh, and his food was in the oven, but he had turned the oven off as it was drying out, and it might be cold now too. Sorry. But he couldn't risk it catching fire. Bye and love, Chris.

Maybe there had just been a mix-up, a misunderstanding. His dad had asked someone to pass on a message and they hadn't done it. Maybe he'd even found Poppea. Yes, that was it. Maybe they were both on their way home, right now, with a bottle of wine and a takeaway meal from the Indian restaurant.

He could see the two of them, bursting in through the door, his dad happy again and Poppea laughing, and the smell of the garlic and coriander coming from the bag, and his dad opening the wine and Poppea putting the meal out and tearing up the Indian bread and giving some to him because she knew he liked it.

It was so quiet when you were alone. He turned off the oven in case the meal burned while he was out, like he had said in the note. The whole place could catch fire and go up in flames. Things like that could happen when you weren't careful. You had to be careful when there was just you. You couldn't just be a child any more and expect someone else to do all the worrying. You had to do some for yourself.

He put his coat on and took his door keys and went out into the night. The rain had gone and the moon was out; there were just a couple of black clouds with grey edges to be seen, otherwise the sky was clear.

He walked to the abbey square, but his dad wasn't there. He spoke to some of the artists who knew him, but they all shook their heads. He went and talked to Scotchy, who was just about to set up his juggling things in the hope that a big enough audience of tourists would make it worth his while, but he hadn't seen Christopher's father either. Scotchy's breath smelt of paraffin. He used to eat fire at the end of his act. Sometimes he singed his eyebrows, and now he didn't have any left.

Christopher went and spoke to one of the waiters at the café. He was standing lighting the gas burners. But he shook his head. He claimed he didn't know who the boy meant. Christopher didn't believe him. He just didn't want to help.

More worried and anxious, he rang home, to see if his father had got back yet, but there was no answer. The phone just rang and rang until the recorded voice cut in and told him there was nobody there.

'Hey, kid, where are you going . . . ?'

He hurried on. There was nobody else his age on the streets. They were adults: young, middle-aged, some students, those who were grown-up and those who thought they were. There were people heading for the bars and the cinemas, then older, more sedate people, heading for the restaurants, the theatre, the concert halls. There was nobody really old though; maybe they were too afraid to go out at night and were hiding at home.

Where to go? He didn't know now. Didn't know any more. Worry turned to fear and that terrible emptiness was there again in the pit of his stomach. It churned it all up again, all the old questions to which there were no answers, things which should have been resolved a long time ago but never were. Why did people leave? Why did people leave you?

His feet walked and he followed them. He just hoped they knew where they were going, that was all.

'Hey son, come here a minute . . .'

He didn't even turn and look. You could tell from the voice that you had to keep going; you didn't even hesitate with voices like that.

Where to? Where were his feet taking him?

He almost wanted to shout out loud, like a child lost in the supermarket.

'*Dad! Dad!*'

And he'd come running.

'*I thought you'd left me. I thought you'd gone.*'

Only you didn't say that. You just got mad or started to cry, and they said, 'Whatever's the matter, whatever's the matter? It's OK.'

The truth was you thought you'd lost them forever, and would never see them again.

His father would be around the next corner. He'd turn the corner and there he'd be, carrying his portfolio and looking a bit sullen maybe, as if he'd had a bad day, because the galleries didn't want his work – or they did, but they wouldn't pay properly for it. But his face would light up when he saw Christopher, and Christopher would know just what to say as they walked back together. He would say back to his father all the things his father had taught him.

'Look at Vincent Van Gogh, Dad, and Paul Gaugin. They weren't famous until they were dead.'

And his father would laugh then.

'I don't want to be famous and dead. I just want to make a living.'

It was a funny notion that – that being famous and recognized once you were dead somehow made up for being ignored and neglected all your life. Van Gogh had died in poverty. Now his paintings sold for millions. But as far as Christopher could see, Van Gogh wasn't a penny better off. None of it would bring his ear back either.

His dad always laughed at that.

'It won't bring your ear back, Dad.'

He'd be right there, around the next corner.

He wasn't there.

Death won't bring your ear back. Death and fame

and money. They won't bring back what matters. Money only buys things. It doesn't bring back people. It doesn't bring back what you love.

OK. One more corner. If his father wasn't there, that was it. He'd go home and ring the police station or go straight to the hospital. Just one more try, just one more corner.

He wasn't there.

One more then.

He turned around it. He wasn't there. He'd have to do it . . .

Then he saw where he was. He was standing outside Mr Eckmann's gallery and a light was burning inside. The sign in the window told him that he was right outside the Gallery of the Art of the Impossible, opening hours 10.00 to 5.30.

He reached up and rang the doorbell. He could hear it echoing through the building. Nothing. Maybe Mr Eckmann wasn't there; perhaps he'd just left a light on for security. He rang again and looked up at the window. He thought he saw a shadow moving, way up at the top where the attic was, where Mr Eckmann had his studio.

Silence again. He rang the bell a third time, a good, long solid ring – the kind that told people you meant business, that you weren't to be fobbed off, that you weren't going away until they answered the door.

He saw some other lights go on. Then he saw a shadow inside, as Mr Eckmann came down the stairs.

'Who is it? What do you want? We're closed.'

'Mr Eckmann, it's me!'

He pressed his face to the window, so that Eckmann could see who it was.

'Go away. Come back tomorrow. We're closed.'

Christopher banged hard on the window.

'Mr Eckmann! It's me!'

'Did you hear what I said? Are you drunk? Do you want me to fetch the police?'

'Mr Eckmann! It's me! Christopher!'

The window separated them. Eckmann peered out, Christopher peered in.

'Christopher, is that you?'

'Mr Eckmann, I've lost my dad.'

'What?'

'Have you seen my dad? He hasn't come home, I've lost him, I don't know what to do.'

'Wait there. I'll let you in.'

The keys turned, the bolts slid back, the security chains were pulled away. Mr Eckmann took no chances. He kept his sculptures under lock and key – several locks and several keys, and one or two alarms.

'Mr Eckmann, I'm worried . . .'

'Come on in. Come up to the studio.'

'I can't find my dad.'

'Come up and tell me about it. When did you last see him?'

'This morning, when I left the house.'

Eckmann led the way up to the studio.

'Here, sit down.'

'I don't know what to do, Mr Eckmann. It's my dad. He's never not come home before. Not like this. I'm worried. You haven't seen him, have you? I mean it's not like him to . . .'

'Whoa, whoa. Sit down now. Let's calm down and go through it, one thing at a time. Maybe there's no need to worry. You mustn't panic. That's the worst thing you can do. Now then – from the beginning?'

Christopher knew Mr Eckmann was right. He sat on the edge of the chair, took a deep breath and tried to calm himself. Mr Eckmann would help. You could see that he wanted to help. Mr Eckmann was a good person. Maybe odd and strange and sad in many ways, but a good person at heart. He would help. You could see that he only wanted to help. It was good of him to give his time, to come downstairs and to open the door . . .

But . . . but then . . . it suddenly occurred to Christopher that it was almost as if Mr Eckmann had been half expecting him. As if he wasn't that surprised to see him at all. That surprise had been a thing he was feigning.

'Excuse me for just one moment, Christopher, I think I forgot to lock the door. I'd better go down and do it. I don't suppose anybody would wander in, but you never know . . .'

He hurried back down the stairs. Christopher heard the clip-clop of his shoes; he sounded like a miniature pony, clattering over a bridge.

Clip clop, clip clop. Who made that sound again? Oh yes. The goats in *The Three Billy Goats Gruff*. No. It wasn't clip, clop. It was something else. Trip, trap. That was it. Trip, trap, trip, trap, over the bridge.

The bridge with the troll.

A troll – small, thickset, muscular, rather ugly maybe, with not much of a neck. Head growing out of his shoulders, but powerful, clever, evil even perhaps.

I'm a troll, fol-de-rol. Trip, trap, trip trap – over the bridge. Little Billy Goat Gruff it was, the small one.

He was no match either for the troll. *Fol-de-rol*.

Christopher looked around, feeling strangely ill at ease. He crossed to the dome which contained the Tiny Dancer. He pressed the button and peered through the lenses. The light came on, but she wasn't there. The dome was empty; there was just the needle, mounted on the plinth.

Trip, trap, trip, trap.

He looked around the room, at the telescope, the arrangements of lenses, the dish of the camera obscura, the clear glass tubes, the electro magnets and condensers and lasers. What was it all for? What was it supposed to do?

He crossed to the other workbench and looked down into the dome containing the tiny city, the replica of the town. It was empty, except for a few specks of black dust. Oddly, they seemed to be moving.

There was the sound of the security chain now, being put back on the door. Mr Eckmann's little feet, clip-clopping their way back up the flights of stairs. The sound of his breathing as he approached.

Then Christopher saw it, tucked out of sight behind a stack of Mr Eckmann's own drawings and roughs. It was his father's portfolio, his battered old leather portfolio, which he had had since he had been a student. Christopher recognized it immediately. There were his father's initials in faded gold – R.M.

He looked away as Eckmann entered.

'Well, well. That's done. I don't like to leave the place unlocked and unattended. You never know.'

Christopher made himself look away. He didn't

want Mr Eckmann to know that he had seen it. He didn't know why. He just didn't.

'So . . . now then . . . what are we to do?'

Christopher wondered if he should challenge Eckmann directly. Or maybe make for the door. Mr Eckmann wasn't any taller than him – heavier maybe, but no taller. He looked strong though; his wrists were thick, covered in black hair, and his fingers were thick and stubby. He was probably strong – very strong. But Christopher was younger, and faster.

Maybe it was time to run. Only then what? He couldn't leave without knowing, could he?

'You . . . you haven't seen him today, have you, Mr Eckmann?'

'Your father?'

'Yes?'

'Me? . . . No. Why would he come here?'

'I don't know . . . I just wondered if you'd maybe seen him . . . in the street.'

'I haven't been out, Christopher.'

'Oh.'

There was something wrong and he wasn't saying. Why wouldn't he say? Why would he lie? Why?

'Mr Eckmann . . .'

'Yes?'

He remained in the doorway. There wasn't a way out.

'Where's the dancer today?'

'The dancer?'

'The Tiny Dancer. I looked in the dome. She's gone.'

'Yes. I moved her for a while. She's quite safe.'

'I think maybe I ought to go now, Mr Eckmann.'

163

'But your father, we were going to talk about what to do.'

'Maybe he's home by now. I really should go.'

Eckmann didn't move. He remained standing in the doorway, studying Christopher's face intently, as if trying to read his thoughts.

'It's a wonderful city,' Christopher blurted out. 'The tiny city. All it lacks is the people.'

Eckmann nodded in agreement.

'Yes, all it lacks is the people. A house is not a home without people; a city is just an empty shell . . . without people.'

He stood away from the doorway and went to pick up the small, domed city and place it inside a cupboard. If he wanted to, Christopher was free to run now. But if he ran, he might never know, never find out, where they had gone.

'Mr Eckmann . . .'

'You know, Christopher, what I think? I think that you're a clever boy. That sometimes you know more than you say.'

Christopher swallowed. His mouth was very dry.

'Mr Eckmann, the Tiny Dancer, it looked just like Poppea, didn't it?'

'You think so?'

'Yes. It was just like her.'

Eckmann followed Christopher's gaze. He saw that he hadn't hidden the portfolio properly.

'Yes, Christopher,' he said. 'It was just like her. She was my model, you could say – more than a model in a sense.'

'Mr Eckmann . . .'

'Christopher?'

164

'Is that my dad's portfolio?'

'Portfolio?'

He looked surprised, feigned it rather convincingly.

'Is it your father's?'

He crossed to it, and slid the case out.

'Why yes, so it is, so it is. Maybe you would be good enough to return it to him.'

He proffered it for the boy to take. It was large and cumbersome for a child to carry, and yet Eckmann was little larger than a child himself.

'Tell him . . .' Eckmann paused to think. 'Tell him thank you . . . but no thank you. That is, I like them, I can see their value, I can see the quality, he's plainly talented, only . . .'

'Only what?'

'I can't see them fitting in to the gallery here. He'd maybe be better off trying elsewhere.'

He set the portfolio down, gesturing that Christopher was to take it. It was his, after all, was it not? Or at least his father's, and in the absence of his father, it fell . . . to the son?

Christopher reached out, unwilling to ask the question. It was almost insulting in its implication, insinuating that Mr Eckmann wasn't quite telling the truth, that Mr Eckmann was a liar, that Mr Eckmann . . .

But he couldn't leave it unchallenged, he had to find his father.

'Ei, Mr Eckmann?'

'Christopher?'

He was already busying himself with other things, tidying up, sorting sketches into neat piles; he was a neat and methodical man.

'It's just, Mr Eckmann, I thought you said you hadn't seen him.'

'Seen him?'

'My dad.'

'That's right.'

'But if he left his portfolio . . .'

'Ah yes. But that was . . . let me think . . . two, three days ago. I said that perhaps I might be interested, but on reflection . . .'

That had to be it then. The portfolio had been gone from the flat for several days, he'd simply not noticed it. Only if his father hadn't gone out to do his rounds of the galleries, where had he gone? And why hadn't he told Christopher somehow – left him a note at the very least? And what about Poppea, how could she also have disappeared? There was still that other thing too.

'Mr Eckmann?'

'Christopher?'

'How did you make the Tiny Dancer move?'

'Ah – the Tiny Dancer.'

'Yes. How did you do it?'

'Trade secrets, trade secrets.'

'That's what you always say, but you know I won't tell anyone. You know your secrets would be safe with me.'

'Is it important – that you know?'

'Sort of. I mean, it doesn't matter if you really don't want to tell me . . .'

'Well, I don't know, Christopher . . . trade secrets, you know, confidential matters. If one of my competitors . . .'

166

'But you don't have any competitors. You're unique. Only you can do it. There *is* only you.'

'Maybe, maybe, but you never know . . .'

'I shan't tell anyone. Promise. You can trust me.'

'You're sure?'

'Yes.'

'Not anyone? Not even your father when he comes home?'

'Where do you think he is, Mr Eckmann?'

'Oh, I'm sure he can't be far away.'

'Do you think he will be back soon?'

'I'm sure he will.'

'How did you do it then – the dancer?'

'A chip.'

'Computer chip?'

'Yes. Very small, very, very small. But the wiring, the connection – virtually impossible to set up and completely impossible to repair. A failure, I'm afraid. It worked for a little while, then burnt out . . . a failure.'

'Ah. That's a pity.'

'Yes. But if at first you don't succeed.'

'Try and try, Mr Eckmann.'

'Try and try, Christopher.'

'Again and again.'

Eckmann smiled, admiring the boy's spirit.

'Yes, and again after that.'

'Never give up.'

'No.'

'I'd never give up, Mr Eckmann, never. Not if there was something I really wanted to do, or to find out. Never.'

'No, I can see that.'

'Mr Eckmann?'

Christopher reached out and took the portfolio. He sat with it on his knee, holding it carefully. It was his father's, after all, almost a part of him, as private and personal as his clothes. He looked up to see Mr Eckmann watching him and, as he saw the anxiety and concern on Eckmann's face, his distrust evaporated. Christopher had been suspicious for nothing. Mr Eckmann was a good man. He wanted to help him. Christopher had known that all along really.

'Mr Eckmann . . . what should I do?'

It would have been easy, even far too easy, to have sent the boy along the same route – the way Robert had gone, the way Poppea had gone, along through a spot of darkness into another, alternative world. There they were, the both of them now, the people Christopher sought, tiny trapped figures in the tiny city, only a few feet away from him, behind the door of a locked cupboard.

It was nighttime for them, dark and black under the glass dome which was their sky. Maybe a little light filtered in through the side of the cupboard door.

It would have been so easy, and it would have made sense – the logical solution to a complicated problem. He'd have had no chance. Eckmann was by far the stronger. Strong as an ox, strong as a herd of them.

And yet . . .

Eckmann stayed his hand. The man, yes, the woman, yes, for after all, hadn't they both conspired to rob him of the one thing he wanted, needed and so essentially lacked . . .

. . . love.

And yet the boy . . .

Was love itself.

'Maybe we should ring somebody, Christopher.'

'You think so?'

'Maybe.'

'The police?'

'Yes.'

'The hospitals?'

'Maybe. But first the police.'

'You think he's had an accident, Mr Eckmann? I thought of that. I asked the other artists, and all the performers.'

'No, no, no. I'm sure that's not it. Or if it is, then nothing serious. But just to be on the safe side . . . to put our minds at rest.'

'Would you call them, Mr Eckmann?'

'Me?'

It was an odd feeling. Eckmann had never experienced this before – another human being reliant on him, depending on him, wanting, needing his help.

'Me?'

'Please – they'll listen to you. You're grown up.'

That was true. He was an adult. Who would know or be able to tell any more than that from the tenor of his voice?

'Please.'

Warmth flooded Eckmann. He couldn't have put a name to it, to the emotion which surged so strongly through him, but it was compassion – the desire to help another and the warm feeling of worth which that brought. Even though he was the sole person responsible for what Christopher was now going through – his worry, anxiety and fear – Eckmann felt compassion.

He felt the compassion of the strong for the weak, of the knowledgeable for the ignorant, and if he could appear to do anything to put an end to all this, to alleviate the pain he saw the boy was going through, his apprehension of loss, his fear of abandonment, his terror that he might have lost the only person he had in the world, the only person whom he confidently, certainly, unconditionally knew loved him . . . if he could do anything, he would do it.

If only for the sake of appearances.

He glanced towards the closed cupboard door. Of course, the true answer, the real solution . . .

But that was beyond his power. To shrink, to miniaturize, yes. To reverse the process – he didn't yet know how, or if he would ever know how. Maybe that part of it was quite impossible.

Even if it hadn't been, would he have done it? What would have been the outcome – for him? She was his now, unattainable as ever but still his. Even if he could have released and returned her to this world, would he have done so?

'Mr Eckmann – please.'

Please. The boy was almost pleading. Eckmann was needed, wanted – desperately so. So yes, he would help, do anything except . . . what couldn't be done. The boy needed a friend, someone to take charge, to be responsible, and there was only Eckmann, no one else.

He thought again of the tiny city, hidden in the half darkness. Sudden, bitter regret gnawed at him for what he had done, for the irreversibility of it, its incurable nature. But then a sense of triumph too, of success, power.

Then the compassion again, towards the helpless child. Eckmann was like some conquering soldier, who slaughters the family of the innocent and then feels sorry for the survivor, gives him a home, and maybe even brings him up as his own.

Brings him up as his own.

Eckmann realized that Christopher was staring at him, hopefully, expectantly, afraid of being disappointed. He seemed so young, so vulnerable. Eckmann could look right into his soul, and see nothing there but innocence and vulnerability and that awful fear, rising to consume him. And it was for Eckmann to pass sentence, to raise or lower the thumb. He had the power of life – and death.

'Of course,' he said. 'I'll ring them now.'

He picked up the telephone and rang the emergency services.

'Police, please,' he said, in answer to the voice at the other end. Then, 'I'm trying to trace somebody who has gone missing. I have his son with me. We're worried that there might have been an accident.'

Eckmann tried to give Christopher a small, reassuring smile. It was almost as if Eckmann had become exactly what he was pretending to be – the compassionate helper, the good Samaritan, the one who does not turn his back or walk away on the other side of the road.

'Don't worry, Christopher, we'll find him.'

And Eckmann believed in it too – in his own kindness, his genuine compassion. It seemed to have slipped his mind completely that he knew exactly where Christopher's father was.

And who had put him there.

At least it would make the boy feel better, knowing that everything was being done, seeing that he had at least one friend in the world, someone he could rely on, one person he could trust – implicitly.

'I'm sure they'll find him,' Eckmann smiled. 'I'm sure they will.'

Christopher nodded, happier now, reassured. He sat, still clutching his father's portfolio, as Eckmann continued the phone call.

'They'll find him, Christopher,' he said again.

Knowing that they never would.

The Pupil

They made a curious picture. A curious couple even, it could have been said. But in truth they were never quite that, with all the unity it implies. No, they were never a couple exactly, never a pair. Just two individuals, thrown together.

Even those relationships which have become disunited, whose partners are on the verge of separation, even they still may have between them a certain obvious, incontrovertible, if decaying, bond.

But in this case that bond simply wasn't there, or at least it was not immediately obvious. The connections were just too difficult to discern. Maybe one bore a sense of gratitude, the other, affection; one conducted himself with a somewhat muted respect and slightly formal politeness, the other listened and watched with pride and love. They plainly knew each other well, and yet, how well, and in what way exactly, it was hard to say.

The taller of the two figures was the younger. He wore the crested blazer and the charcoal grey trousers of an expensive independent school – the local Abbey School, in fact, a traditional but also impressively modern institution, not afraid – indeed anxious – to move with the times. It had even opened its doors to girls, some twenty-five years ago. A bold move back then.

The school was situated close to the abbey and provided its pews with the necessary choristers for Christmas, Easter and other religious festivals. It was considered (by some) to be quite an honour to have been selected for the choir. Christopher had been chosen for it, but he disliked the amount of practice involved and the time it took up.

Eckmann never missed a performance.

Money – or at least the presence of money, if not its actual possession – had given Christopher assurance. He walked along with a long-limbed stride, and the small man beside him had to scuttle to keep up, taking three steps to his every two.

They passed some pavement artists, on their way to a cheap, popular café for breakfast. Once they would have called out to Christopher, asking how he was. Now they just nodded and Christopher gave a vague smile, while Eckmann nodded curtly back, as if to dismiss them, to brush them away like flies from something wholesome, lest they somehow infect it.

He hated Bohemians, especially artists. Most of them were useless. As if art were the sole preserve of idlers, drinkers and wasters. He blamed literature and the cinema for their depiction of the profession. But then a film about a hard-working, respectable artist who paid his taxes and stayed out of trouble would not have found much favour. What the public wanted in its artists was decadence and immorality. They wanted the Moulin Rouge, not the Royal Academy or three-piece suits.

As they walked, each smartly and expensively

dressed, they could, with a stretch of the imagination, almost have been taken for father and son.

On the left, the prosperous professional man, anxious for his son to study and to one day take up the reins of an equally prosperous and respectable profession. And on the right, the son who had outgrown him.

As they did.

You saw them everywhere, this new generation of slender and not so slender giants, towering above their parents, only in their early teens as yet but already looking down upon the balding heads of men twenty or thirty years their senior.

The world was getting taller.

Not that Eckmann minded that. He even took some satisfaction in the disparity in their sizes. 'Look at that man's son,' he could almost hear people say. 'So much taller than his father.'

But he didn't mind that at all. He was proud to be associated with the young man by his side. Proud for people to think that they were father and son. Because in their way, they were perfectly correct. The boy was his son. Or as good as his son.

Christopher saw a boy he knew, walking towards the Abbey School gates in the company of two girls. He raised his arm and waved.

'Rees!'

The boy, tall, languid and blond haired, turned and saw who it was, and made the kind of long-suffering grimace which people do when they see their friends, making out that the pleasure of seeing them is nothing but a pain and an inconvenience.

'Morning, Mallan.'

Eckmann felt a pang. The Abbey School may have moved with the times, but not completely. It retained the archaic tradition of pupils – boys at least – calling each other by their surnames.

Mallan.

How much nicer, how much more appropriate, *Eckmann* would have been.

After all, who paid the fees?

'Better go then,' Christopher said. 'I'll see you later on.'

'All right, Chris – you have everything?'

'Yes, yes. Of course I have. Don't go on.'

Even the irritation in his voice somehow gave Eckmann pleasure. It was a son's irritation with his over-fussy father.

'*Yes, yes, yes, yes, Dad. Now push off, will you, and leave me alone.*'

Not that Christopher ever quite used those words. Or called Eckmann that. His father remained inviolate, sacred, the one person for whom there could never, would never, be a substitute. He still dreamed of him and believed in the possibility of his return.

'Come on, Mallan, if you're coming!'

Rees waited impatiently. The two girls were watching. One turned and said something to the other, who smiled. Maybe they were talking about Christopher; maybe one of them liked him. Maybe they were talking about Eckmann, saying what a funny little man he was. Maybe. Maybe not. Maybe they were remarking on something else entirely.

All water off a duck's back that, anyway. You couldn't live this long and stay that sensitive. At least not on the surface, but inside, inside . . .

'Gotta go, Ernst.'

The sound of his own name both warmed and saddened him. He could never quite get used to it being said or to hearing it in that voice. It was like a cold blast of air and a warming shot of brandy all in one. It almost made him shudder.

For so long it had been 'Mr Eckmann'. For so long he had prevailed upon the boy, doggedly, but not shrilly, insisting, 'Call me something else, Christopher,' hoping the boy would work out what he wanted and make the decision to use the word for himself.

'What, Mr Eckmann? What should I call you?'

'Well, you know . . . not so formal all the time.'

'I can't exactly call you "guardian", Mr Eckmann.'

'No, no. Obviously not.'

They'd both managed a smile.

'But something else maybe. After all, if we're to live together under the same roof now . . .'

'How about . . .'

'Yes?'

Quite why Eckmann was so anxious for that honorary title, he didn't know. Maybe it would have anchored him – given him the appearance of real links with the world. Maybe it would have given him continuity and connection with the whole human race, a man with a future as well as a past.

A man with a son.

'How about . . . ?'

What he wanted to say was,

'*You want to call me "father", Christopher? Well, that's all right. I understand, really I do. And I know, of course, that your own father could never be replaced. But life goes on, as we all know. This is one of the things we have no choice about, the fact of life going on and having to be lived, despite all that has happened in the past. So, Christopher, it would be an honour and a privilege if you wanted to call me . . .'*

'How about I use your first name, Mr Eckmann – if I called you Ernst?'

'Ernst?'

Eckmann hadn't expected this. Frankly, he was shocked. He knew that he might have encouraged it in the past, but then the situation had been different. But then he saw that yes, now it was possibly the best he could hope for. It was the compromise he would have to settle for and be happy with, the only answer to a difficult situation.

'Yes, Christopher. That would be fine.'

And so it was.

Eckmann watched as Christopher hurried to join his friends – so tall, so straight, such regular almost handsome features, such a future ahead, a son to be proud of.

He was everything Eckmann had never been, but had so desperately wanted to be at his age. It was unfair – so grossly, indiscriminately unfair. The way life twisted and scarred you at so young an age. And when that happened it coloured and distorted everything thereafter. You never got over it, ever. Whereas others walked through life unblemished. It really was unfair.

Eckmann felt a physical pang of grief in the region of his chest. He wondered if Christopher might turn and wave goodbye, might remember him once more before he went inside the school gates with his friends.

Eckmann stood watching, waiting, feeling slightly breathless, filled with anticipation, with hope, the same way he had once stood in the same abbey square, looking at the dancer – watching, waiting, with the same anticipation, the same hope of being noticed.

'Hello, Rees.'

'Hello, Mallan. Maths test today, you know.'

'You're joking. I've not revised!'

'Trudy – it's maths test, isn't it?'

'Ignore him, he's trying to wind you up.'

'Trudy . . . I think you're in love with him.'

'Oh, shut up!'

They were gone into the school – parents, home, outside world, all forgotten. Eckmann felt another pang of longing and nostalgia now, for a childhood as it should have been, for the youth he never had.

But then he saw the jaunty way Christopher and his friends walked through the cloister and towards the Great Hall. He saw the way they laughed and joked and bumped and jostled into each other, and he smiled, with familiar indulgence, with parental delight.

Good luck to him. Good luck to them all. For Eckmann was indirectly part of it too now – part of the world of love, concern, care and responsibility.

He too had a family. He too had connections with present, future and past. He had a son.

He moved on, with a light, even jaunty step, and made his way towards his gallery. Before going there, however, he took a short detour and went into the food hall of an expensive department store, not far from the entrance to the Roman baths.

The shelves of the food hall were lined with tins of over-priced produce – there were gourmet soups and jars of caviar amongst the more ordinary items. The fresh fruit and vegetables were beautifully stacked and presented, and priced to match. Each individual apple shone as if polished, the tomatoes were almost violently red, the peppers startlingly yellow, or green, or red again, the aubergines deeply purple. It was an artist's palette – tubes of paint. If you took a purple aubergine and squeezed it, a wodge of purple colour might come out. It was food to paint with, paint to eat.

Eckmann could have halved his bill if he had taken the trouble to shop elsewhere, but he had neither the time nor the inclination to hunt for bargains. He also took a rich man's perverse pleasure in paying over the odds. If he could afford it, why not? Besides, the quality was good, and he was buying for somebody special, was he not?

In addition to tinned food, fresh fruit and vegetables, Eckmann bought a quantity of bottled water. He paid for the goods and then went to the toiletries department where he bought several basic items, along with some things which, surely, only a woman would require. As he paid for everything, the assistant gave him a sympathetic smile. Here was a man shopping on behalf of his wife, no doubt, who was maybe too busy, or perhaps too indisposed, to buy these things for herself.

In this supposition, the assistant was both mistaken and quite correct. The items were indeed for a woman. But Eckmann was not married to her. Nor ever would be.

The bags were heavy. There was enough in them to

last a few days, to tide you over the weekend anyway and into the following week, when you might have more time to do a proper, fuller shop. Yes, the bags were heavy, but Eckmann bore them without effort. His upper body was thickset and strong, and in his determination not to stoop, and to make the most of what height he had, he carried himself erect, and kept his head up, as he walked on to the gallery. He had recently invested in some shoes with stacked heels in an effort to reduce the disparity between him and his 'son'.

The abbey clock was ringing the hour as Eckmann arrived at the gallery. He put the bags down and found his keys. He went to open up the gallery door, but there was some resistance behind it from a pile of freshly delivered letters and catalogues. He managed to squeeze inside and push the obstruction out of the way, then he returned to the street, took his groceries inside, and slammed the door behind him.

As he entered the reception area, the burglar alarm began to bleep. He put the bags down again, tapped the number code into the alarm, and it fell silent. He fetched the post and left it on a table for the girl to deal with when she got in. It was a newish girl, from a temp agency. He didn't like any of them to stay too long. Once it had been different, and he had valued familiarity, but now he preferred a constant stream of new faces. It was inconvenient, as each new arrival had to be shown what to do, and they were not all as efficient as they might have been. But on the other hand, it didn't give them time enough to get too curious or interfering.

He looked at the clock. The girl wouldn't arrive for

181

another half hour. That should give him more than ample time. He hoisted the bags up and headed for the stairs, then hurried up towards his work room in the attic. He stopped halfway to get his breath. He tried to keep healthy and always walked everywhere if he could, but lately he seemed less fit than he had been. Maybe he was just older, that was all. He just needed to take things a little slower. Because he had to look after himself. It wasn't just him now, there were others involved; he was a family man, with dependants, responsibilities, with mouths to feed.

He couldn't help but smile to himself, even to chuckle briefly at the irony of it. He was a man with a family, with mouths to feed. Very tiny ones too, some of them.

It was quite a responsibility, keeping the dead alive.

It takes seven years.

At least in this country.

Different places have different traditions, different customs, other ways. But here, it takes exactly seven years for somebody to die. In the absence of a body. After seven years, they may be considered dead.

Everyone has the right to disappear, of course. It is the privilege of every citizen to vanish without trace, without prior notification and without leaving a note or forwarding address behind; without any explanation. However, in certain circumstances, seven years after someone's disappearance, his family, wife or heirs, may apply to have him declared legally dead and have such assets as he may possess put into probate.

So as yet there was still a possibility that they might

be alive – at least in a legal sense. Three years had now gone by since the day Christopher had come to Eckmann's studio, distraught, afraid, searching for his father. Three years had passed without explanation, without word, without notification of any kind. And still he went on believing in the possibility of return.

Even if, and when, seven years had passed, he would never have sought to implement any legal process which would have had his father and Poppea declared dead. In his mind, they would live as long as he lived, and only die when he did, and perhaps, not even then.

It gnawed away at him, in moments of awful loneliness, which not even Mr Eckmann's kindness could make go away. It was the mystery, the not knowing, and all the terror heaped on terror, that imagination could bring. What had happened to them? Had they been abducted, killed, imprisoned, held captive, tortured, degraded? Were they held in darkness, did they live in fear, in pain, in despair? Better that they were dead, better to think that in many ways. It made it easier to live.

It was an insoluble conundrum. Whichever explanation he chose, there was only pain at the end of it – for him or for them. If they had vanished against their will and had never been in contact, then they were dead or incarcerated somewhere, unable to escape or get word out.

But if that was not so, and they had gone of their own volition, then how, why, could his own father ever have deserted him, without a single word? It would have meant that far from loving his son, his father had hated him. Only vindictive hatred could have inspired such a cold-blooded act of cruelty as to desert a child, your only child, to leave him alone, without a home, or protection, without love.

But he knew that wasn't true. He knew his father did love him, as much as he loved his father. He would have died before doing that. So that meant . . .

Back to the first explanation yet again . . .

Or maybe there was a third. Some physical ailment, some accident, some stroke, some disease, some kind of blow. Maybe his father had been hit by a car, knocked down, had struck his head, suffered concussion and lost his memory. Maybe he had lost any sense of who he was and was wandering around lost.

Maybe, even now, he worked as a street artist, in a square in some distant town, where the unfamiliar ring of other bells brought faint, unsettling echoes to half remind him of other times and other places. But the memories were always just out of focus and out of reach.

Perhaps he had another family now – a wife, another son, a daughter, another name. That was possible, yes. That was an explanation which held in it the chance of forgiveness and reconciliation and return. It was plausible, wasn't it? It held out hope that one day Robert's memory and himself with it, would come back.

Only then, the plausible became implausible by the fact of its multiplicity. Even if Christopher could accept that there had been some kind of accident, that his father had lost his memory . . . what about Poppea? What were the chances of that kind of lightning striking in the same vicinity twice? How and where and why had she also disappeared? Why had she not responded to any of the publicity, the appeal for help, for news of his father and of her?

Somebody must have seen them – or at least one of them. Somebody must have known. Why did nobody say?

Or maybe Poppea had simply gone abroad, as she had always said she might do one day. Maybe they had rowed and disagreed once too often. Maybe she had been offered work in some faraway place and had gone there and decided to settle. Maybe she had children now. Maybe she knew nothing at all about Robert's disappearance. Maybe he was just a memory to her, a sweet, long-ago affair, which lasted a while before she had moved away and moved on.

Maybe, maybe, maybe. Each explanation was unsatisfactory, and Christopher's dissatisfaction with one turned his mind to another, in an unending circle.

Thank god for Mr Eckmann, who had turned out trumps after all. Because sometimes Christopher felt that Mr Eckmann hadn't liked his father. That he'd maybe been a bit jealous of him and Poppea, even though Mr Eckmann was in his own right a successful man. So thank god for Mr Eckmann, and his patience and help and undeniable kindness. If it hadn't been for Mr Eckmann, he didn't know what would have become of him. If it hadn't been for Mr Eckmann, something terrible might have happened.

The school was very different, but time had accustomed Christopher to it. A faint air of ancient obligations and unspecified privilege hung over the place. In the summer the tourists would crowd to watch as the choir traipsed by, in their archaic collars and uniforms, from the school to the abbey. Then, when the procession was over, the watchers would pile in after them, to fill up the pews and listen to the music and the ethereal singing, with a blithe disregard for the signs on the wall reading, *Flash photography within the abbey precincts strictly prohibited.*

At such times, when the choir made the short journey, feeling both slightly foolish in his old-fashioned get-up and also comforted and secure in being a protected member of something unique and special, Christopher would look around the abbey square, and he would remember.

In the mornings he saw Poppea, standing upon the box with the mechanism inside it, which played a timed snatch of music when a coin was dropped into the slot, to set the dancer in motion. Only of course it wasn't her. It was a different street performer, another clockwork dancer, who had rushed in to fill her absence, like air into a vacuum. No unfilled opportunity to make a penny stands vacant for long.

It wasn't her, and yet so like her from a distance, that some mornings an awful wave of longing and almost overpowering nostalgia came over him. It would come so fiercely that he was momentarily overwhelmed, and he maybe stumbled on the hems of the rather ridiculous cassocks and cloaks the choristers wore.

Then Rees's voice would interrupt his reverie.

'*Hey, Mallan, you're standing on my cassock!*'

When there were occasional services in the evening – ones which Mr Eckmann would always attend – then Christopher would recall other images, of other nighttimes.

He would remember Mr Eckmann, in the restaurant in the abbey square, alone at his usual table, with his customary half bottle before him. He would remember the way he toyed with the wine, rolling the dark red liquid around in his glass before finally taking a small, almost imperceptible sip, before starting the whole procedure once more.

He would see the artists setting up their stools and their easels. And here came the ghosts of a man and a boy, walking along the cobbled alleyway. Yes, a moody, dark-haired man, rather sullen looking on a first impression, but once he had thawed out, when you had got to know him . . .

'Hey, Mallan, get a move on!'

The choristers would file on towards the abbey, its open-doored interior glowing with golden light. Above them was the looming buttress of the abbey; columns and spires reached to a moonlit sky and a canopy of stars. Gargoyles climbed a carved stone ladder, maybe trying to get to heaven. Their ghastly faces snarled and grimaced, their stone features contorted into permanent sneers to keep the devils away.

Then, for some reason, Christopher would remember Mr Eckmann, all those years back, standing, leaving money upon the café table to pay his bill. He recollected the expression upon Mr Eckmann's face as he looked towards Christopher's father, packing up to leave the square, and at Poppea who had come to meet him. In recollection, Mr Eckmann's face seemed as strangely contorted as the gargoyles upon the buttresses, and his eyes, under the glow of the gas lamp, seemed to blaze like orange coals.

Or was it just a trick of memory?

'*Mallan! Mind! You've trodden on my cassock again! Look where you're going.*'

The voice shocked him back into the present.

'*Sorry, Rees. Sorry. I was miles away.*'

Or rather years away. And things so fragmentary, mysterious, half-noticed, even incomprehensible, now suddenly made the suspicion of sense.

Was that it?

The look in Eckmann's eyes?

Had Mr Eckmann not liked them – Robert and Poppea?

Only that was impossible. He was so kind, generous, in every conceivable way.

Christopher quelled the thought. It was unworthy of him. Mr Eckmann had been his saviour. More than that, his friend. Where would he be now without Mr Eckmann? Where would he have gone? How would he have lived? What would he have become?

The choristers entered through the abbey doors. Christopher took a last look back. He saw the shape of a dark-haired man, setting up an easel and a stool. He almost dropped his hymn book and fled.

But it was someone else. Just a dark-haired man. Not the dark-haired man he wanted.

He followed the rest of the choir inside. The organ was already playing, and the smell of candles was in the air. There was a small, brief lightning flash as somebody took a picture with their camera of everything that was foreign and quaint.

The City

Eckmann locked the attic door behind him. He went to the window and raised the blinds. The cool morning light filled the attic studio and in so doing it lit up the tiny domed city, the masterpiece on which he had laboured for so long.

Eckmann crossed to the desk and picked up the jeweller's lens which lay there, putting it to his eye. He gazed down into the miniature city and smiled. There they were, going about their business, such as it was. The scene reminded him of the start of a film, a moment of scene-setting, where the camera moves along towards some matter of importance and some major person, and on its way casually comes across peripheral characters going about their ordinary lives. Only here, the two peripheral characters were the only ones there were. They were, for now at least, the only story.

He watched as the woman came out of the house. She carried washing, which she pegged on a line. The man followed and helped her. He passed her the pegs as she hung up the clothes, handing them to her with his minuscule, yet perfectly proportioned hands.

'And how are we today?' Eckmann whispered.

He could not restrain a smile. The sight of them always delighted or even amused him. Sometimes it drove him to anger, when even in their immense vulnerability they seemed determined to defy him, to rub his nose in everything he still didn't have. He could squash them with one snap of his fingers, crush them between finger and thumb, like vermin. Like lice.

But not today. Today they'd had a row.

It entertained him deeply to think that they had fallen out. Because unlike others, they had no alternatives, no one else to talk to, nowhere else to go, no one to complain to about the conduct of the other. It was amusing too, to think of the lovers no longer so in love, maybe starting to apportion blame and experience regret.

'If only you hadn't ... If only I had never ... I wouldn't be here now if ...'

Amusing to see those not actually responsible blaming each other, while the one who was responsible looked mutely on, surveying their little world like a god. A regularly appearing eye in the sky. Their sun, their moon, their light, their darkness, their benefactor, their scourge. What would they do to appease him if he grew wrathful? What if one day he decided no longer to feed them or give them water? If no more manna came from heaven, if no water dropped from the glass-domed sky? What if he made worship a condition of supply? What if he insisted they abase themselves before he sent down so much as one small bottle of water?

But then ... they would probably defy him. And unable to destroy him, they might possibly destroy themselves. That was an option still open to them, one which he could do little to prevent. They'd do it just to spite him, if he made their lives too unbearable.

Carrot and stick, that was the thing. Play them along, like fish on a line. Now give a little, now take. A little punishment, a little reward, the gift of some news, a whole newspaper even, some books, some medicine.

In some ways Eckmann simply could not help himself. He was not, at root, a vindictive man; he was passionate in his way, proud and angry, but not cold blooded. Yet the knowledge of their powerlessness brought out the temptation towards cruelty in him. They were once so envied, so admired by him, but who were they now? Who now was the one with the knowledge, the power? In possession of the one thing that meant the world to them – the boy.

They finished hanging up the washing. Yes, they looked angry with each other this morning. He wondered why, what disagreement had occasioned their moody silence. Perhaps they simply got on each other's nerves now. Perhaps he should miniaturize a book on improving your relationship and send that down.

They'd appreciate that.

Eckmann smiled to himself. What was that someone once said about power corrupting and absolute power corrupting absolutely? There was another facet to that. The ability to deal out cruelty without having to be answerable for it somehow aroused the desire to inflict it.

Like a cat with a mouse, toying and playing, just for the pleasure of it. Like a boy in a garden with the salt cellar in his hand and a slug wriggling by. It would be only too easy to succumb to such temptation.

And yet . . . there was Christopher. If he were ever

to find out, ever to know . . . They were part of him too, as much as he was part of them, and in hurting them, he would hurt Christopher, and in hurting Christopher, Eckmann would hurt himself.

For he had a son now. He was a man with family, with responsibilities, of all shapes and sizes.

Eckmann went on watching. They knew he was there. Must have done. His head above the dome came between them and the light, the partial eclipse of his figure coming between their planet and the real sun outside. In the winter days theirs was a lightbulb sun and a lightbulb moon. If he wanted to punish them, he would turn the moon off early, or turn the sun on late.

The creator of the universe could do things like that, omnipotent, omniscient, all-seeing.

Yes, Eckmann smiled to himself, they'd had a row all right.

Her face was still lovely, but not quite so lovely when clouded with anger and suppressed irritation.

In truth, he felt rather delighted by it.

They went on pegging out the clothes in moody silence.

But then, just as Eckmann was about to put the eyeglass down, the man reached out to the woman and touched her arm. He said something to her and she seemed to dissolve, the irritation went, and a second later they were in each other's arms.

Just as if he wasn't watching, as if he wasn't there, as if he didn't exist, or as if it was all to spite him, to defy him, as if to prove that he, who had almost everything it was possible to have, still did not have the one thing that was impossible – Poppea and her freely given love.

He deliberately kicked the desk. The tremor shot through it and must have frightened them. It would have come as an earthquake in the small, glass-domed city – the city of façades and empty interiors, the city of appearances and replicas, the city of doors which didn't open, of steps which led to nowhere, the city of two inhabitants.

Maybe they needed some company, that was it.

Eckmann smiled again. Someone else maybe? How would that be? One more, two more, then another and another? One at a time – who would notice? People came and went, the world was full of drifters. Who would notice, who would care? One at a time, he could populate his own private world. Lord of creation, master of all he surveyed.

But he could never visit it. Or visit it, yes, but never be able to return. Maybe that was why God came to earth but once, due to the problems of getting home.

He frowned. There was as much disappointment as satisfaction in him. It rankled that he had so far been unable to reverse the process – for he could never bring her back.

He heard a voice call from downstairs. It was the girl from the agency. He went to the door, unlocked and opened it, and called back.

'Yes, open up, if you would. If you could deal with the post, please. I'm just finishing some work.'

He closed and re-locked the door. The last thing he needed was an unwarranted interruption. After all, the animals must be fed.

He smiled again.

'*Look after your pets, Ernst, or you don't deserve to have any.*'

His mother's voice echoed down the passageway of the years. She stood at the end of a long corridor, next to his father, who looked perpetually disappointed in him.

'*Look after your pets!*'

It was time to feed the pets then – to feed them and to clean them out. They would leave out their refuse every day, tied up neatly in tiny black bags, all so thoughtfully supplied in advance.

He picked up the jeweller's glass, for one last look. Exercise and recreation now – thanks, of course, to his grace and favour.

The man was sitting painting. (Miniaturized paints, stool, paper, brushes and easel, courtesy of . . . well, who else?) The woman was exercising, running through a set routine of stretches and turns as she warmed up. (Minuscule leotard, leggings and ballet shoes, courtesy of . . . well, who else?)

So they filled their days. It was strange that what the man painted was often the scenery around him, the miniature city. They were paintings of artifice, like a book about a book, a play about a play, one contrivance based on another.

At other times he painted her. She would sit for him. When they were alone, she would pose for life drawings and sketches. He taught her to draw, she showed him how to dance. They had everything they needed – no, not needed – *required*, to maintain life. What they really needed, they could not have, any more than Eckmann could. They could not return; he could not have Poppea.

All he had of her was the portrait, the nude study, which Robert had painted. It was locked up in the safe at home. He had taken it from their apartment. When Christopher was asleep, he might take it out, view it for a short while, then put it away again, under stout lock and heavy key.

Sometimes Robert painted his son – portraits from memory, of Christopher as he had been, not as he was now – older, taller, thinner faced, his cheekbones more angular, his limbs occasionally too long and clumsy for him. Robert did not know it, but all he painted were memories – portraits of someone who no longer existed.

To begin with they had acknowledged Eckmann. They had waved and looked upwards and shielded their eyes. They had grown both hopeful as well as fearful when the glass dome had first been lifted from the city and they were free to go – but go where? There was nowhere to go, except across the vast wooden desert of the desk, and then to the end of the world.

Eckmann had sent them a letter. Written, then miniaturized.

'*I am sorry to say . . .*'

He was sorry to say that the process was at present irreversible. He did not feel it incumbent upon him to express sorrow over anything else. He informed them that he was working on being able to enlarge as well as miniaturize, but did not hold out any hope of success in the immediate future. And even if he had been able to bring them back, what was the likelihood of his ever doing so?

It was a one-way correspondence, just as it had been a one-way process. When they spoke, he could not hear them – which was maybe just as well. He had to assess their needs and guess what they wanted. The only answers he could give them were to questions he felt they might ask. He sent them what he thought they wanted, told them only what he deemed they ought to know. No more, no less. Sometimes he was wrong, sometimes badly mistaken; sometimes the things he sent were the wrong size, or simply wrong altogether. Sometimes he offended them. He worried what to do if one of them fell seriously ill – all he would be able to send would be painkillers; he could do little other than assist them to an easy death.

Then they had refused to eat. Every day or so he had brought his offerings, lifted the glass dome, started the decelerator, put the things through the process and left their supplies in the usual place. When he returned the next time, they were untouched.

At first he thought that the illness he feared had come. But no. It was a simple refusal to eat, as though a hunger strike were a Get Out Of Jail card in a game of Monopoly. But this was a prison from which there was no escape.

Join the club, Eckmann thought to himself. Walk that mile now in someone else's shoes – the shoes of the outsider, the odd, the strange, the different, the freak.

He kept taking away the old food and leaving new. All they accepted was the water. They both grew thinner, weaker, more gaunt. They spent most of their time asleep, or lying upon the mattresses and such bedding as he had sent them, staring listlessly at nothing, waiting for their refusal to eat to change something. Only there was nothing that it could change. Finally they came to realize this and started to eat again. And besides, there was still Christopher and the promise of the news Eckmann sent them.

'*Christopher is well and has started at his new school.*'

Bits and pieces, dribs and drabs. He fed them news like sugar lumps to horses, little treats every now and again, more grace, more favour. He let them have newspapers, for the news in them was – as far as they were concerned – impersonal. A war here, a conflict there, what did it matter when you were tiny as a dust mite? What difference did you make to things, or they to you?

Knowledge was power though, and sometimes he was sorely, malignly, tempted to lie.

'*Sadly, Christopher is in hospital. A sudden attack of meningitis.*'

A few days of anxiety for them, then maybe, '*Christopher has fallen into a coma. I must rush back to his bedside.*'

A few more days of worry and anxiety.

Then, what next?

Maybe, '*Happily, Christopher has made a full recovery and is expected to be back at school on Monday.*'

Or not so happily. '*Sadly, Christopher passed away last night . . .*'

And how would they ever know that it was not the truth?

It was fortunate for them that Eckmann wasn't that kind of man. It was fortunate that he was a man with scruples, with standards, with morals of some kind. Which, curiously, he was.

Up to a point he told them the truth.

'*I bitterly regret what has happened . . .*' he once began. But he tore that note up. Apologies and regrets were useless. What's done was done. Maybe one day, if he discovered how to reverse the process, it would be undone. But even if he did have that knowledge and ability, how could they ever be allowed to return? Who would willingly release lions? How could he free the very people who had reason to hate him the most?

He kept things on a semi-formal basis. It didn't do to fraternize. He simply relayed news without comment.

'*Christopher is well. Grieving, but well.*'

Then:

'*The authorities wish to take him into care. They are opposing my suggestion that he come and live with me on a permanent basis, even though he has said that this is what he wants, as he knows me and regards me as a friend. Because I am a man and not married they suspect my motives. I find this insulting and outrageous. I shall take the best legal advice.*'

As if his reputation would be their concern, as if they would be boiling with indignation over the slandering of the good name of Eckmann, his imputed motives, and the implication that he was someone of unpleasant character and desires.

'*You will be pleased to hear that Christopher is to come and live with me after all. After extensive and often frankly offensive enquiries into my personal life, the authorities have allowed Christopher to come and live under my roof, on condition that I employ a female housekeeper/childcarer, which I have now done. I do somewhat resent the intrusion and the expense, but nevertheless, as it is for Christopher's sake, I am happy to do it.'*

He almost added, '*It is the least I can do in the circumstances,*' but no, again he managed to restrain the impulse to apologize. Why ask a lame dog to kick itself? Why should he beat his breast and ask their forgiveness, after all? Who needed the forgiveness of such tiny people? What quality or quantity of forgiveness could they give? It would be minute, worthless, infinitesimal.

'*Although Christopher seems happy at present, I have decided, as I am now his guardian, to move him to the Abbey School, where I believe he will receive a superior education. The class sizes are smaller and the syllabus wider and the facilities more extensive – especially in the area of science, which Christopher seems both interested in and adept at.*'

It was almost like sending on school reports to grandparents, or some other interested party.

'*I take it you have no objection. If you do object to this proposal, please do so immediately on reading this. I am watching and will see if you register some form of opposition.*'

It was extraordinary, having done what he had, that Eckmann should still seek approval for what he intended to do next.

No objection came. Maybe they just thought he was mad – totally and utterly insane.

He actually did send on the reports, miniaturized copies.

'*As you can see from the enclosed, Christopher is doing very well at his new school. He has fitted in well and his achievements have exceeded all expectations.*'

He has received several commended-work cards and has won the science prize.'

Then things took a turn for the worse. They needed a father's hand.

'Christopher has not done so well this term. He has been very difficult and withdrawn. He still misses you. He sinks into grief, in long periods of silence and darkness, like an animal in hibernation. He seems to have forgotten for a while, but then everything returns. He still lives in the expectation of news. It is awful for him not to know, and yet how can he possibly be told? The time goes by. One moment it seems to have healed everything, then it is plain that it has healed nothing at all. I worry for him, for what the future holds for him, when his present is so full of longing for the past.'

Then better again.

'Once again, a set of great exam results for Christopher!'

And what was most evident to them was not so much Christopher's achievement as Eckmann's personal pride in them. He could have been writing about his own child, his own flesh and blood, his own son and heir. Which was what he gradually became.

'I am writing to let you know, just in case you are concerned, that I have made financial provision for Christopher in the event of my own untimely death. He will be well taken care of. I am not an enormously wealthy man, but prosperous enough. There will be no need for him to be deprived of anything. I have set up a trust fund on his behalf. Is there anything that you need?'

Once Robert had taken the brushes and had begun

200

to paint in what to him must have been massive letters upon the street of the miniature city. Eckmann had watched through the lens as the letters and finally the words took shape. It was like playing some kind of word-guessing game.

First letter *A*.

He finished painting the huge – yet so tiny – letter, then he paused and looked upwards, as if to say – 'Well? Got it yet?'

But what use was A on its own?

Next came *N*.

AN.

AN? AN what?

Eckmann went off to the bathroom. By the time he returned, the graffiti on the street read *ANTI*.

Still he wasn't sure. He thought he had it. But he wanted to be one hundred per cent certain. He waited for the next two letters to be completed, then he left the room.

ANTIBI.

When he returned from his house, with the tablets in the bag, he was pleased to see that he had been right and had guessed correctly.

ANTIBIOTICS.

He had some left in the bathroom, a five-day course which he had never, in the end, taken. They had to be for her, he guessed. She must be ill and hadn't appeared at all that day. She was resting inside one of the partially hollowed out buildings, lying on the bedding, maybe running a high temperature or suffering with an abscess.

God forbid, that they should ever need surgery or serious dental treatment. What would Eckmann do?

Shrink a surgeon and a whole operating theatre? Miniaturize a dentist?

What had happened in the days before modern surgeons and dentists existed? The world had gone on, people had got by, somehow. People lived and died.

She reappeared after three days, limping slightly. It must have been a splinter or a cut followed by a blood infection.

The word *ANTIBIOTICS* remained upon the street for a long time. It looked like some form of vandalism. There was no rain to wash it off. Finally, Robert must have tired of it, for he painted it out. Then one morning, when Eckmann appeared with the mid-week supply of food and drink, there was an angry message upon the street.

'*SICK LITTLE DWARF.*'

Eckmann reeled away from the desk, dropping the jeweller's lens from his eye. The eye-glass rolled to the floor. There was a pain in his chest, and the sensation of irregular heartbeat. The fluttering lasted only a few moments, then the normal rhythm reasserted itself.

He sat down, faint, distressed. How could they still hurt him? How could they even now have the power to wound him so deeply – these mere specks of people, these nothings, these motes of dust.

In anger he picked up a heavy wrench from among his work-tools and raised it high, ready to bring it down on the roof of the dome, to shatter it and everything inside it to a million pieces.

'*SICK LITTLE DWARF.*'

His heart palpitated once more. He sat down heavily and let the wrench fall from his grasp. He couldn't destroy it, not something so wonderful, so beautiful, which had cost him so much to make in terms of time, energy, devotion, ability – it was his greatest-ever project.

Not only that – he couldn't hurt her.

Or had it been her who had painted that?

No. It had been him. Hadn't it.

But they had to be taught a lesson. They couldn't be allowed to get away with things like that.

There was no food that day, nor water either. They had possibly anticipated some kind of retaliation and had hoarded some from their regular supply. There was no telling how much. Enough for a few days, or for a week or two even. But he could wait it out far longer than they could.

He could wait forever.

He sent a note instead.

'*Paint it out,*' he commanded.

Nothing happened.

He took the dome and returned it to the cupboard, where there was twenty-four hours of darkness every day. They had no other light, he knew that. He was their sun, their moon, their stars, their sky.

It took a long time. Each day he opened the door and peered in. Still nothing. Then finally, after ten days, the first letter was painted out.

'*ICK LITTLE DWARF.*'

Then the next.

'*CK LITTLE DWARF*'

Then two more letters.

'*CK ITTLE WARF.*'

Were they trying to be funny? How funny did they

think they were being? How much more darkness and hunger and thirst could they endure?

'L   ARF'

Was that their idea of a joke?

Then it was finally all gone.

He took them from the cupboard and gave them their light back. But no food yet. He sent them a note.

'Apologize,' it said.

The following morning, written upon the street, was the two-lettered word.

'NO.'

He sent them another message.

'*I can wait*,' it said.

There was silence for a day. Then it slowly began to appear.

'SOR . . .'

And that was all for a day. Maybe things were bad now. They hid inside whenever he appeared, sensing the great shadow of his presence. Maybe they were too weakened by hunger and thirst to finish it. Maybe they had run out of strength, out of paint.

Or maybe they had just run out of anger. For the following morning, there it was.

'SORRY,' it said.

That was better.

He sent them some food then, and some bottles of water. Not too much, just enough. He reduced the food ration. He didn't want them being able to stockpile for a siege.

Sorry. That was better. That was all it took, an apology. He didn't want to harm them or starve and deprive them. He wasn't a torturer. You just had to put your foot down, that was the thing. You just had to show who was boss.

He didn't feel that he had been vindictive; if anything, he had acted with restraint. After all, he could have insisted that they say *Please*, or even have demanded *Pretty Please*.

Funny how they had affected him though. Small as they were, they had burrowed, like mites, right under his skin. He had thought he was over that too, all the insults from childhood, from long ago. But sticks and stones could still break your limbs, and the harsh words went on hurting you, long after the mouths which had said them had fallen silent. People knew that.

He preferred it when their communication only flowed one way.

Eckmann crossed to the window to power the decelerator.

It was quite simple really, despite its complexity. A mere reversal, that was all. As every schoolboy and schoolgirl knew (if they paid attention during their physics lessons), Albert Einstein's theory of relativity states that as objects approach the speed of light, they acquire infinite mass. So what was the obverse of that – the other side of the theoretical coin? What would happen if everything were to be slowed down, if the opposite were to happen. If things were to move . . . at the speed of the dark?

But, of course, the logical objection is that dark has no speed. That the dark is not the presence of darkness; on the contrary, it is the absence of light.

Defined only by omission, not by what it is, but by what it is not.

Or is it? It pleasure, for example, the mere absence of pain? Is darkness only an absence of light, or is it its own entity, with qualities of its own? There is matter . . . and antimatter. There is light, and . . . what could Eckmann call it now? . . . anti-light? Not the simple absence of light, but something else, a little – or rather a whole lot – more complicated. So what now? Ask the question again. If a thing were to move at the speed of light, it would attain infinite mass. But if the opposite were to happen, if a thing were to move at the speed of anti-light – at the speed of the dark – what would happen then?

Its mass might become . . . infinitely diminished? And the closer to the speed of the darkness that it moved, the smaller that mass would become. Having passed through, to the other side of that shadow, then maybe so it would remain until it could be propelled back again.

Only he didn't know how to do that. How to make it run that way. One day, maybe, one day.

Eckmann nodded his head and muttered to himself as he set up the machinery.

'Yes, infinitely small. Exactly. Very good.'

Eckmann adjusted the lenses, the telescope and mirrors. He pulled a switch and set something wonderful in motion. He stood watching, mesmerized, never tiring of it, no matter how many times he saw it happen. He only wished he had a witness, someone to share it with, someone to appreciate the genius of it, but that, of course, was quite impossible. There was only Christopher, and if he were to know . . .

The whirring stopped.

The telescope was now pointed directly towards the pale morning sun. The light entered the large upper lens and emerged from the bottom one, to focus into a sharp, intense pin point. Eckmann carefully adjusted the telescope, so that the light emerging from it travelled on into the strange and wonderful series of prisms and mirrors arranged around the room. He watched with satisfaction as the light was broken up into the colours of the spectrum; he watched as the colours were refracted and reflected back into a single beam of light, which bounced from mirror to mirror again – mirrors of odd shapes and angles. Then the light travelled on again, through polarizing lenses, into thick pyramids of glass which separated out the spectrum and sent it bouncing into a cylinder of spirals and loops.

There was a drone of power as the electromagnet came to life; it spun rapidly, faster and faster until it was no longer even a blur any more. It seemed to have passed the state of motion and to have become solid and immobile again; so fast it was static.

'Now,' Eckmann said, muttering to himself. 'Now then . . .'

Projected from the final lens, on to the far wall, was a dark spot, about twelve inches in diameter. On careful inspection, it could be seen that the spot of darkness was not actually projected on to anything. It wasn't a shadow, or the absence of light; it was the physical presence of darkness. It hung there in the air, like a black ball, a tiny black hole even, an alternative dimension, a small tear in the fabric of time – a hole in the world leading to . . .

A faint blue spark appeared at the circumference of the black disc. It fizzled and crackled, then disappeared.

Eckmann re-focused the lens. The black hole became little more than a pinprick. It hung in the air, not much bigger than a full stop on a page, almost invisible, but with such tremendous power it seemed to draw you towards it, to pull you in, to drag you right inside.

Eckmann removed the glass dome from the miniature city. Then he adjusted the black spot so that it hung suspended just over the tiny street. He looked around the room for the groceries he had bought. He picked up one of the bags and carried it over to the desk.

'Now . . .'

He lifted it up, then slowly lowered it into the speck of darkness.

It disappeared.

He still held the upper part of the bag by its handles, but the bottom section had already vanished, diminished almost into invisibility, sucked into the blackness like smoke into an extractor fan.

He let go of the handles. The bag fell all the way through and could no longer be seen, at least not by the naked eye, as it dropped to the street of the miniature city.

He went and got the next bag. He repeated the process. Then he took the third bag, containing the toiletries, and he dropped that into the tiny pool of darkness too.

It seemed to spin, like waste water going down a sink, as it entered into and passed through the black disc. As it neared the dark hole, it was drawn to it, sucked into it almost. Eckmann could feel the pull, the resistance drawing both the bag and his hand into the small, dark spot.

He quickly released the handles.

If his hand were to enter, if he himself were to tumble into the small, black hole . . . what then? Who would keep them all alive?

'Mr Eckmann? Are you there?'

The voice startled him. It was nearby, right outside. There was hammering at the door.

'Mr Eckmann! Mr Eckmann! Phone for you!'

It was the girl. Thank god he'd remembered to lock the door. He hadn't even heard the phone ringing, and there was an extension, right there in the room. Maybe he had turned the volume down, though he didn't remember doing so.

'Take a message! Say I'll ring them back.'

'They say it's important, Mr Eckmann.'

'I'll ring them back.'

Her footsteps retreated back down the stairs.

Important, Eckmann thought. People didn't know what important was.

He went to the decelerator and shut everything down. It whirred to silence. The black dot remained hanging in the air, like the dot in a question mark, then it faded, like the Cheshire cat's smile, and was gone.

He replaced the domed cover upon the miniature city. Then he took the jeweller's glass and peered inside.

Yes, yes.

He nodded with a kind of benevolent satisfaction, a

paternal approval even, as he watched the two small figures gather up the bags of groceries and provisions from the street. Everything seemed to be fine, all intact today, no broken bottles, no burst-open packages. The emergency, mercy drop of supplies had landed safely.

Good, good. All was fine.

He went to remove the jeweller's glass from his eye. But something stopped him. He leaned forwards again, peering even closer at the two tiny figures who were busying themselves with their groceries – so kindly provided (at no charge at all, like everything else they needed) by the management. Manna from heaven, one might say.

A cold chill came over him. The colour drained from his face. He removed the jeweller's lens from his eye. He wiped it, polished it, wiped his face, put the lens back, looked down again.

No, surely, surely. It wasn't possible, was it? Surely, he had to be mistaken? Surely? Or that meant . . .

He watched as they carried the groceries and supplies to the shelter of an alcove in the street, which acted as their larder. There was a door there, which opened to a small hollow. It was mostly façade. He hadn't actually intended the city as a place for anyone to live in. But there was everything they needed there to survive. He was quite unstinting in that. Some things were difficult to provide, of course, but he did the best he could. There were small bottles of gas to cook with, some small burners. There were cups and saucers, plates and knives, pots and pans. Tiny things, but real enough for them. It was Lilliput. The land of the small.

Surely he was wrong? It was just the shape of her cardigan, which she had put on over the leotard; the way it billowed out and bunched forwards as she leaned over to pick up some of the bottles of water.

Yes, that was all it was. A trick of the light, a deceit of motion. His mistake. Eckmann felt enormously relieved. He took the jeweller's glass from his eye, feeling as though he had just had some kind of narrow escape. Just his imagination, that was all – worst fears becoming realized, worst-case scenarios. But it was all right. No need to worry.

He put the jeweller's glass down into the small, velvet-lined, leather case in which it was kept. He closed the lid, took a last look around the room, then left them to it – to their unpacking, their breakfast, their painting and exercising, however they would pass the day.

He unlocked the door, then closed and re-locked it from the outside, slipping the key into his pocket. Eckmann made his way down the stairs to the gallery, calling to the girl as he went.

'I'm coming. Who did you say called? What did they want? Was it important? Did you say I would ring back?'

And he went about his business, in the ordinary way. It was just another day, after all. Another perfectly ordinary day.

The Unexpected

'Like this, you see, Christopher. Just try it on the match.'

Eckmann's reserves of patience were failing him. He had developed more of that particular virtue than he had ever thought possible, but children were still children at the end of the day. They could soon drink all your patience up, even if you had a whole reservoir of it. They could drink an ocean of it dry, and then complain afterwards about the taste of salt.

Christopher took the matchstick and the scalpel and went to try again. It wasn't a difficult cut, just a very basic carving, but he couldn't seem to get the hang of it at all.

'See here. Look how I do it.'

Eckmann took a match from the box for himself. He selected a fine-headed scalpel and then, with two or three strokes, he transformed the head of the match into Mickey Mouse.

'You see? Now you.'

Christopher tried again. This time he sliced off the head of the match and cut into his finger. Blood dripped into the matchbox, staining the matches with mottled spots.

'Now see what you've done!'

Anger flared up between them. Christopher was angry with Eckmann for making him do this, and he was equally angry with himself for his inability to do it with even the smallest degree of success. He was failing, and he didn't want to fail, yet he felt angry that he should be expected to succeed at something for which he had no natural aptitude.

'Sorry, Ernst.'

'Sorry! He says sorry! Blood – all over the matches!'

If they hadn't both been so angry, the scene would have been comical. Blood, on a box of matches, costing no more than a few pennies, as good as worthless to a man of Eckmann's wealth.

'Well, I don't want to do it! I'm no *good* at it!'

'You're not trying!'

'I'm sick of it. I *have* tried!'

'Not hard enough! You don't put the time into it. It doesn't happen just like that. You have to *work* at it to be an artist.'

'I don't *want* to be an artist! I'm *not* an artist! I was *never* an artist. You're an artist. Dad was an artist. But I'm not. I'm something else. I'm someone else. I'm *me*!'

'Then what *are* you going to do?'

'I don't know.'

'What *are* you good at?'

'I don't *know*!'

'You know how much those school fees cost?'

'I didn't ask to go there. You sent me!'

'For your good. For *your* own good!'

'I was happy where I was.'

They sounded, Eckmann realized, just like a rowing father and son. The adolescent, growing into his own

213

life and independence, the grouchy parent, feeling himself beginning to slip into the past – losing relevance in the world and influence over his child. Instead, he senses the commencement of age, of being supplanted – the intimations of decline.

'I tried to help you – took you in, gave you a home. This is how I am rewarded!'

'Then I'll leave if I'm so much trouble. I'll go. I don't want to stay where I'm not wanted. I'll manage. I'll be all right. I'll find somewhere. I know people.'

'Street people! Wasters, portrait painters, living statues, jugglers, acrobats, fire-eaters – those kinds of people.'

'My dad was a portrait painter – don't you talk about him like that. He wasn't a waster. He was real – true! He didn't sell out, not like you. And Poppea, she was true too. She never did anything wrong! They didn't just care about money.'

Eckmann felt his heart thumping in his chest – he felt the urge to strike the boy rising in his arms and hands.

'Sell out? Sell out? What do you mean by that? I don't just care about money! That's unfair. My art deserves respect as much as anyone's. You think because success comes to a man that he didn't deserve it, that he has sold out. Is failure a virtue then, is that what you think? The only good artist is a failed one?'

'My dad wasn't a failure! He just wasn't interested in money, that was all. He knew there are more important things. Is that how things are measured – by money?

'Are they measured by the lack of it?' Eckmann retaliated. 'What would you know – at your age! I was always true to my art – always. Do you have any idea – of how hard it was – for me!'

Silence. The atmosphere was heavy, claustrophobic. Neither of them spoke. Eckmann went to a drawer, pulled it open, took out some plasters and an anti-septic wipe in a sealed sachet.

'Here – clean your cut.'

He threw the things down on the table. Christopher cleaned the scalpel cut and put a sticking plaster on his finger. He looked up, his face filled with sullen resentment and dogged stubbornness. No one would tell him what to do. He had a mind of his own. He could be determined too. He was his father's son. *Not yours,* he thought, *his. My real father. My father's son. In my blood and in my genes. I can be stubborn too. I know he didn't desert me, I know he'd never do that. Something happened, something bad. Something evil happened to him, and one day I'll find out. I'm not an artist, I can't paint, I can't draw, but I'm still my father's son. Not yours. His.*

The little man was at the window, looking down into the street. Christopher watched him.

See. See how little you are. I'm not. I'm taller than you already. I'm my dad's son.

Eckmann's anger gradually diminished, and was replaced by melancholy. To be hated, by the person you loved. Why did it always come to this, always work out this way? He just wanted what was the best for the boy, that was all. Or was he making too much of it? Maybe, at this stage in his life, Christopher would have treated his natural father in exactly the same way, for all his thoughts and protestations otherwise. Yes, of course he would. He would have

215

quarrelled with his own father too. It was part of the scheme of things, part of life. He was making too much of it. Great mountains grew from little molehills.

He turned. Their eyes met.

Christopher grinned at him, his face suddenly full of unforced, quite spontaneous and genuine affection.

'Sorry, Ernst. Didn't mean to say that.'

It was a smile to melt the iceberg of even Eckmann's heart.

'I'm sorry, Christopher. My fault.'

'You know, Ernst . . .'

'What is it, Christopher?'

'Well, you know, you're so good at what you do, and it must come so, well, relatively easy to you . . . you can't imagine how difficult it is for somebody else, who's got no aptitude like that.'

Eckmann sat down, both flattered and contrite.

'Let's just agree that you're never going to be an artist of the miniature – huh?'

'Yes. Let's agree on that.'

'No more quarrels.'

'No more quarrels.'

Eckmann stood again.

'I'm going to the studio – do a little work. You'll be all right on your own?'

'I'll be all right. Besides, Lucy's here.'

The housekeeper had her own separate flat in the basement. She was at home tonight, staying in to watch television.

'Ernst?'

'Christopher?'

'I'm sorry for what I said. I am . . . I am grateful. You've been very kind to me. You have.'

'I . . . I was glad to help, Christopher.'

The boy took a few steps towards the door then,

'Ernst . . .'

'Christopher?'

'No news, I suppose?'

Eckmann stood tense, his body stiff, apprehensive.

'No, I'm afraid not. The reward still stands, of course, but no . . . nothing.'

'No.'

'I'm sorry.'

'You don't think . . .'

'Think what, Christopher?'

'No. Nothing.'

'No – think what?'

'I just thought, if we increased the reward maybe . . . someone might come forward, with something . . . some information . . . or something.'

'Yes, we can try that, Certainly, yes, we can try that.'

'I don't like to ask, you've done so much.'

'No, no. Not at all. I'll see that's done. We'll increase the reward. We've had some strange responses though, have we not. False sightings, false hopes and alarms.'

'Yes, I know. And I know it's been a long time, but you can never tell . . . it might have been amnesia, he might have been mugged, wandered off, not knowing who he was. Someone might have seen him. Or he might get another blow to the head and it all might come back to him, just like in the stories – you know, like in that film we saw. Something could happen, at any time . . .'

Eckmann let the torrent pass. He had heard and endured it many times before.

'You never know, eh, Ernst? You never know.'

Eckmann nodded solemnly.

'You're right. Christopher. We never know. I'll see the reward is increased.'

'What did you think would . . . ?'

'We'll double it!'

'Double it? Are you sure? Is it all right? Can we afford that?'

Eckmann did not miss the shift of phraseology in his speech.

Can *we* afford that. *We.* They were *us* again now, a unit, united in common enterprise, with bonds of mutual affection. We. You and I. The collective means of expression. The first person – plural.

Eckmann nodded.

'We can afford it. I'll see to it tomorrow.'

'Thank you, Ernst. You're very kind.'

Eckmann grunted, nodded, and went towards the door.

In many ways he was generous, that was quite true. But in this particular instance it was very easy to be generous, for it was an inexpensive matter to double the value of a reward which you knew, for an incontrovertible fact, would never be claimed.

'Oh, Christopher . . .'

'Yes?'

'If not art . . . science maybe?'

'Yes. I like science.'

'Maybe a scientist one day then?'

'Maybe, yes.'

'You think you'd like that?'

'Yes, I think I would.'

'Let's work towards that then.'

'Yes, OK.'

'Make that our goal.'

'Yes.'

'And Christopher ... No more matchstick carvings.'

The boy held up his bandaged finger and grinned.

'No more matchstick carvings! That's a deal.'

A spot of blood was visible under the plaster.

'Goodnight, Christopher.'

'Goodnight, Ernst.'

'Not too late to bed now.'

'No. Not too late.'

Eckmann left the room. Christopher was growing up all right, faster and faster, every day. His features were changing; he looked more and more like Robert. He had even developed some of his father's mannerisms. There was no doubt that he was his father's son. Yes, he was that all right.

Eckmann slipped out into the street and followed his customary route to the gallery. It was a fine night. Some seagulls had wandered inland and were vying with the pigeons in the abbey square for a share of the tourists' bread crusts. Signs around the square beseeched the visitors not to feed the birds.

'*Pigeons are vermin and carry disease*,' one of the signs bluntly and uncharitably announced. But as was so often the way with signs, most people took little notice of them. There was even a man with a small stall, selling bird seed. Eckmann looked at him, disgusted – wasters, chancers, street people, hand-to-mouth merchants, living for the day – the man was one of those.

At the café, Eckmann stopped for a glass of wine. He had already eaten with Christopher and wasn't hungry. He lingered over the first glass, then ordered a second, but when the waiter approached and asked if he would like the empty glass refilled again, Eckmann declined. Two glasses were quite enough if he was going to work that night. They were enough to relax the body and the mind and to help the work go well, but any more than that . . . and he'd start breaking things.

He paid his bill and waddled on his way.

A tourist at a nearby table spotted him and, once Eckmann was out of earshot, suggested to his children that they should feed Mr Eckmann some bread crusts, along with the other birds, as he seemed to walk like a duck.

The children laughed obligingly at Dad's joke.

Eckmann heard the laughter.

But it was water off a duck's back.

The arrows could no longer pierce his skin. He seemed to have grown a suit of armour. The laughter meant nothing any more.

Eckmann went into the gallery and up the stairs. He entered the attic studio. He had left a low-wattage light burning. It was maybe a little gratuitously cruel of him to consign them to unnecessary darkness, and of late he had taken to leaving on a light.

He went to the desk and set out his work things. In a strange way, the proximity of the tiny city was company; he liked to have them near him.

Like pets? The thought again flashed into his mind. Yes, maybe just a little like pets.

He started to work. It didn't come so easily to him these days. There were enough exhibits in the gallery and on reserve to keep him and it going for a long time. He felt that he had covered so much ground now, what else was there? What was different enough, original enough, to put on display . . . except . . .

He looked at the dome. What were they doing in there tonight? How did the time pass? Quickly? Heavily? Did it hang in the air like miasma, like fog?

He got on with the latest sculpture. He peered down into the lenses of the microscope and began to carve a replica of Rodin's famous statue, *The Kiss*, from a grain of rice.

The grain split.

He shook a second grain on to the glass slide and began again.

It was basmati rice, Indian, good quality; he preferred it to other kinds. Some varieties were round and fat, but this was longer, more slender.

Patience, that was what it took; infinite amounts of it. Patience, dedication, and yet more patience. Almost as much patience as children.

He felt an uncomfortable tightness in the lower part of his chest, just above his diaphragm. He moved around until the pain eased off. It must have been indigestion or heartburn, or maybe the wine – a little too acidic perhaps. He concentrated on the sculpture and began to carve an outline of the form depicted in the photograph in front of him.

The work went well for a time, then he needed to take a break. He filled the coffee maker with water and, as it warmed, decided to take a look into the dome to see how they were faring. Was it coffee time there too? He'd sent some coffee, hadn't he? Same brand – with his compliments. He sent them wine sometimes, when he was in the mood. And he tried to remember birthdays. These little things mean so much, when you are, after all . . . such a little thing.

He'd sent them a radio. He didn't think it would work, but he sent it, as an experiment. He never saw them listening to it though, so it couldn't have survived the miniaturization, as he had suspected it might not.

He put the rice sculpture aside and moved the microscope over to the dome. That was better. The jeweller's glass was good, but this presented a more powerful, more detailed image. You could even see the signs of ageing with this – the deepening lines on Robert's face, the furrows in his brow, the anger, the lack of resignation.

Ah yes. There they were. Sitting reading. They had quite a library now. Maybe one of them might need spectacles one day. That was going to present a problem; any physical ailment presented a problem. Or if anything were to happen to Eckmann, what would happen to them? Like the Pharaoh and his slaves entombed in the pyramid, like the Indian noble and his wives upon the funeral pyre – would they all die together?

He sharpened the focus of the microscope. Yes. There they were, the two of them, sitting on the steps of the tiny abbey, reading and talking until it was time to sleep. She seemed very relaxed tonight too, happier than she had been for a while. She appeared to be thriving really, despite it all – blooming in her own way. And she had put on a little weight – no bad thing, as she had always been slender, verging on too thin.

He watched as she put down her book, stood and then made an enormous stretch, her arms reaching up to the sky, standing on the points of her toes and then rolling back again. The loose dress she wore rose and fell with her movement, clinging to the contours of her body.

At first Eckmann's mind refused to accept what he saw.

'Poppea, Poppea,' he murmured to himself. 'You're starting to get fat.'

It had to be the life in there, not enough exercise, not enough to do, the boredom, too much food consumed as something to break the monotony.

Her arms fell to her sides. She stretched again and pirouetted. The dress again outlined her shape as she spun.

'You're getting a bit of a stomach, my dear.'

Then she crossed to where Robert was sitting reading. She sat beside him, took the book from him, put it down upon the step, took his hand and guided it to her stomach and placed it there, covering it with her own two hands so that it did not slip away.

No.

Not her stomach.

Her womb.

Eckmann held his breath, just as he did when he was carving that last, most difficult cut on an all but finished piece – like a diamond cutter, making the crucial incision into a priceless stone. He held his breath, second after second. His skin felt cold, then clammy. Perspiration appeared on his forehead.

She was pregnant.

They were expecting a child.

How dare they! Without his permission! Without God's permission!

He turned away in a complex turmoil of emotions – angry, wounded, worried, concerned, outraged, afraid, insulted, humiliated – yes, humiliated. They had humiliated him. It was like . . . like coming home to find your wife in bed with her lover, in the marital bed, *your* bed. Someone else lying there – with your wife! It was immoral, an outrage, an insult – an outrageous insult to him, an act of unbelievable defiance. After all he had done for them. After all he had *done*!

The water in the coffee maker hissed into the filter and dripped into the pot. The contraption bubbled and spurted for a full five minutes, until the last of the water was through. Eckmann stood, on the verge of an explosion of temper. He so nearly reached out and knocked the tiny city, and its glass-domed sky, its inhabitants and inhabitants-to-be, to their destruction. It would have taken so little, the merest gesture, but somehow the eruption did not come. But the anger went on pounding through him, like a pulse. Then he recognized the final ingredient in the emotional soup that was bubbling inside him. Envy. Green, bitter envy. He was jealous of them.

Even now, even as things were, he still hadn't won.

She was expecting a child – *that man's* child. Not Eckmann's child – *his* child. And who had locked them away together? Who had made it possible? Who had, in effect, made any other outcome virtually impossible? Eckmann had. He had done it to himself. The only real amazement was that it hadn't happened sooner.

A half-brother, a half-sister, for Christopher. *His* child too.

He had to punish them for this. In a suitable manner. A revenge to fit the slight. Payment in kind.

For what could exceed the joy of a child being born, other than the grief of one being taken away? An eye for an eye, a tooth for a tooth, a child for a child.

He would tell them that Christopher was dead.

Let the joy of that news fall directly upon them, like a ton of tiny bricks.

Rage

Hope deferred
Maketh
The heart sick.

Yet, in Christopher, hope remained. In the circumstances it was more along the lines of an unrealistic and unsustainable optimism, or possibly even a minor form of madness. But the fact that his hopes were not realized nor his dreams fulfilled, did not destroy them for him. He just went on hoping and believing that one day his father would return.

In the meantime, there was Mr Eckmann. Christopher's feelings towards him were ambivalent – gratitude, yes; respect, yes; affection – even that too. But love, well, that was difficult. Mr Eckmann was not a man who easily inspired that emotion in others, and this was not, at least in Christopher's case, anything to do with his physical appearance. He had long since seen beyond that – if he had ever much noticed it at all. Mr Eckmann was just . . . well . . . Mr Eckmann. That was how he was – his blatant ugliness, his deformity, his stature, his shuffling, waddling walk, the timbre of his voice, the powerful breadth of his shoulders, the strong stubby fingers, on the surface of it quite incapable of any fine or delicate work. All this was indeed Mr Eckmann, yet it was none of him too.

Christopher saw someone else – a man of great generosity and kindness, a man full of affection and consideration, but under that again, he detected – though he could not have put this into words – a man with an irreparably damaged soul.

It was as if at some point in his life, Eckmann's alienation from the rest of the world had inflicted a fatal injury upon him. Something had broken and never properly healed, and now it would never be right.

There was rage in him, an awful, terrible anger. It was anger at the way the cards had been dealt, at the hand he had received. The fact that others had received even worse cards was no consolation.

At first Eckmann had wanted to mete out some instant retribution and punishment to his captives. Some petty deprivation – to lock them in the cupboard maybe, leave them in the darkness.

But even as his hands reached to pick up the miniature city, he realized the immense pettiness of such a course and how in implementing it he would only degrade himself.

He left the city where it was.

Instead, he took a sheet of paper and quickly wrote on it. Before it had just been an idea, a mental exercise of power, but now he would do it for real.

'*I regret to inform you that Christopher is dead. There was an accident in the street. Eckmann.*'

He went to power up the decelerator, to miniaturize the message and to send it to them, but then he stayed his hand.

They wouldn't believe it. It was too sudden, too convenient, too implausible. They would know it was a revenge upon them, an abrupt, immediate retaliation. They'd know. They weren't stupid. He examined the note. No. It was farcical. There was too much of the playground in it. He could hear a refrain echo in his head. *Na, na, nee, na, na – you're pregnant so he's dead.*

No, no. Quite out of the question.

He crumpled up the paper and threw it into the bin. Then he feared that perhaps someone might unravel it and read what was written there, so he retrieved the ball of paper and tore it up into many pieces.

No, it would be best to do it a little at a time, to drip feed the information. First a little note – *Christopher not so well today so staying off school.* Then a second note, a few days later – *Christopher still off school, I'm afraid. Am taking him to see the doctor.* Then a third, a few more days after that – *Christopher back at school but still complaining of feeling unwell – bad headaches. Doctor suggests tests.* Then some silence, just to keep them guessing. Then in a while – *Went with Christopher to hospital today. Have been referred to consultant. Concerned about scan. Headaches v. bad. Again off school.* Then, when they were nice and worried – *I do not know how to say this but have no other way. Christopher is seriously ill with an inoperable tumour of the brain. Its growth very sudden and rapid. All we can do now is pray.*

That should give them grief and anxiety enough for a while.

And then he'd leave them incommunicado, frantic and desperate.

Leave them to sweat.

See what joy they got from the child in her womb then.

That would teach them.

Let a few more days go by, then a briefly scribbled note, half illegible, with all the hallmarks of haste and tiredness – *Have just come from Christopher's bedside. With him almost every moment of the day now. Just left him to send you this. He drifts in and out of consciousness. Has been in horrendous pain ...* (Yes, that was a nice touch. That would twist the knife in his father's heart, the little incidental information about the horrendous pain.) ... *but thank god the morphine seems to be working at last.* (Or was the *at last* an embellishment too far?) *Must go now. We are all doing everything we can.*

Then he would leave it again ... how long this time? Two more days? Two more long, eternal days?

No.

Make it three.

Oh, go on then.

Four. Or five.

No.

Make it six. That would be perfect. Then the final communication. (Possibly with a few drops of water dripped on to it to simulate the tears he would undoubtedly be shedding, and to make the ink run convincingly.) *With deep regret I have to let you know that Christopher passed away this morning. I was with him to the very end. His last thoughts and words before he drifted into final unconsciousness, were of you, and his wish that one day you would be reunited. You have my deepest sympathies and most sincere*

229

regrets. I will see to it that Christopher receives a decent and proper funeral. I wish I could properly convey my sorrow at everything that has happened. I wish I could reverse the process. I have tried and tried but cannot do it. Maybe one day, one day soon. Again, with my deepest sympathies. Eckmann.

That would do it. Nicely.

That would finish and sour their joy forever.

Yes, knowledge was power all right. In fact, it was more than power, it was a weapon. And what a pity that knowledge should be power when power corrupted so absolutely.

Maybe a few days afterwards he'd send them a copy of the funeral order of service, showing the hymns sung, the extracts read out. Maybe even a small lock of Christopher's hair. Yes, that would be a nice touch – a little keepsake, a lock of hair. Something of the artist in a touch like that.

Calmer, reassured, with a suitable revenge now in mind, Eckmann felt more able to forgive. He even tied the blind open so that they could enjoy the moonlight, then he left the attic room, locking the door behind him, as always.

He walked home. The streets were deserted. It was after one in the morning. He passed the entrance to the Roman baths – closed, secured, tourist free. He thought back to two thousand years ago, the Romans in occupation. Was there a man like him then, just like him, making his way through the deserted town as the wild dogs barked and the wind softly blew between the pillars and columns?

If the rebel was older than the kingdom, how old was the outcast, the misfit, the solitary figure making

230

its lonely way home? As old as the world probably, as old as civilization, as old as the men in the caves.

Eckmann let himself into the house. He removed his shoes, put on slippers and walked carefully up the stairs. A light was still burning in Christopher's room. The door was slightly ajar.

'Christopher . . .'

He spoke the boy's name in a whisper and slowly opened the door. Christopher was in bed, his head on the pillow, his eyes shut, a book still in his hand. He had fallen asleep while reading. Eckmann went to the bed and took the book from him, marked his place by folding down a corner of the page, then placed the book on the bedside table. He glanced at the cover to see what it was. It was *The Catcher in the Rye*. Eckmann had read it himself once, a long time ago. He remembered it as a wonderful book, but he could never have read it again. It was a book to twist knives in your heart.

Eckmann looked down at Christopher, asleep and vulnerable. It crossed his mind that he could go and fetch some scissors and cut the lock of hair now, and have it ready for when it was needed.

Christopher's breathing was deep and slow. His eyes moved behind his closed lids, following the picture show of some dream. Eckmann contemplated the boy's face, its regularity, its conventional handsomeness, so completely unlike his own with its jarring difference, its ugliness.

He would never have a son. Nor a daughter. Nor anyone. He would never have a wife or a child or a family. Never. This was his family. Adopted, borrowed, taken by trickery and force.

Had that been it all along then? Eckmann wondered. Had it not been Poppea he had wanted so much as the idea of what their union might bring?

A child?

Had that been what he wanted? Continuation? A thread joining him to the future as well as to the past.

His lips formed words.

'My son,' he whispered. 'My son.'

He reached out and brushed the hair away from the boy's forehead.

After all, that was right, wasn't it? Christopher was his son – his to love, his to be responsible for. His. And no one else's. His son, his heir, someone to carry a memory of him into the world beyond his own death, someone who would remember him – with affection, with gratitude, maybe even with love.

'Goodnight.'

He said the words softly, turned off the bedside lamp and left the bedroom, making his way to his own.

He sat on the bed and lit a cigar. He rarely smoked, but tonight he needed to feel the light-headedness it brought, the way it seemed to distance him from reality.

Eckmann knew that he couldn't do it now. He couldn't punish them. How could he? They were the two people in the whole world whom Christopher loved. And he loved Christopher. How could he hurt the people who meant so much to the boy? Indirectly, he would be hurting Christopher too – not that he would ever know, and yet . . . it would sour everything between them. It would surface somehow, manifest itself in some way, like a bad conscience, bad blood.

232

The jealousy and envy seemed to have risen like the smoke and dissipated into the air. He'd have to make plans now, take practical steps, think of all the things they might need – books, clothes, mineral supplements maybe; she might need those. Then there would be the labour itself. There was only one person to help deliver the baby and did he have the first clue how to go about a thing like that? There was so much to think of, so many things to plan. Still, at least there was plenty of time. No immediate hurry, that was something.

Eckmann lay back upon his bed and exhaled a stream of smoke up towards the ceiling. Then he reached to place the cigar upon the ashtray on the cabinet and to pick up the remote control for the television. It was very late, but he might catch some news.

Then he felt it.

It began in the centre of his chest. It wasn't so much pain at first as a sensation of pressure. Then it began to spread. It radiated outwards and upwards – into his left shoulder and then down along his left arm.

He felt fear. The sensation of panic. All the same, he also seemed to remain outside it, as if watching it all happen to someone else. His skin felt clammy again. Sweat was covering him, especially his upper body. It was cold and chill. The sensation of pressure was becoming one of pain. Not severe, not agonizing, but constant, rhythmic pain.

He knew what it was and he was afraid.

He decided it was best not to move yet. If he remained where he was, maybe it would pass soon. Or maybe he would die. Here, now, tonight. He had no fear of death at all. Fear of the pain increasing, yes, but of death, nothing. He was quite indifferent. Let it come if it wanted to, what did he care?

Frankly, he would be glad that it was all over. He had done what he had wanted to, accomplished what he could. What remained now was just serving time.

Then he thought of Christopher, of his responsibilities to him, of the two – no, the three – lives dependent upon him, the lives of those dwelling under the glass dome of the tiny city. Only he knew of their existence, only he knew how to use the decelerator, how to keep them alive.

God was a hard game to play.

But then God, of course, was immortal.

God's heart did not give out.

Eckmann remained lying still upon the bed. There was a hand upon his chest now, pressing harder and harder. It belonged to someone of considerable strength, and he was afraid that if the hand pressed any harder . . .

. . . it would crush the life out of him.

He watched as the smoke curled from the cigar. He watched as the cigar grew dull and burnt out, as all good, expensive cigars, untainted with saltpetre, did.

He watched. Waited.

The pressure on his chest increased. Any harder and there would be the crack of bone as his chest burst open, as the unseen hand reached into the cavity and closed its grip around his heart.

Still no fear of death though, just a willing, almost cheerful acceptance, tinged only with regret that he hadn't made better provision. The money was not a problem; Christopher would get all that. No, no, it was the dome. He needed to tell Christopher, needed to explain, needed to be . . . forgiven?

'Christopher!'

He called his name, but he called so faintly that the boy could not possibly have heard. He tried to call louder but the pain prevented him.

No deathbed confession then. No last words. Nothing.

He should have left a letter, something to be opened – *in the possibility of my death*. No. That was being unduly coy. *In the certainty of my death*. Too abrupt? *In the event of my death* then? Yes. That would do it. That was the convention. A letter for Christopher, the words written upon the front of the sealed envelope, *To be opened only in the event of my death*. Put that in the safe here, or at the gallery, or better still lodged with the solicitor who had drawn up the will. Or was there the risk that someone there might look at it – just a little peek perhaps? No, no. They were professional people, with standards, reputations. Anyway, who would believe a story like that?

Apart from Christopher.

But too late now to write any letters or make any startling disclosures.

How long he lay there, Eckmann did not know. But gradually the pain diminished and, as it did, he lost consciousness. He awoke some hours later, somewhat surprised to find himself still breathing. His skin was as grey as the dawn; he was exhausted and drained of all strength and the pain had subsided to a dull ache.

He thought to telephone an ambulance. Then decided to leave it. He would wait until morning, then visit the doctor. He undressed and lay between the

235

cold sheets. He turned on the electric blanket and fell asleep with it on. He woke up hot and turned it off, then slept again. He felt curiously at peace, oddly happy. In a way he felt relieved now, knowing that one day soon he might die.

In the morning Eckmann felt perfectly well. He went downstairs to find Christopher already at the kitchen table, having breakfast with their housekeeper. He said his good mornings and took the coffee that was offered to him.

'I'll walk in with you this morning,' he said. 'I need to call in at the doctor's.'

Christopher looked across the table at him, worried, concerned. He, who had lost so many people in his life, instantly panicked at the faintest possibility of losing one more.

'Nothing serious, I hope,' the housekeeper said, in the tone of one who knows in advance that it couldn't possibly be.

'No, nothing serious,' Eckmann said. 'Just need to call in – regular check-up.'

Over the coming days, the doctor arranged tests which told Eckmann what he already knew.

'You've had a heart attack,' the doctor said. 'I'll arrange for you to see a consultant. He'll be better able to interpret the ECG trace.'

There was another slight delay, another appointment, another examination, more tests, with Eckmann on a treadmill, wired up to a dozen electrical connections.

'It's scarred,' the consultant told him. 'Part of the heart is dead tissue. You may even have had other attacks in the past and not noticed.'

'That's possible?'

'Yes.'

'And what of the future . . . ?'

'Well . . .' the consultant hesitated, wondering what kind of a patient he was dealing with, how well-informed Eckmann already was, and how much he needed – or indeed wanted – to be told.

'I believe most people who experience one attack, experience another.'

The consultant hesitated before nodding.

'Yes. That's right.'

'Which I might do?'

'Yes.'

Another silence.

'Could it kill me next time?'

The consultant was used to matters being put in more oblique terms.

'I'm afraid you have a congenital heart weakness,' he said. 'I'm surprised it wasn't picked up before. It's more than likely due . . .'

How to put it tactfully?

'. . . to your stature.'

Ah.

Eckmann sat a while. He didn't say anything. The doctor handed him his shirt. He pulled it on over his short, muscular arms. He buttoned it up over his powerful, barrel chest, which was matted with black hair. He looked strong enough to lift a small mountain.

Betrayed, he thought sardonically to himself, from within. Undermined. And he smiled. Treachery, that was what did for you, treachery from inside. Each

237

man kills the thing he loves. And as each man loves himself more than anything, that is usually where he starts.

He stood to tuck the shirt into his trousers and looked up at the consultant.

'You can operate?'

The consultant looked doubtful.

'A new valve perhaps? A pacemaker?'

'That's not the problem.'

'Diet then? More exercise? Less exercise? Drugs? What? Or can you do nothing for me at all?'

'I'll give you something to thin the blood. And a nitrate spray, to help if there's more chest pain – just direct it under your tongue. When it runs out, go back to your own doctor. We'll call you in for regular check-ups and monitor things closely.'

'How long then?'

'How long?'

'Before I die?'

This directness was a little too much for the consultant's liking. He appreciated bluntness, but things could have been just a little more imprecise.

'You'll live for years,' he said, smiling professionally but without warmth.

'How many?'

'Hard to say.'

'I need four.'

'Four?'

'I have responsibilities. A son. He's fourteen. I need four years Then he'll be old enough – at university. I need four.'

'Mr Eckmann, you might live another thirty years.'

'I don't need thirty on the basis of "might". I need four – guaranteed.'

The consultant peeled the rubber gloves from his hands, dropped them into the bin, and went to the sink to wash – though surely his hands were clean?

'I'm sorry, Mr Eckmann. I wish I could guarantee things – for all my patients.'

'So you can offer me thirty but you cannot guarantee me four?'

The consultant washed his hands.

'I can't even guarantee myself four, Mr Eckmann.'

He smiled his thin smile again.

'No,' Eckmann nodded. 'I suppose not. That is life.'

'That is life,' the consultant agreed. 'Now, I don't wish to hurry you . . .'

But he had another patient.

Eckmann called in at the chemist's to pick up a few things, then he went in to the gallery. The girl was behind the reception desk and the place was half full of tourists.

'Busy this morning, Elena?'

'Pretty much.'

'I'll be in the studio.'

'All right, Mr Eckmann.'

She watched him go as they all watched him go, and thought what virtually all of them had thought.

'Funny little bloke.'

They said the same when they got home at night.

'Got sent on a new job today.'

'Who're you working for?'

'Funny little bloke.'

What was especially funny about him that morning

239

was what he was carrying. Poking out of the top of his bag was a baby's changing mat and a red, plastic rattle.

As he went on up the stairs, the rattle dropped down inside the bag. It sounded like a maraca as he shuffled on up the steps.

The Ruffian

Time came and went. The explanations of former years no longer sufficed and, as Christopher grew older, he questioned more and more what he had once so willingly accepted. As he grew, a sense of unease grew with him. There was something wrong in what he had been told; somewhere a mistake had been made.

He would cast his mind back, over and over, to the tiny dancer pirouetting upon the top of the pin; the way she had looked, the reality of her tears, how she fell and lay still and seemingly broken, like a rag doll dropped upon a bedroom floor.

It was so long ago that sometimes Christopher felt that he must have imagined her. But he knew he hadn't. He had seen her. Seen her dance – not like the mechanical dancers in music boxes, but sadly, as if she had no choice.

Then she had disappeared. And then there had been Mr Eckmann's almost dismissive explanation of how he had finally succeeded in bringing motion to his sculptures. 'Chips – computer chips – teething troubles – didn't quite work out.' He had never mentioned it again, nor, to Christopher's knowledge had he attempted to rectify the early faults or improve the process.

Which made no sense at all. He would have tried again, surely. For all its failure, it was still an astounding, almost miraculous success. To have brought such fluid animation and such lifelike, genuinely human motion to a figure of any size would have been remarkable. But to have brought it to a thing so tiny . . . it was almost . . . a miracle.

So why hadn't he tried again? Why had he given up? It made no sense. Mr Eckmann wasn't the kind to give up. The evidence of his trying and trying again was there, in the glass cases in the gallery; there, under the microscopes for all to see.

Yet it was impossible to talk to Eckmann about it. He blustered, grew irritable, changed the subject, muttered that he had lost interest, that it had been a wrong turning, a dead end, a false trail. He had better, more important things to do. He was concentrating on this, he was working on that, he had other projects on his mind. He was working on another process, to achieve a different result. Only what it was, he would never say.

There was only one explanation Christopher could come up with. It was Poppea. The heart had gone out of Eckmann when she had disappeared. He had lost interest in things and didn't wish to pursue them any more.

From the perspective of adolescence rather than childhood, and in experiencing emotions and desires now which he had not previously known, Christopher saw the reality of how the past had been. Eckmann had loved Poppea, been infatuated with her. It made sense of so many things. His coldness towards Robert, his lap-dog-like devotion to Poppea, his instant attention to anything she might need or want, her occasional suppressed, but nevertheless quite obvious, irritation with him.

He had offered her love and she simply didn't want it. Friendship was as far as she was able to go, but friendship only prolonged Eckmann's agony by offering him the hope that it might develop into something more, while from her perspective it plainly never would.

Then there was the job in the gallery. It was as if he had been trying to buy her. But Poppea was never to be bought. Perhaps Mr Eckmann had come to realize that in the end. Perhaps he had even been the reason for Poppea's going away. Some argument, some demand, some impossible situation.

Yes, there was no denying it, Mr Eckmann was a strange and complex man. As Christopher grew up, he realized that he frankly did not understand him. He sometimes wondered if Mr Eckmann even understood himself.

Christopher wondered about his own mother too, why his parents' relationship had foundered, why she had left them both, where she was now, if she ever thought of him, longed to meet him, wanted him back.

He and Eckmann still quarrelled sometimes. Once Christopher had almost struck him. It had been an argument about a piece of homework. Eckmann had found it, half completed, on the floor of Christopher's room. Assuming the worst, he had taken the homework and gone to find Christopher, who was sitting in front of the television, watching a programme he had promised himself that he would see.

Eckmann waddled in furiously, small and angry, bubbling like a pot. He threw the homework down and demanded an explanation of why it had not been completed. Then, without waiting for one, he launched into another tirade of what he had done for Christpher and the boy's ingratitude.

'You know how much it costs me? The fees for that school? You have any idea – *any* idea? I send you to this school so you may have the best, and this – *this* is how you repay me! You can't even do the homework you're set. You sit here, in front of the television!'

There was a simple explanation but Christopher wasn't prepared to give it. Eckmann's entire manner and approach, the very fact that he was standing between Christopher and the television, preventing him seeing what he wanted to, coupled with the fact that Eckmann had simply walked into his room . . .

This time he had gone too far.

'What do you think you're doing? What the *hell* do you think you're doing, going into my room, reading my work, picking my things up off my floor. Do I go into *your* room? Do I interfere with your work? Do I?'

'There's a difference!'

'*What* difference!'

'I pay for your school. You don't pay for mine!'

'Then I'll go to another school. One you don't have to pay for! All right? Happy? Now get out of my way. I want to see the television.'

'You are not watching the television until you have done this homework.'

'The homework does not have to be in until next

week. That's why I haven't finished it. Because it doesn't need to be done yet. OK!'

But it was too late now for Eckmann to back down.

'I don't care about that. I want it done *now*. This is *my* house. *My* work, *my* money – it pays for *everything*. You take it all for granted. I get no respect. You will do this homework and you will do it *now*! You will do as I say!'

'Why!'

'Because I am your father!'

Christopher stood. He was shaking with anger. Eckmann looked up at him, apprehensive, afraid.

'You are not . . .'

The words wouldn't come. His voice was cracking with emotion. He swallowed, breathed deeply, fighting for some control.

'You are not . . . you are *not* . . . my . . . father. And you never will be.'

He turned and left the room.

Eckmann sat on the sofa, the blood pounding through him, his heart racing. He sat fearing a second attack – that this time his heart would give out for good. He took the nitrate spray from his pocket and sprayed two short blasts under his tongue. That was better, better. He sat back, counted slowly to twenty, absorbing himself in the numbers. Yes, he was right, of course; Christopher was right. He had no business going into the boy's room. He knew very well that Christopher was a conscientious student and needed no prompting or overseeing to complete his projects on time.

Why then had he done it? Why had he been motivated to provoke the stand-off, this fight for control?

He didn't know. Maybe because Christopher was growing up, no longer a child, no longer so compliant or biddable. Maybe because he would leave soon, and Eckmann would be alone again, with no one, just as before.

Eckmann apologized. He went to Christopher's room and tapped on the door.

'Christopher . . .'

'Go away!'

'You're programme's still on.'

'I don't want to see it.'

'Christopher . . .'

'What do you want? Go away. Haven't you done enough damage!'

'Christopher . . . I'm sorry.'

And he was. For so many things, that he only wished he could tell him about.

He was about to go when the door opened.

'Ernst . . .'

'Yes?'

'I'm sorry too.'

Christopher extended his hand awkwardly. Eckmann reached out and took it. Then, in a clumsy, embarrassed manner, Chistopher put his arm around Eckmann's shoulders and gave him a brief, gruffly affectionate hug. Eckmann tried to respond, but Christopher was already moving away.

Later that night Eckmann realized that it was the first and only time they had ever embraced. It was years and years since anyone had shown him affection him like that. He fell asleep, feeling sadder than he had in a long while.

*

The child was born one night in summer. Eckmann had not been there to witness the birth, though his curiosity had driven him often enough to the studio in the small hours of the morning, just on the off-chance, just to see, for he knew that the time was near.

Evidently there had been no serious complications, for if there had been, Robert would most probably have been unable to cope with them, and the child – possibly even the mother – would not have survived. Giving birth, like dying, was, when it came down to it, still a pretty primitive business.

Eckmann stared down through the microscope. He made no conscious effort to control or direct his emotions. When feeling came, he recognized it as a sense of awe, of wonder, not only at the fact of new life appearing, but of the fact that it had done so here, in this place, in this . . . dimension.

Life was a flower that could grow anywhere. In deserts and wastelands, in tundras and wildernesses. It was ferociously strong and immensely delicate. So tenacious that it would hang on grimly to the slightest hold, and prolong itself through awful suffering rather than surrender to death. Yet it was so fragile too, that a breeze could destroy it; a gust, a shower of rain, and it would wither and fade as if it had never been.

Eckmann felt rather proud. He began to have visions of his entire miniature city, with bustling streets and busy citizens, all going about their business, their heads full of concerns other than to get back to where they came from.

Life was life, surely, wherever it was. Large or small, gigantic or microscopic, it went on in the same way.

Size, as people say, doesn't matter.

Maybe they could call the place Eckmannville.

It turned out to be a girl. Eckmann would have been as happy with a boy. But then, of course, he already had a boy, so a girl was nice too. Of course, none of this was actually so, neither of them was actually his, and Eckmann did not literally see it in this way. It was more a game he played – a game of possession. And of course, in terms of responsibility, they were his indeed.

He became a diligent father. Maybe too much so. He grew less careful about how and when and where he bought supplies. On one occasion he left a packet of pink-labelled nappies sitting in the kitchen. Christopher had wandered in and seen them, and had looked at them first with amusement, then with puzzlement.

'What are these?' he asked the housekeeper.

She looked at them with equal perplexity.

'Ernst must have bought them.'

He came in to find the two of them contemplating the package.

'Ah,' he said. 'There they are. I promised to get them – for the girl – at the gallery. She asked me if I'd mind . . . picking them up.'

It seemed incredible. Mr Eckmann, doing his receptionist's shopping for her? And since when did she have a baby?

'Her sister . . .' Eckmann said, and without further explanation, and with his face colouring scarlet, he took the package and left.

Nothing like it happened again.

'Hope he's not going soft in the head,' the housekeeper had said. Christopher gave her a severe look,

248

as though this were no way for her to be speaking about her employer.

But it had been a strange thing to buy.

Eckmann busied himself with his responsibilities and his charges. The right food, the necessary medicines, the correct supplies, toys, picture books; all were shrunk and sent to the city. He sent extra bags for the rubbish to cope with the additional waste, and they were left out, and he would remove them, picking them up with a pair of flat-headed tweezers, the jeweller's lens screwed into his eye so that he could find them and take them away. He didn't want any infections spreading. He was everything now, doting nursemaid as well as dustman.

He sent them champagne. And two wide brimmed glasses. He watched as they drank, hoping perhaps that they might raise their glasses to him, and give a toast to him, a small libation to the gods – such as they were. But no.

He wondered sometimes how much they hated him. It was probably impossible to quantify.

In a moment of generosity, or maybe it was guilt, he sent them photographs of Christopher and copies of his most recent school reports, so that Robert could see for himself how his son had progressed, how he had changed, how Eckmann had not neglected his responsibilities.

Christopher had found Eckmann in his room, looking for the reports. Eckmann had immediately apologized for being there.

'Christopher, I'm sorry, I just wondered if you had

your last reports. I just wanted to make some copies, in case, you know, something happened to them.'

Christopher began to wonder.

He began to wonder if Eckmann had a mistress.

It wouldn't have been impossible. Eckmann was small, squat and ugly, but he was still a man. And he was wealthy enough. Money could sometimes buy what age or appearances prevented being given freely. Maybe that was it. Maybe that was where he disappeared to so frequently at night. Maybe he wasn't working at all. Maybe he had got her pregnant. That might explain a lot of things. Maybe Mr Eckmann had a secret, other life that no one else knew anything about.

But then so did Christopher. He had a girlfriend of his own – Trudy, from school. He didn't tell Mr Eckmann what he did, and Mr Eckmann didn't confide in him either. Neither asked any questions, and neither was told any lies. It was a reasonably satisfactory arrangement.

And then there was the letter.

Eckmann had a copy on the computer in his room. He had it protected under a password, and he also kept a paper copy in the safe, next to his will.

'*To Christopher. To be opened in the event of my death.*'

This document had, over time, had various guises. Eckmann constantly re-wrote and re-worked what it contained. Every now and again he would print out the new version, destroy the one in the safe, and the revised letter would take its place.

'*My dear Christopher, I know you will find this hard to believe and difficult to forgive but . . .*'

Or,

'*Dearest Christopher, Please find it in your heart to forgive me and, if possible, not to hate me for what I have done but . . .*'

Always the '*but*'. No way around that.

Or maybe an entirely different approach:

'*Christopher, I know you will find this difficult to accept, but . . .*'

No, no. The '*but*' again. How could he avoid it?

He couldn't.

Eventually, he gave up trying. Then one day, in the August after Christopher's final term at school, it came for him, as he was on his way up the stairs. It came, it happened, as simply as that. Without any warning or any formality at all. He was carrying a birthday cake at the time, which he had ordered specially from the patisserie a few doors down from the gallery.

And suddenly, there it was.

The birthday cake was for a child. Eckmann had selected a design with the number 4 piped upon it in pink icing. He had asked that the words '*Love To Maria*' also be piped upon it, in the same pink icing, and that four candles, set into sugar, rosebud holders, should be placed at each corner. In addition to the cake, he carried some birthday cards. One was written out to the same name – Maria. '*From Uncle Ernst*,' it said. The other cards were blank, as if he had bought them on behalf of somebody else, for them to fill in themselves, at a later time.

And he was laden with presents.

Maybe that was how he had lost his footing.

He had so many presents, he could barely carry

them all. There were books, toys, colouring crayons, clothes, soaps, jigsaws, hair-bands, a box of balloons, some games, some beads, a box of chocolates . . . Some of the presents were wrapped, and the gift tags upon them carried the same message as the card – 'To Maria, Happy Birthday, With Love From Uncle Ernst.' The other gifts awaited wrapping and, for this purpose, Eckmann carried rolls of wrapping paper, gift tags and Sellotape.

As he hurried up the stairs, he missed his footing on the step to the landing. Had his arms not been full of presents, he might have managed to retain his balance, but as it was, that would have meant letting go of everything, and he didn't want to drop the cake.

She'd been expecting the cake. She'd been told about it, promised it. She knew about Uncle Ernst and how the world worked. Maybe when she got older, they'd tell her the truth. But for now, it was like Santa Claus – someone to believe in for a while. Uncle Ernst, up in the sky, the man who came when she was asleep, or pretending to be, and brought the presents.

No, he didn't want to drop the cake. It would fall from the box, which would burst open on impact, the pink ribbon unravelling, the candles breaking, the icing cracking open.

Madam Life's a piece in bloom.
Death goes dogging everywhere.

As he fell backwards it came into his head, out of nowhere, out of the past, out of his schooldays years and years ago; a poem by someone whose name he couldn't even remember. They were words he didn't even know that he knew.

He fell back, still holding on to the presents. He was

252

afraid that he would break his neck, but no. He landed heavily on one of the steps, but instead of stopping, he rolled and fell back again to the step below.

She's the tenant of the room.

He had to hold on to the presents though, Eckmann thought. Just dust them off, straighten them up. Musn't disappoint her. Keep hold of the cake and the presents. They'd have told her there would be a cake. No friends, perhaps, not like for other children; no real party, no clown, no magician, no conjuring tricks. But presents and a cake. And a special present from Uncle Ernst.

He fell again.

He's the ruffian on the stair.

He had saved the cake. All intact. He'd saved the cake.

For his little girl.

Little, little, oh so perfectly little . . .

Girl.

Then the ruffian got hold of him and twisted his heart.

With his kneebones at your chest.

Punishment, maybe, for all he had done.

And his knuckles at your throat.

Only this time, there was no calm, no resignation. This time Eckmann tried to fight it, willed it to go away. He wanted to live, *had* to live. He *had* to get up to the studio, to the attic room. It was someone's birthday, somebody special, someone who mattered to him, somebody . . . he loved.

She was expecting Uncle Ernst to bring her presents. His little girl. His darling. You never saw him. Never saw Uncle Ernst. If anything, he was like a cloud, a

253

big, vague cloud in the sky. But one day, maybe one day . . .

He put the presents down carefully and stretched his hand out towards his pocket for the spray.

The ruffian got hold of his arm and twisted it. Eckmann couldn't reach, just couldn't quite reach. The ruffian had him now, on the stair.

Right there.

On the stair.

Was that in the poem too? No. That was another song.

The ruffian had his very heart. Eckmann was strong, strong as a bull, with shoulders like an ox, but this was stronger. Or maybe it was his own strength he was fighting, and not the ruffian at all. He tried again to reach for the spray, but his hand couldn't find it. His hand was a wizened claw now, contorted against the pain.

Then the pain stopped. And there was darkness. And the ruffian had what he wanted, and he moved on. He tiptoed down the stairs and let himself out of the gallery – though nobody saw him go. He slipped through the door without opening it. He went out into the street, blending into the crowd. And he began to follow somebody else.

Madam Life's a piece in bloom.

Or she was. Once. Now she festered, she withered in the vase.

Eckmann lay amongst the presents, the tags, the wrapping paper, the bags, the colouring crayons.

He still held the cake. It was quite intact. He had saved the cake. For his perfect little girl. Only now, there was nobody to send it to her.

The Letter

Christopher found him. He had news of his own. His exam results had come. They hadn't been due until tomorrow, but he had dropped in at the school on the off-chance that they might have arrived early, then had rushed home, a smile on his face. He called out, his voice echoing through the house.

'Ernst! Ernst! I got them!'

Straight As. In everything.

'Ernst! Ernst! You there?'

Only Eckmann wasn't back. Must still be at the gallery. Christopher could have rung but he wanted to tell him in person, so he grabbed his keys from the lock and left the house, the door crashing behind him. He half ran, half jogged to the gallery, the letter in his hand. He couldn't help grinning. Eckmann was going to be pleased. Not as pleased as Christopher though. He could pick and choose now – any of the offers. Straight As. He was thinking of what he would say when he got to the gallery; tease Eckmann a little maybe, make a joke of it.

'Ernst, you remember once you said something to me about not doing homework, and how you were paying all these school fees and I was wasting your money? Yes? Well now, I don't want score any points or anything, but if I could just show you this letter . . .'

He'd be on the defensive at first. He'd take the letter, a little worried, a little wary. Then he'd see, and the smile would spread across his face too. And then he'd want to celebrate. Out to eat. The café in the square. Or maybe Christopher could actually persuade him to go somewhere else for once in his life. Maybe he'd invite Trudy. Better ring her, tell her too, see how she'd done. And Rees.

Maybe he'd be grown-up too tonight, tell Eckmann what he thought, about him having someone, a mistress. It could all be out in the open. Tell him to bring her too. Eckmann and the secret woman, Christopher and Trudy, and straight As, all celebrating together. University in October then, the one he wanted – the one that wanted him. Ernst would be proud of him.

His dad would be proud of him too. Would have been . . . proud.

But don't let it spoil today.

Today was a good day.

Tonight they'd have wine. He was old enough to drink it. He'd let it roll around the glass, just the way Eckmann did, the way he had always seen him do it, right from way back, when he was just a small boy, sitting having his portrait painted to bring in the customers.

The gallery was locked. He rang the bell, but there was no answer. He used the rusty door-knocker to hammer a funny *rat-a-tat-tat*, just to let Eckmann know there was a happy joker at the door. Nothing. He had to be up in the studio then, and couldn't hear, or thought it was some unwanted caller and wouldn't bother to come down.

Christopher took his bundle of keys and sorted through them to find the one that fitted the gallery door. He unlocked the door, and hurried inside.

'Ernst! Ernst!'

There was a strange silence. He went towards the stairs. Something compelled him to look into the exhibition room. Everything was dark and silent. The unseen, microscopic sculptures looked back towards him. The polar bear, no bigger than a grain of salt, looked out blankly. Nothing stirred at the pyramids. The Sphinx remained inscrutable. The camel still stepped through the eye of the needle, on its way to the kingdom of heaven with all the rich men.

'Ernst! It's me!'

He went on up the staircase, his long legs carrying him up, two, three, four at time. He was tall now, at least six feet, well built, at the start of manhood. He was intelligent, able, considerate, kind, humorous, loyal, honourable . . .

A credit to his parents and teachers and to those who had brought him up.

'Ernst! Where are you?'

He rounded the staircase, and there was Eckmann, lying like a child, fast asleep among its birthday presents, at the end of a long, lovely day.

'Ernst . . . Ernst . . .'

Christopher knelt beside the body. He put his hand to Eckmann's face to feel for breath. There was none. He took his wrist and felt for a pulse. There was nothing. He felt his forehead. The skin was already cold.

'Ernst . . . Ernst . . . wake up, Ernst . . . I brought my results . . . got my results . . .'

Christopher picked up the dead man and cradled him in his arms. Pathetically, he tried to show the letter to him, holding him up, refusing to believe what his senses told him, that he was already cold, already dead. As if the letter were a jar of smelling salts and might revive him.

'Ernst . . . see, Ernst . . . look . . . came today . . . I got them from school. I just looked in on the off-chance, on the way home. I went cycling. All day. With some friends. We went along by the river, rode for miles. See . . . see the letter . . . it's my results . . .'

He held the letter closely, near to the dead man's eyes.

'You see. I did well, Ernst. I did work. I know you thought I didn't always, but I did. I hope you're proud. I tried to repay you. I did. You see, Ernst – straight As. You see that? You are pleased, aren't you?'

The dead man's head lolled down and his chin slumped to his chest.

But Christopher wouldn't let him do that.

He wouldn't let him be dead. He'd lost too many people in his life to let another go so easily.

'I knew you would be pleased. I wanted to show you, you see, Ernst. I just didn't know how to . . . how I felt. I'll get into university now. You can come and visit. And I'll come home, every holiday. Bring my friends. Show them the gallery. Your sculptures . . . Ernst, please don't die . . . please don't . . . you're my family . . . you're all I have . . . please don't die . . . I love you.'

The words which Eckmann had waited a lifetime to hear fell now upon deaf, dead ears. It was all he had ever wanted to be told. That he was loved.

And he was. By his son.

The paper with the results on it fluttered to the floor. It lay there amongst the presents. Christopher sat, still cradling the dead man's body, his arms around the small, misshapen form. He held him, swaying softly, like a parent bringing comfort to a hurt and injured child.

He began to cry. Not just for now. For everything. For what he had lost, for all the times past, for his mother whom he had never known, for Robert, for Poppea, for his childhood, for his past, for the Tiny Dancer who had fallen and lain like a rag doll, immobile upon the ground.

He cried for the memory of a million scenes and memories and feelings which he would never experience again. The way it felt to sit in the square as his father drew his portrait and the way the tourists clustered round. His father's hand holding his, his stubble as he kissed him goodnight, the smell of Poppea's perfume, the scent of her hair as she kissed him goodnight too. The sound of them making love when they thought he was asleep.

He wept for his life, and for the loss of everyone he had ever loved. And among those he had loved was the little man whose cold, dead body lay in his arms.

At length he stopped. The crying subsided. His eyes cleared. What to do? Something.

Then he saw the gifts, the wrapping paper, the gift tags, the cards.

'Ernst?'

The cake.

He gently laid the body down, trying to position it so that it might have some dignity. He picked up the box and undid the ribbon. He opened the lid, and looked inside.

Love to Maria. And the number 4. And four small candles, set in sugar rosebud holders, at each corner of the cake.

'Ernst . . . who's Maria?'

It was a birthday cake, for a little girl.

He explored the presents. He opened the unsealed envelope and looked at the card. *To Maria, Happy Fourth Birthday, With Love From Uncle Ernst.*

It made no sense. None at all. Why here? Why was he taking the things upstairs?

He stood and looked up towards the landing at the door of the studio. An awful coldness filled him now. But he made himself go forwards, one step at a time, up to the attic door. When he got there, he paused, then he made his hand reach out and turn the handle of the door. It was locked.

He went back and took the keys from the dead man's pockets. He found the one to open the studio door. He undid the lock, turned the handle again, and went inside.

It was still light. It was summer and wouldn't be dark until well after ten. He looked around, apprehensive, expecting something frightening and unfamiliar. But there was nothing. Just the light flickering upon the camera obscura, the drone of the traffic from far down on the street, and there upon the desk . . .

Oh yes.

The tiny city. The replica. Eckmann's great project,

his masterpiece. Funny, he hadn't mentioned it in a long time. In fact, come to think of it, Christopher hadn't actually seen it for a long, long time. For years.

He crossed to it. There it was, under the glass dome. He remembered it as an astounding piece of work, so detailed, so exact, so true to life, so perfect.

He walked away from it, to try and find some clue as to why Eckmann would have been coming up here with presents for a child. He looked around, but there was nothing. Then he saw the microscope, placed near to the tiny city as if positioned at the ready, for easy and familiar use. He moved it out over the dome, then he adjusted and focused it to suit his eyes. Then he looked down into the city.

There were the familiar buildings and sights. There was their house. There were the Roman baths. There was the crescent of Regency houses, all the exteriors perfect in their detail. There wasn't a flaw. There was the river walk and the river, fashioned from a sliver of mirrored glass. There was the rugby pitch. There was his school. There was the gallery. There was the abbey and the abbey square where his father had once painted portraits, where Poppea had once stood, as a living statue, only moving when someone dropped a coin into the box to set the music off. And there . . .

There she was.

There was Poppea.

Crossing the square.

There was his father.

Crossing the square.

And there was Christopher.

Crossing the square.

Holding their hands.

261

And as they crossed the square, they swung him between him, and he giggled and laughed and shouted for joy and begged and demanded that they do it again.

Only it wasn't him. It was a girl. A little girl, about four years old.

Crossing the square.

He felt the onrush of what could only be madness – total, absolute madness, the loss of all understanding and mental control. Everything in his field of vision turned to the colour of blood. Then it slowly cleared, and he saw at long last what had happened. He saw it with awful, terrible clarity.

Remnants

There was dust. Faded and unfaded patches too, like the rings left by glasses and cups on the tables of cafés and bars. Outside, a torn poster flapped in the wind, the rain scurried along the street, and some tourists stood in disappointment, staring at the sign in the window, which read *Closed*.

One shielded his eyes and peered inside. The floor was strewn with unopened letters and possibly unpaid bills. Yet, knowing Christopher, all that would have been taken care of. He was never one to leave a bill outstanding, or to shirk his responsibilities and obligations.

A car appeared. It was large and expensive, probably leased. It was there as evidence of success. The estate agent who drove it left it parked on a double yellow line and hurried to meet the man waiting for him by the door.

'Be all right there for a while,' he said. 'Hope I've not kept you waiting.'

He extended his arm to shake hands.

'Only just arrived,' the man told him.

'Good. Now I have the keys here . . . if I can find the right one.'

The estate agent tried the first of several in the lock. The fifth one opened it.

'Got so many keys in this business. But there we are. Come inside.'

The other man was staring up at the fascia of the building.

'The Gallery of the *what*?' he said.

The agent looked up at the sign.

'Oh that. "The Gallery of the Art of the Impossible".'

'And what was that exactly?'

'Oh . . . miniature sculptures, I believe, that kind of thing.'

'So what happened to it?'

'Don't really know.'

'Not lack of visitors, I hope?'

'Oh no, no. Far from it. First-class location. Prime site. Tremendous walk-past trade. But let's go inside. Ideal premises, actually. You'll see for yourself.'

They walked in. There was some resistance from behind the door. It came from a pile of junk mail. Some of it was addressed to the Gallery of the Art of the Impossible, or some variation thereof, other items were personally addressed to Mr E. Eckmann, or E. Eckmann Esquire.

There was a faint odour of damp, an atmosphere of emptiness and the beginning of decay.

'Needs airing, of course.'

'Been standing empty long?'

'Not that long. Few months. Sorting the estate out, that kind of thing.'

'Musty, isn't it?'

'Just needs the heating on and some windows open.

Doesn't take that long, I'm afraid, for things to seem musty, but they're as quickly fixed. What's your line, exactly?'

'Oh . . . candles, you know, soaps, perfumes, luxury items, that kind of thing.'

'Well, perfect position for that.'

'Yes, we've got one shop already elsewhere, in another town. Just looking to expand.'

They went on into the gallery itself. The plinths and stands remained, but the domes which had once sat upon them, containing Eckmann's finest and most delicate work, had all gone.

'I'd watch your feet there. Seems to be a bit of broken glass.'

'What happened here?'

'Must have dropped something when they were clearing the place out. Removal men. You can get some cowboys.'

'Huh. Tell me about it.'

'Yes, well, it's fairly spacious, as you can see.'

'And there's an upstairs?'

'Yes, yes. Several levels. Quite extensive – storage, offices, what used to be a studio.'

'Shall we go on up?'

There was a shattered pane of glass in one of the windows. Some rain had entered, and there was a patch of damp upon the bare, uncarpeted floor.

'This was the studio, was it?'

'I believe.'

It was cold, damp, soulless.

'Great potential.'

'Yes . . . yes.'

The would-be purchaser looked around. There

were marks on the floor, of the desks and tables which had once stood there. In the corner, something remained.

'What's this dish?'

'It's the base of what I believe is called a camera obscura.'

'Oh? Is there any more to it?'

'Probably was once.'

'But that's all gone?'

'All gone now, I'm afraid. Yes.'

'Pity.'

'Yes. Still. You could maybe get something sorted out, if you wanted to get it working again. I mean, it's quite a feature really.'

The man sounded dubious.

'Hmm . . .'

But then he didn't want to admit to anything that might indicate that he liked the place particularly. He intended to put an offer in well under the asking price. You never knew, maybe the owner who had inherited the building was anxious to sell. He might even be desperate to get rid of the place.

The day after the funeral, Christopher had returned and broken each one, quite methodically, without any evidence of anger or malice. He simply went to the exhibition in the gallery and destroyed Eckmann's life's work. Even as he did so, he didn't know that it was in any way the right, or even justifiable, thing to do. The sculptures existed as wonders and things of beauty in themselves. In a sense they had long since ceased to have any connection with their creator, and even if, in another way, they still had enduring links to him, well, was the art to blame for the faults of the artist? Were the sins of the father to fall on the son?

Apparently they were.

He removed each dome from its stand and dropped it to the floor. If it did not shatter immediately he picked it up and hurled it across the gallery until it did.

Then he ground its contents underfoot.

He would eradicate every trace of Eckmann. It would be as if he had never existed.

He picked up the dome which contained the camel in the eye of the needle. He remembered the first time he had seen it – as a child. How he would come to the gallery first thing after school and how Eckmann would let him in for free. He remembered how he would gaze with wonder and delight at the tiny, beautiful sculptures, enraptured by them, lost in them, for what seemed like small eternities.

Maybe he should keep one, if only for the sake of the past.

He held the glass dome a moment, then released it and let it fall. It broke into a thousand pieces. He ground them under his heel. He worked on, patiently and methodically, until he had broken and destroyed them all – except one.

There was one which, of course, he could not destroy – not without destroying himself along with it.

That night, after finding the body, Christopher had sat for long hours, staring down into the tiny city. He watched them as they moved, as they slept. He watched them as they woke in the morning. He saw the lines on his father's face, how he looked older now, how his hair was flecked with grey. He saw how Poppea had aged too, still lovely, still beautiful, but moving as all living things did, ineluctably towards age and, one day, death.

And then there was the girl.

The girl.

Whose birthday presents hadn't come. Whose cake had not arrived. Whose knowledge and understanding of the world was . . . what? That the world was a small city, with a glass-domed sky, which defined the boundaries of the known universe.

And in this world were two other people only, her father and her mother, and nobody else – apart from the provider. Yes, the great and good provider, who sometimes, often, came to see them – a good, true, wise, munificent god.

And sometimes the hand of God would come down and lift the roof from the sky, and there were all kinds of wonders then – gifts and water and good things to eat. But no children. No one else ever came, or visited. There was no one else at all, except in the books, which told of another world, somewhere.

Somewhere out there was this other world, with people on it, just like her, or so the books said. But she didn't believe them. It was quite impossible – nothing but fantasy and dreams. She asked her mother, who said that one day, when she was older, they would tell her everything. One day, when she was old enough to understand.

Christopher sat and watched her. He heard a voice speak softly.

'My sister . . . my sister . . .'

He realized the voice was his own. Then the person

the voice belonged to remembered a name, a name he had seen, picked out in pink icing upon a cake.

'Maria . . .'

He watched her move across the street. She had a skipping rope. She skipped a while, then grew bored with it, and stopped to sit and tie knots in the rope, and then untie them.

'Happy birthday, Maria . . .' he whispered. 'Happy birthday.'

All he could think was that she must have been so disappointed that her birthday had passed and nothing had come. And into this small incident he invested all the anger and grief and pain of his young life, and he found himself weeping, and the tears fell upon the roof of the dome.

She looked up. She ran to get her parents. She brought them to the street and pointed to the sky. They too looked up and saw the rain fall. They watched as the drops hit the glass sky, and then ran down the side of it, leaving streaks of moisture.

'Dad . . . Poppea . . . it's me . . . it's Christopher . . . it's me. I've found you. I've found you. After all the years.'

They watched – the girl delighted, the adults per-plexed – as the rain fell and fell and fell, until it seemed it might never stop. It seemed as if it might even shatter the glass, flooding the whole city and sweeping them away. The girl grew tired of watching and went back to her skipping. But the man and the woman remained where they were, looking up to the sky, as the rain went on falling. Falling and falling.

Afterwards, Christopher went to the stairs. Eck-mann's body lay there, his skin with a bluish tinge to it now. He reached down and closed the man's cold, life-less eyes. It was impossible to know what to feel, so many emotions conflicted in him, like clashing rip-currents and tides.

'How does it work, Ernst?'

Christopher prodded the prone body with his foot.

'How do I make it work?'

He squatted down beside the body. He realized that he had nearly trodden upon one of the presents and he moved his feet away. He reached into Eckmann's pockets and took out what was there. He rifled through his wallet, but there was nothing there to help him. He took Eckmann's keys and compared them to the ones he had himself. There were several extra, which he did not have. One of them bore the name of the maker of the house-safe.

'I'll be back.'

His voice, then his footsteps, reverberated through the gallery. He let himself out of the front door. It was early morning by then, just after dawn. He hurried back to the house and let himself in. Then he went to Eckmann's study and rifled through the drawers and his private papers. Finding nothing, he took the picture down from the wall and used the key to open the safe. In it was, amongst other things, a cash box. There was also a painting of Poppea, his father's painting, the one which he thought had been lost.

One of Eckmann's keys fitted the lock of the cash box. Christopher opened it. He found the letter addressed to him, *To Christopher. To be opened in the event of my death*, along with a document titled *E. Eckmann, Last Will and Testament*.

Christopher took the letter and sat at Eckmann's

desk to read it. He read it through several times. It was several pages long. He read the pages slowly and carefully, setting each one down before picking up the next. It made sense, and yet no sense. There was one phrase, interminably repeated – '*if you can find it in your heart to forgive me . . .*'

But he couldn't.

He left the letter upon the desk, stood and went to the safe, and lifted out the file which the letter had directed him to take. It was bulky, full of handwritten notes and emendations, all in Eckmann's distinctive writing. The card on the spine of the file read – *Decelerator*. He went back to the desk and sat to read it. For now he just needed to know the basics – how to make it work, how to keep them alive. Tomorrow he could begin to work on the cure. He was not discouraged by the note on the final page.

'For all my best efforts,' Eckmann's writing said, 'the process seems to be irreversible.'

Christopher put the letter into the pocket of his coat. He picked up the file, left the house, and returned to the gallery. The post had arrived. There were some tourists by the door, peering in through the window.

'Are you opening up now?'

'Sorry, we're closed today,' Christopher told them.

'But it says you're open.'

'We're closed. Sorry.'

'Will you be open tomorrow . . . ?'

Christopher hesitated. He had not yet decided, but now he knew.

'No,' he said. 'We won't be opening. Not again.

271

We're closing now – for ever. There's nothing to see. Sorry.'

'But we've come from the USA . . .'

'Sorry. I can't help you. Excuse me.'

He closed the door.

He walked past the body without a glance at Eckmann's face. But in passing, he saw the cake. He picked up some of the presents and the cards, and took them on up with him to the studio. He went inside. He sat and wrote a letter. Then he removed the glass dome from the city, went to the decelerator and turned on the power.

It was simple enough. Exactly as described. He focused the black dot, so that it just hovered over the street of the city. He sent them the presents and the cards. Then he took the letter and he dropped it through into the blackness. It disappeared from his sight.

He went to the microscope and watched as they read it. He watched as they looked up towards him. He watched as they held each other and cried – in hope perhaps, in joy. The girl went on opening her presents, absorbed in her day-late birthday. He'd have to get her a fresh cake later, and a present from himself.

He left them and went to the phone. He dialled the emergency number and requested the ambulance service.

'Hello? Listen, I've just discovered someone . . . lying on the stairs . . . they were missing overnight and I came looking here . . . no . . . no . . . I think they're already dead . . . have been . . . for quite some time.

Yes. Heart attack I think. Yes, thank you. If you would.'

In time the house was sold. It released a considerable sum of money, as did the sale of the gallery. Eckmann had owned the property outright, it wasn't leased or mortgaged. He had built up quite a portfolio of shares too, and had investments in bonds, cash and other property. There is no doubt that his sculptures would also have raised a considerable sum, but they were gone now, destroyed.

Apart from a legacy to his housekeeper, Eckmann left his entire estate to his son . . . well, his adopted son . . . Christopher, who was suddenly an extremely wealthy young man. But if anyone had expected him to indulge himself in fast cars, or travel, or one of a thousand other distractions, they were proved wrong.

He accepted the place offered to him at one of the leading universities, and he went there to study physics. He proved to be a diligent and committed, if somewhat solitary and friendless, student. Some thought that he was even a little eccentric, especially in his attachment to a souvenir he possessed of his home town – a small replica of the city he had been brought up in, which sat under a little glass dome. It was the kind of thing you often saw for sale at Christmas time. You could imagine that if you shook it, you would see snowflakes fall. Only there were no snowflakes, nor the liquid in which they would have been suspended. It all seemed to have drained away, or dried up, or otherwise disappeared.

Last Word

And that's where the manuscript ends. I don't know if that was supposed to be the end of it. Maybe there was more to come, but if there was, it never got written and that was all there is.

So there you are. That's the story Christopher Mallan left behind him; that's all that remains. I couldn't say if it's a good story or something of a sorry one, but it's what he wrote, word for word. I haven't changed a thing.

It's a touch Gothic for my taste, and heavy on the suspended disbelief, though I have a touch of sympathy for the characters. It's a representation of some kind, I'd guess, a metaphor or a parable maybe. He was trying to touch a nerve there, and this little story of his represented larger issues and bigger things, though I couldn't rightly say what, as I've never been one for deep literature and prefer a good thriller or a crime story myself.

I think it was maybe just the past coming out in him, all the loss and abandonment and the feelings which must have remained, and this was his answer to it, a kind of therapy you might say – a search for meaning.

So, these whizz-kids, huh? Too clever for their own

good, I call them. Up like rockets, but down like stones. They sure burn bright while they're burning, but they don't burn for long. Fireworks, that's all, and shooting stars, streaking across the sky, then sizzling out in the ocean like a hot coal dropped into a water barrel.

When they find they can't cut the mustard, they start to crack up. It's the one-way ticket to the funny farm then. Yup, I'm afraid so.

So me, as I say, I've seen them come and I've seen them go. Christopher, he was a nice enough kid, but he couldn't hack it, see, just couldn't stay the pace. All those big plans and schemes of his must have come to nothing; those dreams of that decelerator of his, they were small pies in a great big sky. He just couldn't see it – though I could have told him. Until one day he finally did realize how impossible it all was, and he just couldn't take it any more and cut loose.

It's a crazy story he wrote, right enough. I can only imagine that he was halfway to cracking up when he wrote it. But at least it got it out of his system. Better out than in maybe – or there again, maybe not.

So what can I tell you? He's gone without so much as a forwarding address. So I've just got to finish clearing his desk out and then the next new whizz-kid will be in to take his place. And how long's he going to last? (Actually, I believe it's a she this time. Not that it makes any difference. They're still all whizz and fizz and then they fizzle out.)

But me, Mr Nice and Easy, that's my way. Take it steady, take it slow. Nothing flashy, just plodding along, good solid work, nothing too inspiring maybe, but useful stuff. Ole Mr Tortoise and ole Mr Hare, and we all know who won that particular race.

So.

That's it then.

Or I thought it was.

Then I found the second letter, at the bottom of the heap, inside a box file, with my name on the front.

'*Dear Charlie,*

Well, you've read what happened now and I guess you know what I'm going to ask of you. What I'm asking is a lot to ask of anyone, but I think you're a good, kind man, someone people can depend on. You might be a bit gruff and on the surly side, but your heart's in the right place.'

(Well, shucks.)

'*If you've read the manuscript, you'll know what I'm going to ask – I'm going to ask you to look after us. The decelerator is quite simple to use. The instructions are all here in this box file and the extra equipment is in the lab, locked in the cupboard marked CHRIS'S STUFF. It's so simple you wouldn't believe it – only you have to believe it. You could build one in your garage or your work room. It wouldn't cost you much more than the price of a decent sound system. But I couldn't leave it any longer, Charlie. I couldn't go on waiting and waiting, trying to work out how to un-fire the gun. They're getting older, and who knows how long any of us has got. I thought Dad looked pale and ill, and I was afraid he might die. I had to take the chance, Charlie. I had to. I kept putting it off, leaving it another day, thinking I might work out how to do it, but I can't. Time's against me.*

Against us all. We only have so many days. All we can do is choose how to spend them.

It's all in the file here – how it works, how I've tried for years to make it run the other way. We should be all right for a while, I've been stockpiling for a long time. I've hoarded all sorts of things to try and make us self-sufficient – things to grow, ways of extracting moisture from the air for water – we ought to be able to keep going for a good long time. But there will always be things we need, and a friend to send them – maybe someone to try and finish the work I couldn't complete. Maybe you can do it, Charlie. Maybe you can succeed where I failed. You're a whole lot smarter than you tell people. Maybe one day you could bring us back. Remember when you invited me to your house, Charlie, to meet your wife and your kids? I'd like to return that compliment one day. I'd like you to meet my dad, and Poppea, and my half sister. I'd like that so much, Charlie. I'd like you to meet my family too. Because I do have one, you see, I really do.

Thank you for everything. I hope you don't feel that I've given you a responsibility you don't want. If it's all too much, don't worry – we'll have to get by, somehow. No one lives for ever.

Goodbye. Yours, Christopher.'

What can I say?

I mean, I remember, you know, when my old man died . . . and I'm not saying we always got on or anything . . . but I can remember that day even now, and the times since when I'd wished the one thing I could do was to see him again and talk to him again and . . .

277

Am I going crazy? Even starting actually to believe this? What a joker! I mean, he had me going there good and proper. He nearly had me getting the microscope out and looking into the little dome, just to check it out – that's how much he got to me. There's one born every minute and I reckon one of them was me.

Tell you what, If there's any of you ladies who like the sound of this guy, get in touch and I'll send you down there. You can help in the colonization of Planet Dome. Would you like that? Starting a new race of little people? Being one of the aliens out there? Only thing is, it's a one-way ticket, there's no coming back.

He almost had me swallowing that one. Nearly got me getting the microscope out and looking.

Tell the truth . . . he did.

I did look.

What can I tell you?

I felt . . . so small. Yes, small. In this great world of ours, in this vast universe. I felt . . . so small. To see them, these people, whom he wanted so much to be with. I felt . . . tiny . . . insignificant . . . humble . . . even ashamed. I felt like kneeling down and saying a prayer . . . and I don't even believe in anything.

Here's a thought now. This is the choice given you. I've been wondering how to put it, and this is the best I can do. I'll spin this coin and see which way it comes up. This is the heads or tails of it – to spend your life in this world, with everything it has in it except the people you love. Or to spend your life in another world, with the people who mean everything to you – able to hold them and talk with them and cry with them and laugh with them and even fight with them. Able to be with them, but never able to come back.

What do you choose?

Take your time. Think about it. What do you choose? There's no guarantee, there's nothing certain – except that you can never come back.

It's a hard one, huh? It takes some thinking about. I'll be back to hear what you've decided. I've just got to do a few things. You know, little everyday things, routine maintenance. I've got things to look after, various responsibilities, mouths to feed. I've got a project to keep me occupied too. And I've got to pick up a present or two later. For a little girl. Nine years old soon. I guess if I don't get her something, nobody else will. She's not my little girl. She's just related to a friend of mine. He'd buy her a present himself, but he can't get to the shops.

That coin's in the air. See it spinning? Have you got any closer to deciding? It's a hard decision right enough, and life's not getting any longer. What're you going to choose? It's heads or tails, and yet that isn't really it either, it's your head or your heart – heads or hearts. I guess it's a tough one. It always has been. That's all there is sometimes, the ticking clock and the falling coin, and knowing you have to decide. Like Christopher. It's having the courage to know your own heart. Once you know that, there's nothing else you can do.

I guess the choice is already made.

I'm a busy man now. A man with a mission. I've got things to do, people to look after. There's a trigger out there and I've got to learn how to un-pull it. They're all depending on me, I'm all they have, I'm the only one who knows about it. So that's my epitaph, I reckon. That's how I'd want to be remembered – as the man who un-fired the gun. The man who un-exploded the bomb. The man who dropped the pieces of glass upon the floor, and they all joined up together again.

See, I've joined the crazies. Yes I have. Isn't that right, Chris? It doesn't take much. It's quite an easy thing to do really. We've gone and joined the crazies, who believe the weirdest things.

The coin is spinning, slowly falling to the ground. He was right, you know. Christopher was right. *Time's against us all. We only have so many days. All we can do is choose how to spend them.* That's all we truly have. Just as he said. Our days, and how we spend them. And the people we love. The rest hardly matters. We have to go where we most need to be, to follow our hearts to where they take us. Perhaps we travel there in fear and in unknown darkness, yet maybe we journey towards the light.

Yes, I think we do.

I hope we do.

We journey to the light.